Promises Beyond Jordan

PROMISES BEYOND JORDAN

VANESSA DAVIS GRIGGS

BET Publications, LLC
http://www.bet.com

NEW SPIRIT BOOKS are published by

BET Publications, LLC
c/o BET BOOKS
One BET Plaza
1900 W Place NE
Washington, DC 20018-1211

All Kensington Titles, Imprints, and Distributed Lines are available at special quantity discounts for bulk purchases for sales promotions, premiums, fund-raising, and educational or institutional use. Special book excerpts or customized printings can also be created to fit specific needs. For details, write or phone the office of the Kensington special sales manager: Kensington Publishing Corp., 850 Third Avenue, New York, NY 10022, attn: Special Sales Department, Phone: 1-800-221-2647.

ISBN: 1-58314-467-6

First Printing: February 2004
10 9 8 7 6 5 4 3 2 1

Printed in the United States of America

To my mother, Josephine Davis, and father, James Davis, Jr.

PROLOGUE

Chosen in the Fire of Affliction

December 31, 1970
Winston-Salem, North Carolina

Lena Patterson looked up at the silver-haired nurse with tears in both her eyes and her voice, and softly said, "Haven't you ever loved anyone so much there was nothing you wouldn't do to keep them from hurt?"

"Lena, that doesn't answer my question," Nurse Hayes said. "Who can we contact to let know you're here? It's been a week now; someone needs to know your whereabouts. Surely there are family . . . friends who are worried about you? I'd like to call them." Lena looked away. "Then, here." Nurse Hayes held out a news article. "When I saw this, I realized it was about you. Go on. Read it."

Lena's hand began to tremble as she held tight to the paper. Her eyes fell where Nurse Hayes had pointed. Lena noticed herself as she began to shake even more. Not from the pain that definitely racked her body, but the impact and reality of just two paragraphs printed in the newspaper dated December 25, 1970.

* * *

WINSTON-SALEM, NC: December 25 is supposed to be a day of celebration. For one family, at least, this is not the case. Last evening, a fire totally engulfed a duplex home, critically injuring a woman as she apparently attempted to save the life of two children she believed to be trapped inside the house. Firefighters say they are still investigating the cause of the fire, but it appears to have begun with a live Christmas tree. "People need to be careful around this time of the year," Chief Houston said. "It only takes fifteen seconds for a dry tree to blaze—consuming anything and everything daring to stand in its way."

As to the condition of the twenty-year-old black woman, one doctor (who wished to remain anonymous) said, "It will be a miracle if she even pulls through. I hope she has a strong family. She's going to need more than we can ever give to survive the extensive third-degree burns suffered on her upper and lower body." One fireman was reported as saying, "We tried to stop her, but she broke loose! Don't know how she made it into that inferno, let alone made it out. But she did . . . and with a little child wrapped in her arms." Names are being withheld pending family notification.

Lena couldn't feel the tears that ran down her bandaged face. And as much as she didn't want to, she knew what she had to do.

Richard Jordan came to the hospital an hour after Nurse Hayes called him. Standing next to Lena's bed, he wondered what decision she had come to.

Unable to say the words, "I'll sign the papers," she only nodded her answer to him.

Richard was twenty-one and had so much to offer the world. Besides being 6'1" and a beautiful dark brown, he was smart, kind, mature, and responsible. He was already aware of his life's calling: to help the hurting. And as bad as things looked for her, Lena knew how much he loved her, knew he would do right by her. And yes—knew he could be trusted to keep his word.

"All right," she whispered, then swallowed hard. "But just until I'm better."

"Of course," Richard said, fighting back the tears. "That goes without saying. And you *will* be better soon. Then you . . . me . . ." He couldn't speak anymore. *Who am I kidding?* Even the doctors were shocked she had made it this far. They knew it was sheer will keeping her alive. But how much longer could she truly keep up the fight? "Lena, I'm sorry," he said. "So sorry."

She handed him the folded article. It was getting harder for her to get her words out. "Keep this also. For me. Safe. I want it back. Some day. Promise me, Richard. Promise . . . you'll keep this . . . and give it back . . . to me . . . some . . . day."

He knew what she was doing: making him hold on to something. She had to know in her heart *he* believed she would make it through. To know she knew how much she had to live for. Keeping the article—promising to return it—would be evidence of his faith. "Promise me," she said as she closed her eyes.

"Lena, don't you worry." He put the article inside his coat pocket.

Reaching out, she tried to touch his hand and form a smile. "Oh, I'm not worried." She stroked his hand. "Remember, Richard. Just until I'm better."

He leaned down and softly kissed her bandaged forehead. "I promise." Wiping at a tear that had somehow managed to escape from his eye, he tried to give her his most confident smile. "Just until you're better. Just until you're . . . better."

CHAPTER 1

Casting Down Imagination

December 2000

"Have you ever loved someone that you never had?" George Landris said as he stood tall, looking down upon his wife-to-be.

"What?" Theresa Jordan said, more confused now than when they first began this conversation some ten minutes ago. "George Landris, what in God's name are you talking about? We're getting married in less than two weeks. Nine days. December 30th, 2000, George. And you come here to tell me you *have* to go to Alabama? Then when I ask why . . . why you *have* to go, your only explanation is about loving someone that you've never had? I'm sorry, but, no . . . no, I don't understand."

George pulled her closer, realizing he should have told her something else instead. "Theresa, I'm not trying to hurt you. My going has nothing to do with us. It's just something I have to do. I know I'm not explaining this very well. You're just going to have to trust me on this. I'll call you when I get there—"

"And just *what* do you propose I tell my family? My friends? The people at church, should anyone ask? Did you even think to mention to Deacon Thomas that you might not be back in time for Sunday services?"

"Theresa, Sunday is three days away. Don't you think you're making a big deal out of—"

"Well, what do you expect? Exactly how am I supposed to act? Tell me, Pastor Landris. Please tell me. What *is* the correct way to respond when the man who has promised his love to you informs you he's about to up and leave, just like that?" She snapped her fingers. "Better still, what's the correct way to respond when it appears he's leaving you to see about some other woman, in some other state, *and* . . ." she held up her index finger, "he didn't even ask if you'd care to go with him?"

"She's not some *other* woman, Theresa. She happens to be someone who . . . needs me right now. Surely you can understand and appreciate that? Things like this come with my job. You know this. You also know needs don't bother to make appointments." He bent down slightly to look into her light brown eyes. "And *had* I asked, what would you have said?" His own eyes now forced her to be fair and honest with her answer.

"Okay," she said, turning away from his gaze before turning back to his warm hazelnut-colored eyes. "I realize I told you just yesterday I'd be too busy this week and next to run around with you on your visits or otherwise. But George, the whole reason I took off from work was *because* I have so much to do."

"And that's fine, Theresa. But any of those visits would have been to people here in Atlanta. I honestly can't say how long it will take me in Alabama."

"I know, George." She could only let out a hard sigh. "And *had* you asked, I wouldn't have been able to go. Not on such short notice. Not with Christmas coming Monday, planning our wedding . . . getting my hair done before Sunday—" She sighed again. "It's just that—George, she's not even a member of our church! We need you *here*. Your congregation . . ." she pressed her lips tight before pouting them out, ". . . me."

"Well that's a very Christian way to go about it. We can only see about people who are part of our congregation?" He half-teased, then became serious. "Theresa, I don't want to make this any harder than it needs to be. I'll call you when I find out something and be back as soon as humanly possible. I promise."

Theresa stepped back from George and tilted her head to one side. Tears began to slip from her eyes. "Yeah, sure. And you always keep your promises. Right, George? So does this mean at least I'll see you at the altar on our wedding day?" She smiled, attempting to make him feel she was okay. "Tell me, Pastor Landris, are you the one, or should I have waited for another?"

George stepped back over to her and took her hand; her venture to joke didn't fool him any. "Theresa . . . I do understand this probably makes no sense to you; I'm not sure I'll ever be able to explain it—totally, anyway. Alabama's not all that far. Let me get there, find out what's going on, and we can go from there. All right? Just please, please don't cry." He wiped at her tears. "In your heart of hearts, you know this is something I must do." He lifted her head up by raising her chin.

"Yeah, George. In my heart, I know." Theresa smiled and stepped back from George. "Drive carefully, okay?" She began to twist and fiddle with the engagement ring on her finger. She had received the two carat, pear-shaped diamond just six months ago from George, the charismatic, dynamic, powerful, forty-year-old Wings of Grace Faith Ministry's pastor. The dreadlocks-wearing, Word-teaching, brand-new-mercy-preaching, handsome pastor led the three-thousand-and-still-growing membership church. "I'll wait," she said. "Here."

George picked up his overcoat and slid it on. "I *will* call you when I get there and know something." He searched her face, trying to see if she would give him an okay-to-leave-me smile.

She didn't . . . couldn't bring herself to look at him, but rather continued to twist the ring on her finger—the token that pledged she was soon to become Mrs. George Landris. The ring was a symbol of that which has no beginning and no end. She glanced up at him, desperate to muster her best smile. But the hurt was all that labored through. And George couldn't help but see it all over her face. He opened the door and walked out, closing it softly behind him.

Theresa flopped down on the couch and began to cry. "If only I hadn't shown him that article in the paper this morning!" she said, repeatedly beating both fists on the couch's seat cushion. "He probably wouldn't have even known it yet. Now, instead of happily planning the beginning of our life together, he's off to see about some famous Johnnie Mae Taylor." She punched her fist twice into a back pillow before grabbing it, using it to muffle her moans. "Oh, God! What do I do?" She cried louder. "What . . . do . . . I . . . do . . . now!?"

The past two months, George had begun to see a difference in Theresa. He had, indeed, prayed about marrying her before popping the question. She appeared to have a heart for the church and the ministry. She'd come in, on day one, with her sleeves rolled up to work with the youth and the Drama Ministry. In fact, she'd worked wherever she was needed. But something was starting to unravel with her, although George didn't know what . . . or why. When he asked her about it, she laughed—blaming anything and everything on the pressures of planning a wedding, a "major production." A ceremony, she insisted, was a "must have."

George popped in a Kirk Franklin CD as he sped down I-20 West from Atlanta to Birmingham. He had tried to reach someone in Alabama to find out more information than what the four lines in the newspaper had reported. He hadn't been able to get in touch with anyone who could tell him anything of substance. The article said it was a car accident, critically injuring three people. No other details were, as yet, available. There was too much left George didn't know.

Theresa had no idea when she showed the article to him that he would react the way he did. He hadn't really shared a lot about his past with her—that part of his past, anyway. She had no way of knowing that he even knew the up-and-coming author, although Theresa had bought and read both her books.

When George saw her reading Johnnie Mae's latest book, he didn't bother to tell her he knew the author personally, even though he knew it would have been a thrill for Theresa to have met Johnnie Mae: she had voiced that much to him at least twice. Still, he never mentioned how he could get her a personal audience with the newly famous writer. One day, he had told himself, he would most likely surprise her with a special meeting. But, as he drove well over the speed limit of seventy, he wondered if he ever really would.

Getting from Atlanta to Birmingham, George knew, would only take him about two hours. But even that seemed too long a time for him to learn the answer he so desperately needed to know right now. *Johnnie Mae, her baby girl—Princess Rose—were they both all right? And Solomon . . . what of Johnnie Mae's husband?*

He pressed the eject button of the CD player, thinking he needed some true quiet time. Time to be able to *really* talk to God. Time to pray . . . to seek God's face. *Am I doing the right thing by going to Alabama? Especially right now? And how will Johnnie Mae react to my coming . . . my being there after some two-and-a-half years?*

The radio instantly blasted, "This is V-103, and you're rocking the box with Portia Fox." The radio seemed to mockingly stick out its tongue at him as Patti LaBelle crooned, "If only you knew . . ." Reaching to silence the music, he quickly drew back his hand as though someone had—without warning—hit it. Almost by instinct, he found himself, instead, singing along with Patti, ". . . do love you."

Passing the Anniston exits, he knew he was only forty-five minutes outside of Birmingham. "Dear Lord," he prayed aloud, "let all be well. Please, Lord. Please. Just let all be well."

CHAPTER 2

The Spirit of the Lord Is Upon Me

Since George hadn't been able to get anyone to tell him anything over the phone, he had driven to each hospital and spoken with someone at each information station face-to-face. Birmingham has at least nine hospitals; he was up to number six and was beginning to wonder if maybe he should try something different altogether.

"Excuse me, Miss," he said to the middle-aged black woman behind the area with the word "Information" spelled out at its base. "I pray you can help me. I'm looking for someone who may have been admitted to University Hospital after a car accident this past Monday night or possibly Tuesday morning."

"What's the name, sir?"

"Johnnie Mae Taylor. Might be listed as J. M. Taylor."

She searched the computer. "Sorry. No one here by either name."

"Then could you try Solomon Taylor?"

She typed away and looked up at him. "And you are?" she said.

It was at that instant he knew he had located the right hospital. *Finally, after driving all over the city.* "George Landris," he said. "L-a-n-d-r-i-s."

She looked at the screen again. "I'm sorry. Looks like there's not a Solomon Taylor listed either."

George knew what was up. That was why he hadn't been able to get any information over the phone. To keep people from bothering them during this time, the hospital probably had received strict instructions not to release any information other than to approved persons. His name, apparently, wasn't on the list.

"Miss, look. I happen to be a friend of the family. I came over from Atlanta about five hours ago. If you could possibly speak with someone in the family, let them know I'm here . . . I'm positive they would give you permission to tell me what room number—"

"You know," she said, almost smiling as she cut him off, "you look so familiar. I know I've seen you somewhere. I've been trying to place you since you walked in. Would you happen to be a preacher?"

"Yes, I am."

"I knew it! I knew you looked like someone I'd seen before. You come on that . . . that TBN channel, don't you?" Her eyes were almost laughing. "You're that pastor me and my husband watch every Sunday evening. Well, every Sunday evening we don't have to go back to church, that is. We have a lot of church programs, but I love to watch you when I get a chance. I love your teaching!"

"Thank you," he said. "I appreciate that."

"Pastor Landris . . . why, of course! Don't know why I didn't put it together sooner." She began quoting his TV slogan: " 'Taking Life to a New Level with the Power of God.' Oh, and please forgive me for having to lie to you earlier. There's a notation that states only people listed can be given any information. Unfortunately, your name's not here. An oversight on the family's part, I'm sure."

"Believe me. I do understand."

"Since I saw that teaching you did called 'Integrity in the Workplace,' I know it wouldn't be proper to disclose this information . . . even to someone like yourself."

George continued trying to maintain a smile. *What could I say?* "Well, do you think you might be able to check with someone . . .

let them know I'm here asking? They may give you the go-ahead. Then neither one of us would be compromising our integrity."

She grinned again. "Of course." Picking up the receiver, she made a call. "Pastor Landris?" she said, no longer smiling. "No one is answering the number they have listed. But I'll keep trying it." She began to smile again. "I still don't believe this! I actually got to meet you! Glory . . . and in person! Right here, on my job at that! Just wait until I tell my friend Maggie. She's going to flip! She watches you all the time. Never misses you. Videotapes you, even."

George looked at his watch. He didn't quite know how to respond. He'd been getting this type of reaction a lot lately—one of the things that seemed to come with the territory of being on television each week. He was truly honored by people's comments, but he had only considered this as part of his commission to go into the highways and byways . . . to spread the Good News.

Television had certainly been a runway for him getting the word out. That was when his ministry really took flight. By beating the bushes and hitting the streets, he had managed to grow the congregation from thirty-seven faithful members to one with over fifteen hundred members. Shortly after he began broadcasting over the airwaves via radio and television, a flood of people began pouring in. Now, there were almost thirty-five hundred members—three thousand consistently filled the pews each and every Sunday. God had certainly been faithful.

"Pastor Landris?" The woman interrupted his thoughts. "Would it be *too* much trouble if I were to ask you for your autograph? I mean, I think you're just as much of a celebrity—if not more so—as those Hollywood stars."

George took the small pad and pen she held stretched out. "It would be my pleasure, Mrs. . . . ?"

"Dawson," she said. "Jewellene Dawson. Jewellene has two els."

George smiled and handed the autographed paper back to her. He didn't want to rush her, but he really couldn't think of much else other than learning what he had come all this way to find out. "Mrs. Dawson—"

"Jewellene."

"Jewellene, do you think you could try that number again for me, please? Or maybe there's someone who can authorize your releasing that information?" He started to stress the fact that he *was* a man of God. *Surely there must be some loophole in their rules that would accommodate someone in my type of position. After all, visiting the sick was a part of what I was called to do.*

"Yes, of course." She called, but there was still no answer. The other person she called told her that a family's instructions were to be adhered to completely. When Jewellene tried to explain the unique situation, she was told it didn't matter if it was the Pope himself! So Jewellene tried calling that contact number again. "Pastor Landris," she said, "I'm sorry . . . *still* no answer. But I did reach the nurses' station. They said they would try to get a message to someone in the family. If you like, you can wait over there. I'll let you know as soon as I hear something."

George looked at the seating area, which was a good distance away from Jewellene's station. "Thank you, Mrs. Dawson," he said. "You've been most kind." He sat on a couch that ended up being quite comfortable. A good thing, too; he was there for over an hour.

"Pastor Landris?" Mrs. Dawson said. He stood up. "I've not heard back from anyone yet. But you know, I was just sitting there thinking. I'm due to get off in about twenty minutes, and I'd really hate for you to have to wait *here*. So it occurred to me, there's a perfectly good waiting room . . . across the street. Just go straight out that door," she pointed, "over to the Jefferson Towers Building. Nothing says you can't wait in *that* waiting room. Maybe you can talk to one of the nurses there. Who knows, someone might be able to relay something of importance. After all, a waiting place is a waiting place."

George looked at her and smiled. He took her hand and patted it twice. "Thank you, Mrs. Dawson. You're an angel. And may God bless you for all the kindness you've shown. You and your family will certainly be in my prayers."

She blushed. "Well, Pastor Landris, it's like I always say: University Hospital might be known throughout the world for many great accomplishments, but at the beginning of it all, a waiting place is still just a waiting place."

George strolled out the door and quickly made his way across the street. As he pulled the door open, he almost caused the person coming out to lose her balance and fall forward. "Oh, I'm so sorry," he said.

"George?" the woman said, taking a closer look. "George Landris? Is that you?"

He couldn't believe it. More than two years had passed since he was last in Birmingham. And *who* would be the first person he runs into? "Honey? Honey Benefield," he said, as though they had actually left on the best of terms. They had disagreed on *ships:* she desiring a relation*ship*; he only offering his friend*ship*.

She looked him up and down. *Umph, umph, umph. Still fine as ever, I see.* She smiled while popping her chewing gum. *And check him out, he grew back his dreads. They're even longer than the first time we met.*

He could feel her stare measuring him up. Honey always had a way of making him feel self-conscious about his body. He was physically fit, the result of working out practically every day. It never seemed to bother Honey how transparent she always was in displaying her hunger for him. Noticing her eyes were now frozen on his hair, he allowed a tiny chuckle to slip past his lips. "It grew back," he said to her. "Stronger and longer than ever."

"Yeah, I was noting that fact. Some say hair is an outward sign of spiritual growth. I liked you with the bald look, but dreads have started to grow on me. And I really am sorry about my son getting all that green gook in your hair that time. I realize how difficult it must have been for you to have had to begin again."

"Beginnings are a part of life. Often we find we must end one thing in order to begin another . . . or anew." He didn't want to be rude and was fully aware this was still probably a sore spot for Honey—but he had to ask. "How's Johnnie Mae? There was a brief article in the *Atlanta Tribune* about the accident, but not enough details were available to answer the questions I had. It didn't say who was hurt, how bad, or how anyone was doing. So I—"

"Had to come," Honey said, finishing his sentence. She didn't blame him, only wished someone cared about her even a third as much. Curious about what he'd been up to lately, she decided it best not to ask. Unsure of exactly how much she should tell him, she said, "George, Johnnie Mae got banged up real bad, but she made them release her anyway. Solomon and Princess Rose both are in intensive care. Princess Rose is over at Children's Hospital—another reason why Johnnie Mae was not going to be confined to any hospital bed. But George," she said, "between you, me, and the light post . . . it doesn't look so good for either of them right now. Johnnie Mae has practically slept in waiting rooms since they released her. I don't know how she'll feel about you being here, but I do know she can use all the support she can get."

The weather was cold as they stood outside. George gave Honey a little hug. "It really is great to see you. Is anyone with her?" George wasn't as certain now that his being here was the right thing to be doing. But it was too late to turn back.

"Yeah. Someone is usually around, except when official visiting hours are over. Her brother, Donald, just arrived. Hopefully, he's still with her. Of course, her mother has been with her from the beginning. Johnnie Mae made her go home about an hour ago to get some rest. You know, it was just two-and-a-half years ago that Mrs. Gates lost her own husband. She doesn't cope so well in hospitals. Johnnie Mae knows that. Our friend, Sister, was here earlier. Do you remember her? Anyway," she said, not giving him time to answer either way, "she went home about two hours ago. It's generally around this time of day that everybody starts heading back. I've got three left at home to see about myself. Oh, and I'm *still* single. My oldest daughter is away at college now. Can you believe that? I actually have a child who's attending college!"

"God is good, Honey."

She pulled herself back and tilted her head the way black women do when, without having to utter a word, they're asking, "What you talking about?!"

"George Landris . . . did you just say what I think I heard? Did you just say the word 'God'?"

He laughed. "I happen to say the word 'God' a lot these days, Honey. You see, I'm a minister—"

"You're a what?! You're a minister? Oh . . . now I *know* there's a God somewhere!" She laughed. "So tell me, when did all this happen? Better yet, *how* did it all of this happen? I can't believe it! George Landris, a minister? You? Of all people? A minister?!"

"Okay, okay. That's enough. Let's not get carried away. I mean, I wasn't *that* bad." George smiled before glancing downward at his wrist. He had been at this hospital for two solid hours.

Honey saw him peek at his watch. "Oh well, gotta run! It's freezing out here! Maybe we'll see each other later? Then you can fill me in on your great conversion. How long were you planning on staying? In Birmingham, that is, not the ministry?"

"Truthfully, I hadn't really thought about it. I pretty much got in my car around one o'clock Atlanta time and just drove over. They're not exactly dispensing information, including where Johnnie Mae is. I brought a few days' worth of clothing just in case it took me longer than I calculated to find out anything."

Honey tried to look serious. *Translated, that means as long as Johnnie Mae needs you,* she thought. "So, George, or should I say . . . Reverend Landris—"

"Pastor Landris."

"Oh, pastor. So it's pastor, huh? Okay, Pastor Landris. Well, have you jumped the broom yet? Started yourself a family?"

"I'm engaged," he said. "The wedding is set for December thirtieth."

"Whoa! That's not but . . . eight . . . nine days away."

"So I've heard."

"Uh-huh."

George started back toward the door. "I suppose I should see about locating Johnnie Mae—check out how she's holding up."

"Well, George, you know how strong she is. Hasn't shown the first sign of breaking down yet. She's in the MICU waiting room, on the left." Honey bundled tighter and began to walk away with a swish. "You take care now," she yelled without looking back. "Uh-huh," she said under her breath. "George . . . getting married? And in less than two weeks?" She continued talking to herself. "But you're up here seeing about Johnnie Mae? Yeah . . . okay, Pastor Landris. Well, you can send me an invitation to this wedding."

George took a deep breath and slowly pushed the door open to the waiting room. He scanned the room, but found it completely empty. Letting go of the breath he had held so tight, he sat on a chair by one of the two walls of windows. Fifteen minutes passed. Thirty. Forty-five. Then the door slowly opened. He looked up.

"Johnnie Mae?" he said, rising to his feet.

She stood as though she had permanently taken root in that spot. Staring as though this was something her tired mind had simply manufactured to help keep her sane, she finally found her voice. "Landris?" she said.

He smiled. And she—not being able to stop herself—began to cry. "You came," she said in between sobs. "But how? How, Landris? Tell me. How do you always seem to know when I really need . . . someone?"

He pulled her close and held her softly, as though she might somehow break. "Shhh," he said. "It's all right. Everything's going to be all right." Seeing her built-up reservoir of tears continuing to flow, he eased her into a chair.

Sitting next to her while still holding on to her, he repeatedly ran his hand down her hair. "Go ahead," he whispered. "Let it out. Just let it all out."

CHAPTER 3

Let Not Your Heart Be Troubled

Theresa looked at the clock. It was a quarter past eight P.M. George had been gone for over seven hours, and she hadn't heard a word from him. She had tried his cell number, but apparently he had his phone turned off. *What could have happened to him?*

B had called from the beauty shop to say she would be getting to Theresa's place later than she had originally planned. B's real name was Bellona Conlie (Bellona after the Roman goddess of war). Bellona never did like her first name, so she made everybody call her B. "Just B."

And B could cold do some hair: waves, scrunches, twists, rods, feathers, braids, peacock tails, and French rolls. You name it, she could do it: natural, press, perm. "Just tell me what you *want*, and you *won't* go home disappointed!" was the line she used when anyone inquired of her services. She and Theresa had been friends since they were twelve. Even back then, B was working her craft.

At age sixteen, B found herself pregnant. She married the guy, even though they had only known each other for two months. A month after the baby was born, they separated. A year later, their divorce was final.

"His name should have clued me in on the type of person he really was," B had said. "Tyrone Conlie." She pronounced his name like it was bitterweed.

"How can a name tell you anything about a person?" Theresa asked.

"Tyr is 'tired.' Then there's the word 'one.' See? Tired one. But the biggest clue was in his last name. Con for 'con artist.' And lie for . . . well, 'liar.' There it is . . . right there! Bright as a full moon!"

"B, you don't really believe you can tell things just from a person's name?"

"Try it sometime. You'll see. You can save yourself a lot of headaches by paying attention to what's in a name. 'A rose by any other name' . . . my foot!"

"*Your* name's Conlie now," Theresa had said. "So what does that mean?"

"Oh, that will change soon enough. I'm gonna find me a good man, take on his name. Hey, let's check the phone book and see how many single men are listed under Goodman."

"Girl, you're too crazy!"

Theresa had thought about what B said when she first began talking to George Landris on a serious basis. All she found in his name were the words "Land" and "is." "Land is" seemed a good thing. Unless it was a deserted island.

B was coming over to fix her hair tonight. That was one of the benefits of having a friend who did hair. Usually, Theresa would go down to her shop, but it was always busy leading up to any major holiday. Christmas was on a Monday this year, and every woman of color was trying to get her hair done as close to the days right before it. B had told Theresa she'd come to her apartment Thursday night so they could also work on some final details of her wedding while she did her hair. B didn't want folks all up in their business, watching their mouths every time they opened like they were waiting for planes to emerge. Friday and Saturday, B knew she'd be *slap* worn out!

Theresa curled up on the couch; her mind needed a rest—just a few minutes of . . . rest . . .

A three-year-old little girl cried out, "Mommy, Mommy! Flames! They're all around me! I'm trying, but I can't seem to get out. The flames are so hot. Have I died? Am I dead, Mommy? Is this that place you called hell? I don't want to be here. You promised angels would watch over me—encamp round about me. You promised! Oh please, God. Send me an angel. Send an angel to bring me out of this place. Lord, save me. I want Jesus as Lord of my life. Please . . . give me a chance."

The little girl began to cry harder, though no tears seemed to flow. "Send an angel to deliver me," she said. "I promise. I'll be good. I'll be good. I promise. Please."

Suddenly, her body lifted straight up; and it was no longer hot. Able to open her eyes, she looked around. She had been delivered! "Where's my angel?" she asked. Then in the distance, she heard a bell ring. Then again. And again . . .

"Ring!" The phone rang a fourth time. Theresa bolted straight up.

"Huh? What?" She looked around, rubbed her eyes, and stumbled toward the phone. Five rings. She answered it just before the answering machine did.

"Hello."

"Hey. I was just about to hang up," George said. "Where were you?"

"Oh . . . George. It's you." She was still trying to get herself oriented.

"Were you asleep? Did I wake you?"

"Sort of. Not a deep sleep though. Just deep enough for a weird dream."

"What about?"

"Fire . . . trying to get saved . . . being delivered. There was even an angel. I don't know; it was crazy. Must have been something I ate," she lied; she hadn't eaten yet.

He laughed. "Sounds like a sermon to me. Maybe I can use it."

"Yeah. Maybe." She looked at the clock. It was a little after nine in the evening. "Where are you? Why are you just now calling? Nothing's wrong, is it?"

George leaned his head against the top of the pay phone at the hospital. "It's a long story."

"I have time," Theresa said. "I tried calling you, but your cell phone must be off."

"It's probably the battery. I need to get a new one so it will stay charged longer." He thought a second. Actually, he hadn't remembered to turn it on.

"Did you find out anything? Ms. Taylor? Her family? Are they all going to be okay?"

"It took me awhile, but I did locate them. Johnnie Mae's pretty much okay. Better than the others. Her husband and child both are in intensive care."

"Oh, George, no," Theresa said with genuine sincerity.

He let out a deep sigh. "Theresa, it's pretty serious. There's a lot of praying being done here. A lot. The doctors are doing all they can; but even they know, ultimately, it's still in God's hands."

"You don't sound too confident."

"Look, I'm not going to talk long. I just wanted to call and let you know what was happening here."

"Are you going to be home later tonight?" Theresa asked as she bit down on her bottom lip.

"No. I don't feel like driving back tonight. I'm going to get a room here."

"But it's only a little past nine. If you left now, you'd be home by eleven. I cooked something for you."

"Theresa, listen. I'll give you a call tomorrow. So get yourself some rest. Oh, and Theresa?"

"Yes," she said, almost smiling. *I knew it; he wouldn't fail me. He's going to tell me he loves me.*

"Stay away from those bad dreams," he said, trying to sound cheerful.

"George?"

"Yes?"

"I love you," she said. Without thinking, she held her breath.

"Sleep tight," he said. "And sweet dreams. I'll talk with you tomorrow."

At nine-thirty, B was leaning on Theresa's doorbell. Theresa opened the door.

"Girl, these women are a trip! Trip, I tell you!" She strolled past Theresa, who hurriedly closed the door. "They be asking why it's taking so long for them to get in and out of the shop. If I would turn most of them down when they start with all that begging after I already done told them I'm booked up, then they wouldn't *have* to be in the shop waiting at all! I be telling them, 'I can't take no more,' but they beg and plead, 'Can't you work me in? I don't mind if I have to wait.' Yet they be the main ones complaining that they've been there for three or four hours." She began pulling things out of her jumbo tote bag: comb, gel, rods, shampoo.

"And I *know* they don't think I'm gonna make my people, who did right by making their appointments early, be the ones to have to wait. So when they say, 'Work me in,' I really do *work them in.* I don't play that! Cause them same folks that be complaining the loudest, you won't see their heads again until the *next* major holiday. I can't make no living off them kind of customers." B turned and looked at Theresa who had, by then, flopped down on a bar stool.

"So, what's up with you? You look like you just called off your wedding the day you were supposed to walk down the aisle."

"B . . . why did you have to say that?"

"What? I'm just playing. Dang! You sure are touchy tonight." B looked toward the kitchen. "What you got in there to eat? I know you cooked, and you know I'm starving. I need to hurry up and get on your hair, too. I got a long day ahead of me tomorrow. Did you get that? A-head." B noticed Theresa was busy staring hard at nothing. "Theresa? Theresa," she sang. "Hey!" She walked over and bent down in front of her. "What's wrong with you?"

"George went to Birmingham today."

"England?"

Theresa looked at her and held her head to one side as she twisted her mouth. "No. Alabama."

B started laughing. "Dang. The way you're acting, who'd know he'd gone just two hours away? What you gonna do when he really goes far? And you know you won't be going everywhere he goes, either. Especially after those little munchkins come along. You're thirty-three; need to hurry up and get started."

Theresa didn't want to hear about her late start in having children. "B . . ."

"Okay, okay, okay. Well, it's apparent something's bothering you. George went to Birmingham . . ." B thought for a second. "Oh . . . now, don't tell me he got stopped on his way and is being detained. You know, this racial profiling stuff has gone too far! Can't a black man drive a brand new Mercedes in America without being pulled over or harassed?"

"B, it's not anything like that. You were closer when you were joking about my wedding being called off."

"No. No . . . you . . . are not! I know you are not getting cold feet—"

"It's not me."

"George? You mean, George is getting cold feet? Pastor Landris—"

"Look, B. I shouldn't have even brought it up. Nobody's getting cold feet. It's just, he went to see about a friend who was in a car accident the other day."

"The man is a saint! A saint, I tell you!"

"He couldn't find out any information on her—"

"Her? What *her*?"

"His friend is a woman."

"And he went to see about her? Did I say saint . . . or Saint Bernard?"

"Yes, he went to see about her. Apparently, they were once *quite* close."

"So he dropped everything? No warning? No planning? Just rushed off to Birmingham? To see about a woman? A woman he *claims* is just a friend?"

Theresa shook her head and laughed. "Funny, it sounds *so* much worse the way you put it."

"So what did he tell you when he got back?"

"He's not back yet."

"Then why are you here, instead of there with him? I mean, your hair ain't *that* raggedy, girl. And whatever hotel he's staying in, I'm sure they have more than one room. Since y'all claim you're saving yourselves until you're married."

"B, it's not like that. She's married." Theresa adjusted her body. "You remember the book I added to our Sistah2Sistah Book Club list a few months ago? The one by Johnnie Mae Taylor?" B nodded. "It's her. She's the friend."

B pushed Theresa, causing her to lean over and pop back up. "*Get out*!"

"I kid you not."

"Get . . . out . . . of here! Your fiancé? Your soon-to-be-husband? Heck, our Holy Ghost-filled, tongue-talking pastor? He knows *her*?" She smiled. "Dang!"

"And never said one word to me about it. I know he saw me reading her book. I even mentioned to him I hoped to meet her if she ever came to Atlanta."

"Well . . . I'll . . . be! So, did he say how she's doing? You know, I really did like her first book."

Theresa looked at her sideways. "B, no you didn't. You said you didn't get what she was trying to do. That it was too *hard* for you to read." Theresa started laughing. "Girl, you *know* you need to quit!"

"I said I didn't *get* it; not I didn't *like* it. There's a big difference, you know."

Theresa got up and started toward the kitchen. "Let me fix you a plate. I cooked some of George's favorite foods thinking he might be hungry when he got in from his trip. No need in us letting good food go to waste." Theresa stopped and turned around. "But on the serious side, B. From all George told me when he called, her husband and child really need some serious prayers."

"Oh, I'm gonna pray for them," B said. "When I get home—"

"B, you *know* you're lying. You're not even thinking about praying for nobody. You're going to go home and fall over into your bed. How you can even manage to sit there and form your mouth to lie like that is beyond me."

"Girl, get out of my business! You don't know what I do. Besides, my name *is* Conlie, remember? I realize I only acquired the name through a series of misfortunes, not counting my son, of course. But I guess that's why I married Tyrone in the first place. We were more alike than I knew. I believe people, more often than not, get together with people who mirror some of themselves."

"Oh, no. Not that name thing again. Maybe I ought to pay a little more attention to your theory. You seem to have given much study to it. Me, I'm still stuck on the opposites attract theory."

"Cliché, girl. Whose theory was that? Einstein's? I mean, have you seen *his* hair? You'd best to let go of that old school, and get with the new program."

* * *

That night, Theresa prayed a long, fervent prayer for Johnnie Mae Taylor and her family. Only she couldn't help but wonder—in her heart of hearts—was she praying for Johnnie Mae's sake? Or, was it really for her own?

CHAPTER 4

Cast Not Away Your Confidence

George was at the hospital when he called Theresa on Thursday night. Although he had intended to leave Friday, he couldn't seem to make himself go. Physically, Johnnie Mae was exhausted. Solomon was in a coma. And Princess Rose was being kept sedated. Visiting hours for both were limited, only fifteen minutes each time, and to a small number of visitors at a time. George couldn't leave Johnnie Mae knowing how hard it was for her to maintain the front she was displaying for family and friends.

He told Theresa, when they spoke Friday, that he would definitely be back by Saturday night. She said she understood, but he wasn't so sure she did. Landris and Johnnie Mae's mother, Mrs. Gates, kept a prayer vigil in the waiting room. He'd been in to see both Solomon and Princess Rose twice. The second time, Johnnie Mae asked if he would pray and lay hands on them. He did.

Johnnie Mae had known Landris was changing. Shortly after he left Alabama back in July of 1998, he started attending a church just outside of Atlanta. Moved by a minister who spoke and taught on spiritual things that could be used in practical, everyday life, he decided to give his life to Christ. When Princess Rose was born, Landris had sent Johnnie Mae roses along with a note he knew that she alone would understand. But Johnnie Mae called him after she got home from the hospital and asked him to "please not do anything like that again."

Honey had always been suspicious of their relationship, not quite buying into their claim of just being close friends. And Solomon was beginning to catch the little things Honey or Sister would "accidentally" say. Johnnie Mae didn't need the added hassle of dealing with Solomon having doubts about their own relationship, or the paternity of their child. Johnnie Mae knew, no matter what the truth, when a man starts to doubt, it's hard to make him believe differently.

Landris had called about a month before she had her number changed and kept it as unlisted. It hadn't been changed because of him, but because of the half-million-dollar book deal she had just signed. When word got out, people started calling from everywhere. And everybody and his brother had a soon-to-be-best-selling book they needed her to help them birth into the world. By the time Johnnie Mae realized she hadn't given Landris the new number, Landris himself had moved and gotten an unlisted number.

Johnnie Mae knew he had been called to preach eight months after Princess Rose was born. Three months later, he was asked to pastor a small church with a loyal membership of exactly thirty-seven. That was about the last time they talked. But Johnnie Mae knew that anything Landris truly believed in, he would give his whole heart and soul to.

And Pastor Landris was diligent about getting into the streets and harvesting lily-ripe fields. After that, the church grew faster than he alone could keep up with, forcing him to get a private number.

It wasn't until Johnnie Mae turned on the television (she rarely watched TV) one Sunday evening about two months before that she found her lost friend. She couldn't believe it! But she was even more impressed with his anointed persona. Johnnie Mae wasn't into many televangelists; it was just too easy to spot the phony, money-hungry ones. For her, anyway. She felt sorry for those who believed so much that they would send their hard-to-come-by money in exchange for a miracle or breakthrough from someone who was clearly a scam artist. Some televangelists were sincere, though. And she was glad to see that George Landris could be counted among that small but faithful few.

"Why didn't you or somebody call me about the accident?" Landris asked Johnnie Mae on Saturday night as they sat in the Children's Hospital cafeteria a little after six P.M. He had finally convinced her to break up her routine—MICU at University, then PICU at Children's Hospital, and then back to the waiting room—for a bite to eat.

"Landris, besides my not having your number, I didn't think about calling anyone. All I've truly thought about is my husband and little girl getting better—having Solomon look at me and smile and Princess Rose call me Mommie. Everybody who found out got the news from either my mother or Donald. Donald even went as far as to get the hospital to not release any information except to the people he had listed."

"Yeah, I'm familiar with that list. I called from Atlanta before finally having to drive over. It was as though you guys didn't exist. I checked with all the hospitals I *thought* you might be in but still came up empty. Finally, when I did locate what turned out to be the right hospital, my name wasn't on the list. So they still couldn't tell me anything." He took a sip of soda. "The woman in information tried calling the number listed, but no one ever answered it."

"That's Donald, all right. I don't know why he did that. Trying to keep people from bothering us, I suppose. But I love that people care enough to check on us. I did have the hospital take that note off. And I'm sorry you had to go to so much trouble. Going so far as to have to drive all the way here."

He smiled. "It's no problem. I'm just glad I found you. I had to be sure for myself that you and your family were okay."

Johnnie Mae asked Landris about his life these days. He told her about the church. How much he and the church had grown both spiritually and physically strong. How much he *loved* what he was doing. And how much having Jesus as the center of his joy had not only changed his whole life, but his whole outlook on life.

"Have you gotten married yet?" Johnnie Mae asked.

Landris smiled. "Not quite."

"Not quite? What does 'not quite' mean?"

"I'm engaged. Set to be married this December thirtieth."

"Wow, that's great! I bet she's a wonderful person. Has to be."

Landris grinned. "Yeah, most folks think so. She's been in the church all of her life. Knows the Bible from Genesis to Revelation. She works with the youth and the Drama Ministry. Her father is a preacher . . . the Bishop Richard Jordan. Her mother's really nice, too—Beatrice. Everybody keeps telling me how fortunate I am to have snagged her. Theresa, that's her name. Theresa Jordan. Anyway, I believe we'll be happy."

"Believe?"

He looked down, shook his head, then looked back at Johnnie Mae. "That's why I don't like talking to you."

"Why? Because I know you so well?" She tried not to smile.

"No. Because you *think* you know me so well."

"Let me ask you a question, Landris. Or should I call you Pastor Landris now that you're this big pastor of this big-time church?" she teased.

"Landris is fine. I'm still, technically, the same person. Just got brand new hands, feet, tongue, heart, and changed my hanging-out partner."

"This Theresa. Tell me: Do you love her?"

Landris pushed a fry in his mouth and took another sip of soda. "Now, what kind of a question is that to ask?"

She bowed her head, let her chin rest on her fist, and leaned forward. "One that you really should know the answer to without having to stall for time."

"Theresa," he began, "is a *very* special woman. She's smart, funny, a great cook. She would make any man proud to call her his wife. And like I said, when it comes to church stuff . . . she's on it."

"Landris, the question is a simple one to answer. Do you love her? Did you pray about her becoming your wife?"

He looked at her. "Johnnie Mae, I'm going to be honest with you. I did pray. I prayed hard. But here lately . . . in my spirit—"

Just then an announcement boomed across the intercom. "Mrs. Johnnie Mae Taylor, please report to the PICU nurses' station immediately. Johnnie Mae Taylor, you're needed at the PICU nurses' station immediately!"

Johnnie Mae jumped up. "Princess Rose!" she said. "I've got to get up there!"

Landris was right with her, racing toward the elevator. She pressed the up button several times as though that would make the elevator arrive faster.

"She's going to be all right, you know," he said, trying to calm her. "Don't panic now. You've got to keep your head about you."

"Landris, I don't know what I'll do if something happens to my baby. That little girl has completely changed my life."

"I know," Landris said, stepping into the opened elevator. It slowly began to rise; he wished it would go faster.

They hurried to the nurses' station. "I'm Johnnie Mae Taylor—"

"Thank God you were close," Nurse Brown said. "Dr. Shuller needs to see you immediately. He's on his way up now. In the meantime, we need help in getting blood of your daughter's type. The problem: supply is generally low during the Christmas season. When people think of giving, they don't consider the gift of life. Your daughter is type A negative, which means she needs to be matched with another A. Were she type O or AB, it wouldn't be such a task, because both O and AB will successfully transfuse from any type. We had a hold on her type when she came in, but some things happened—tornadoes, bad weather, and this time of year it's not easy to get her type. Unfortunately, time is not a luxury."

"What about my blood type?" Johnnie Mae said. "My blood should match my own daughter's, shouldn't it?"

"We called over to University already to get your type; you're O positive."

"Then I'll find somebody. I'll get some bodies in here. Someone has to match her. I'll do whatever it takes—" Johnnie Mae said, then looked at Landris.

"Mrs. Taylor," Nurse Brown said, watching a young doctor striding quickly their way, "here's Dr. Shuller now. Dr. Shuller, this is Mrs. Taylor."

Dr. Shuller took Johnnie Mae to an area where he could explain what was going on without interruption. Landris stayed at the nurses' station.

The doctor told Johnnie Mae that Princess Rose might need a whole blood transfusion, as opposed to separated blood. With massive internal bleeding, if they didn't operate within the hour, Princess Rose would essentially drown to death in her own blood. Then there was the cause of her bleeding, which needed attention. But without blood on hand in case of complications, it would be risky to operate. "A risk, Mrs. Taylor, I feel necessary and am prepared to take."

Johnnie Mae began to rub her head. All of this was too much.

"Mrs. Taylor, I'm not trying to upset you; I just want you to know how serious it is. I can't promise how things will turn out with this particular surgery, but I can tell you this: Without it, your daughter won't make it through the night." He moved in closer. "Mrs. Taylor, I want you aware of what needs to be done in what will be a short amount of time. Certainly, not the time for me to play word games. I'm not holding anything back. Is there anything you need to ask me?"

"Doctor, is my baby going to be all right?" Johnnie Mae was shaking. "She *just* celebrated her second birthday. In fact, we were coming home the night of the accident after her birthday party at Chuck-E-Cheese's. She loves that place. Her birthday was Monday,

December eighteenth. It snowed Sunday . . . can you believe that? Snow in the middle of December in Alabama?"

Dr. Shuller could see she was slightly losing it now. "Mrs. Taylor—"

"Monday night there were still slick spots. Our car slid onto a sheet of black ice. We were doing fine, until an eighteen-wheeler hit the same ice and slammed dead into us." She saw the night just as it had unfolded, recalling Solomon slumped at the wheel . . . not moving. *Princess Rose?* She couldn't turn around to see about Princess Rose. It seemed like it took such a long time to be freed from the wreckage. Sirens, loud . . . everywhere. The jaws of life. The ride to the hospital. "I had Princess Rose buckled in her car seat in the back seat, but I couldn't turn to see her. I was so scared."

"Mrs. Taylor, I promise we'll do all we can to ensure you'll be taking that little angel home soon. Having her in the back seat of the car, secured correctly in an approved car seat, actually saved her life." He shook his head. "You have no idea how many times I have had to tell a parent their child didn't make it because of either no car seat or an incorrectly installed one." He took a breath and let it out slowly. "Now, let's see about you signing some papers so we can get her all fixed up—good as new. And let's hope Nurse Brown has some good news about that blood we're in desperate need of."

"Dr. Shuller, if we don't get a match for her blood type—"

"Then let me make sure you completely understand this: Your daughter *must* have surgery within the hour. If there's no match available, we're going to have to take our chances and deal with that then. Mrs. Taylor, it's so serious that I'd rather take our odds with not having the exact blood type on hand, than the odds of losing her while we try and find a match. We can't wait while she continues to bleed internally like she's doing now. We may have to use saline or pump her wide-open with type O. We'll just have to see."

"Well, I'll see what I can do to find someone to match her . . ."

"Regardless, I plan on performing the surgery within the hour," he said. "With or without a match."

When Johnnie Mae returned, Landris was nowhere to be found. She couldn't believe it, but figured he had already left to go home. Deep down, she hated that he hadn't stayed just a little longer, just a little while longer. But there was no time to worry about that now. The only thing of importance was locating a blood donor now. Anyone. Anyone who would safely match Princess Rose. For the doctor had just made it undeniably clear that the tide set against them was steadily rising . . . with each passing moment.

CHAPTER 5

Cry Aloud, Spare Not

Everyone Johnnie Mae could get in touch with, she had called. Six people had come and were willing to see if their blood type would match, when Nurse Brown informed Johnnie Mae fifteen minutes before Princess Rose was to go into surgery, "There's no need. We have a match," she said. "A perfect match!"

Johnnie Mae let out a sigh.

"You must have a direct line upstairs," Nurse Brown said. "I mean, it wasn't fifteen minutes after I told you about the blood problem that the people in the lab were calling to tell me someone had shown up wanting to donate blood. And, don't you worry, they always screen donated blood for AIDS as well as for hepatitis. The blood checked out fine, so everything is a go."

"I don't know about a direct line, but I certainly am grateful my prayers were heard. I can definitely use all the help I can get down here." Johnnie Mae smiled.

A room full of people were in the waiting area as Princess Rose was whisked into surgery. It was only then that Johnnie Mae wondered again why Landris had left when he did without so much as a good-bye.

More than an hour had passed since they had taken Princess

Rose in. Johnnie Mae was so restless, she decided to take a walk all the way down to the other nurses' station. The two nurses on duty smiled at her as they continued their routine. The blond-headed nurse was frowning as she spoke nonstop to a handsome, bald, black male nurse.

"I'm telling you the truth! You know how fast things travel through the hospital grapevine," the blond nurse said. "Nurse Brown said they had this patient who desperately needed type A negative blood for a possible transfusion. Now you *know* how difficult that is to come by, especially this time of year. No one wanted to tell the mother that the chances of finding a match weren't likely." She wrote something on a chart. "Anyway, Nurse Brown said there was this minister who just *happened* to be hanging around at the time."

"Oh, I know where this is going," the male nurse said.

"No, now . . . just listen. Anyway, he asked Nurse Brown a few questions about blood type and about relatives matching. Then he asked where one could find out what type blood one was and about possibly donating. But then," she said, lowering her voice, "Nurse Brown said he asked the strangest thing."

"What was that?"

"He wanted to know how you would go about specifying who your blood goes to. Of course, Nurse Brown told him. The next thing she knew, they were calling her with a match for her latest request. And . . ." she said, smiling, "that it was *specifically* requested to be used for, ironically, the same little girl who needed it, with less than a half hour to spare! Nurse Brown believes it was from that minister."

"God does work in mysterious ways! I mean, what are the chances that a total stranger would be hanging around with the same blood type as someone needing it that same hour? Now you *know* that was God!"

"Oh now, it's not as big a deal as all that. I should have known you'd go get religious on me. But I did think it was interesting how all that played out so . . . so . . . oh, all right . . . so divinely!"

Johnnie Mae covered her mouth as she began to cry. "Landris," she whispered. "It had to have been Landris. But how—"

Dr. Shuller came over and saw her crying. "Mrs. Taylor . . . it's over." He began to smile. "Everything is functioning just as it should now. And that blood, whoever the donor was, came in right on time. Turns out, she needed it after all. I was thankful. That was one less crisis we didn't have to work through."

Johnnie Mae began to cry harder. "Oh thank you, Doctor. Thank you," she said. "When can I see her? When can I see my baby?"

"You can look in right now, if you'd like. But we can't stay but a minute." He led her to Princess Rose. She looked so peaceful. "My guess, she'll be coming out of it in another hour or two. I know she'll be glad to see you."

Johnnie Mae began to laugh through her tears. *My baby would be opening her eyes soon! She was going to be all right.* Johnnie Mae went into the waiting room to share the good news. It was after nine o'clock, and she understood that all her friends and family had to leave. Each one promised to come back tomorrow after church. She just knew *she* wasn't about to budge tonight.

"You sure you'll be all right here alone?" her mother asked as they stood downstairs in the lobby. "Now, I don't mind staying. . . ."

"Yes, Mama. I'll be fine. You go on home and get some rest. I'll see you tomorrow. One of my prayers is close to being answered. Now if only Solomon would just—"

"He will," her mother said. "He will. The doctors are doing all they know for him. Didn't you say today when you were there that everyone said he was showing steady signs of improvement?"

"That's what they said. I'll check on him first thing in the morning. Maybe when I tell him about Princess Rose . . . especially if I can tell him she has opened her eyes, he'll fight even harder himself."

The family left together, Donald making sure all the women were safe inside their vehicles.

Johnnie Mae went back upstairs to the nurses' station. "I'll be in the waiting room for a few minutes," she said, her voice sounding a bit tired. "If my daughter so much as twitches, please come let me know."

They smiled. "Will do, Mrs. Taylor."

Johnnie Mae walked into the waiting room, frozen as she let go of the door. "Landris? But I thought—"

"How is she?" Landris asked, trying to force a smile of confidence.

Johnnie Mae grinned. "The doctor says she's going to be fine. Better than fine. In fact, he said she could awaken within the next hour."

"That's good to hear."

"So . . . where did you disappear to?" she asked.

He looked at her sideways. "I had some business to take care of. Something that couldn't wait."

"Landris, I know what you did—the blood. But how? How did you know?"

He sat back against the chair. "Let's just say, I was praying it would." He looked at her. "Johnnie Mae . . . you know you and I need to talk, don't you?"

"I know, but not now." She sat down beside him. "So . . . when are you going back to Atlanta? I know you have to be at your own church tomorrow."

"I can leave about five in the morning; that'll be six o'clock in Atlanta. If I get home around eight or so, I should be at the church by ten, piece of cake." He smiled. "Look . . . I already turned in my room key earlier. So, I figured if you don't mind some company, I could just hang out here with you until the morning."

"Landris, you know you don't have to do this. I'm fine."

"I know. But what are friends for? And I can drop you off on my way out at University so you can check on Solomon—if you'd like." He grinned. "Since I did bring you here in my car today, I would *technically* be leaving you stranded if I didn't drop you off."

"Walking's good for people. I wouldn't mind if I had to walk." She looked up at the ceiling, leaned her head back, then looked at the floor before glancing at him again. "Would you like to go in with me and sit with Princess Rose? I don't want her to wake up and I not be there."

"Sure. If you don't mind my infringing on family time."

"I don't think now is the time to be getting technical. From what I hear, your blood may have helped to save her life," Johnnie Mae said with a laugh. She stood and stretched her neck from one side to the other.

Landris looked at her. He could see she was tired, and he was even more impressed with the strength of a woman. It was almost eleven in Atlanta now. Theresa would surely be asleep. He decided against calling, possibly waking her up again. At church tomorrow, he would see her. Maybe by then, he would be better able to explain why he had stayed in Birmingham for what would be three whole days. That conversation, he knew, would come . . . soon enough.

CHAPTER 6

Lay Thy Foundation with Sapphires

At Sunday morning services, almost everyone was wondering where Pastor Landris was. It was Christmas Eve day, and they just knew he would have a powerful message ready to set their hearts on fire.

Theresa knew this was serious. George didn't miss a service. Minister Huntley, an associate minister, did a nice job. No one suspected he had only learned he would be preaching at six that morning. Pastor Landris had called him after speaking with Deacon Thomas.

"Seems an emergency Pastor Landris had gone to see about out of town, took an unexpected turn," Deacon Thomas said during announcement time. "Pastor Landris had intended to be here this morning, but something beyond his control transpired. He asked that I wish you all a Merry Christmas, and to remind you of the importance of counting all your blessings this holiday season."

Of course, Minister Huntley was thrilled to be chosen to fill in. He knew the church would be packed. There were just certain days when folks made more of an effort to show up at church, like Christmas and Easter. Minister Huntley didn't really care why they had come, he was just glad he'd get the chance to deliver a message he had written months ago. He'd already fine-tuned it, and even practiced it in front of the mirror several times. Today was the day he got to hear it bounce off a congregation and come back to him. And he did like what he heard! Seems the people did, too.

Theresa sat there the whole time trying to look as though she knew what was going on, although she had no idea George wasn't going to be there. He'd told her he would be back no later than Saturday night. Yet there wasn't a call, a message, or anything from him. *What is he trying to prove?* she wondered while continuing to pretend everything was fine. *What is going on?*

All eyes turned toward her when the secretary read the announcement regarding the "special ceremony, our own Pastor Landris and Sister Theresa Jordan's wedding being held at the church on this Saturday, December thirtieth, at two o'clock in the afternoon." People grinned and nodded in her direction as she plastered a smile on her face. *Oh, yeah. George has a lot of explaining to do!*

"Ready for your big day?" Sapphire said as soon as the benediction was uttered and she could reach Theresa. Sapphire didn't bother with a last name. Most folks didn't realize she even had one. She and Theresa were tight, so of course Theresa knew what it was: Drummond. Sapphire Renee Drummond.

"Girl, your hair looks *gooood!*" Sapphire said, standing back to get a better overall look. "B knows she can put the hurt on a hairstyle. I should let her do something different with mine one of these days. When I'm ready to change, that is."

Sapphire was a beautiful, dark chocolate woman, with dreadlocks down to the middle of her back. She'd been growing her dreads for over fourteen years—back before it was fashionable or acceptable. That was what Theresa liked about her: She didn't care what people thought, or whether or not they approved of what she did or did not do. Yes, she was a black woman, with dreadlocks, and a first name but no last, who used her anger to fuel her purpose and desires, practiced the best form of revenge, called "succeeding," and was as smart as they came. This thirty-five-year-old was intelligent. She was somebody going somewhere to happen!

Theresa was the caramel colored, traditional perm-and-curls (except when B got in one of her funky moods and tried something new on her head) type, who wore curls, twists, scrunches, rods, scrimps, waves, and occasional French rolls, was dubbed the Goody-Two-Shoes of the bunch, hardly caused any problems, and who not only liked to—but usually did—get her way. Most believed her mother, Beatrice, and father, Bishop Jordan, were the cause of her being so spoiled. But she did love God, Jesus, her church, and her pastor, and knew the Bible as though she had been the one to painstakingly translate each word of it into English.

B was more of a mahogany tone—like a nice stain on strong wood, the only one who didn't make you think of food when you saw her (although she was a beautiful size fourteen), but rather something that belonged in your home to admire and be comfortable in. B liked braids, but it "wasn't nothing but a thang" for her to whack off her hair, slick it down, or bush it out. She was the free spirit of the bunch who would definitely tell it like it t-i-s, tis! Just don't make her mad. And if there's ever a fight, you'd be wise to make sure you're on her team, because B could grip a thing and tear it to shreds with her bare teeth.

Theresa was the shortest of the three—5'5"; Sapphire, the tallest at 5'9"; and B stretched in at 5'7". When people saw them out somewhere together, they were often teasingly asked, "So, what's the name of your little group?" B was the one who would respond, "Five-Seven-Nine, and we can't help it that we're fine!"

Sapphire and Theresa stood just beyond the steps outside the church. "What time should I come over?" Sapphire asked.

"Come over?" Theresa said, nodding as people spoke.

"Yeah, for Christmas. You remember your folks invited me to share Christmas with all of you at their house? I was wondering what time you were planning on being there."

"Oh, yeah. Tomorrow *is* Christmas, isn't it?"

"Theresa, what is wrong with you lately? You aren't getting nervous about the wedding, are you?"

Theresa returned a wave to Sister Velma. "No, just got a lot on my mind."

"I suppose so. First Christmas, then this gargantuan wedding. How many people are you expecting again?"

"About three thousand for real. Most of the church will probably be there. That's why we had to rent the center for the other reception. After we have the traditional reception here at the church, we're going over to the center for the sit-down dinner. Of course, that's the one by invitation only."

"Yeah, I know. I just love hearing you talk about it. It's going to be some wedding! You'll definitely end this year with a bang. Then begin it with the man of your dreams."

"You're such a sap!" B said as she walked up behind Sapphire and gave her a hug. "You know there's no such animal as a dream man or such a thing as happily ever after! Sorry, Theresa. Not trying to zap the positive energy out of your new life to come. I just hate folks that walk around in Paradise Island."

"B, just because *you* can't get a man and keep him doesn't mean that's everybody else's problem. You change men like most women change their stockings," Sapphire said.

"Yeah, you're right. Every time one gets a run in it, I throw the sucker out! No need in going through life looking tacky because of some uncomfortable old habit." B picked up a strand of Sapphire's hair and let it fall back down. "And you *know* what I say about a man who is no longer servicing my needs."

"And what's that?" Sapphire said.

"Next!"

"Oooh, you ladies are cold," Maurice said as he walked over and kissed B on the cheek. "Sapphire, My Queen. You look lovely as ever." He directed his loving attention to Sapphire's long legs that ended at the hem of her miniskirt.

"Maurice," Sapphire said, pretending to turn up her nose at his cute self.

Theresa looked away. She'd been searching for an opening to get out of this conversation and over to her car. It was hard for her to concentrate while she wondered where her fiancé was. She could not *believe* George hadn't called to tell her he wouldn't be at church. And now, standing before her smiling, was the last man on earth she ever wanted to talk to—in this lifetime, anyway.

Maurice touched Theresa's arm. "Say, T . . . I said, how's it going?"

Before she had time to think, she had snatched her arm away, like he was acid or something. "I've *asked* you not to call me T," Theresa said. *In fact, I've asked you not to come around, talk to me, or look in my direction.* That was what else she wanted to say, but didn't. "Look, people . . . I've got things I need to handle. Sapphire, I'll see you tomorrow around one. B, I'll talk with you soon."

"What about me? You gonna dis a brother, just like that? You know, I knew you when—back before you were about to marry some big-time preacher."

"Maurice, don't take this personally, but the only thing you *really* got going for you—in my humble opinion—is that you happen to be B's brother. Merry Christmas, all!" Theresa said, then strolled away.

"I don't know *what* you did to her, brother," B said, "but I'd say she *definitely* hates your guts."

"Girl, now you know better than that. You know what they say . . . there's a thin line between love and hate."

"Well, all I know is, Theresa is hardly ever rude to anyone. I sure wish I knew what you did."

"Maybe it's not so much what I *did*, but what I *didn't* do. You ever think about that, sister dearest? You always think the worst about a thing, B." He sighed hard. "See the sandwich as half-left instead of half-eaten, why don't you?"

* * *

Theresa threw down her purse when she walked into her apartment. She checked her answering machine. No messages! *Where is he?!* Now she *wanted* to be mad. That way she could tell him exactly how she really felt. But she was also worried that something bad might have happened to him. Minister Huntley did say George called him this morning and asked that he fill his shoes today. So if anything had happened, it would have been after he called Deacon Thomas and Minister Huntley this morning. *And just why did he call Minister Huntley and Deacon Thomas and not me?* she wondered.

Deacon Thomas had mentioned he spoke with Pastor Landris early this morning, saying, "Pastor expressed his sincere wish for all to have a wonderful Christmas." *If he cared so much, then why wasn't he here to tell them himself?*

And everybody seemed to want to talk about the wedding. But Theresa wasn't so sure there was still going to be one. Not until she and George had a heart-to-heart talk. From the looks of things, those premarital counseling sessions they attended for twelve weeks didn't seem to have helped their relationship much. It was billed as a time for them to get to know the *real person* they were about to commit their lives to. Now that she thought about it: *How well did she really know Pastor George Landris? Really?*

For sure, she never would have figured him to have up and left to see about some friend—who happened to be a woman, famous or not—and not return for three days. That's one she would have flunked, had it been on a test.

Oh yes, Pastor Landris just might find himself good and embarrassed come Saturday. Let him explain why there will be no wedding. I love him and all, but I don't have to take crap off nobody. And I mean that thing, too! Being the doormat gets old after awhile. Oh yeah, we're going to have a good long talk! And he'd best be on better terms with me before we go to my folk's house tomorrow. Cause he knows . . . Daddy doesn't play, when it comes to his little girl!

* * *

At five that evening, the phone rang. Theresa snatched it up, just knowing it was George on the other end. *Finally! Finally!*

"Hello," she said roughly.

"Theresa?" a woman said.

She sounded familiar, but Theresa couldn't quite place her voice. "Yes?"

"How are you? This is Lena."

Theresa sat down and rubbed her head. Lena Patterson. *Lord*, she thought, *I do not need this now!* "I'm fine, and you?" she said in a much friendlier tone.

"Doing fine. Getting ready to catch my bus what leaves early in the morning."

"Your bus? Where are you headed?" Theresa really didn't care, but it didn't hurt to let her think she did.

"Why, I'm on my way down there. Beatrice . . . Jordan invited me for Christmas. I thought she and Richard had told you."

"My mother? My mother invited you for Christmas?"

Lena was quiet for a second. "Yes, Richard's wife." Lena always felt the extra effort Theresa seemed to make in expressing her love and protection for Beatrice. Whenever Lena mentioned her, it was as though it gave Theresa added pleasure in being able to let Lena know *precisely* where her heart and loyalty lay when it came to her mother.

"I just wanted to call before I left and wish you Merry Christmas. I usually call early Christmas morn, but my bus won't pull in until around 10 A.M. It leaves here around 2:00 A.M. It's not *that* far from Winston-Salem to Atlanta. There's just that Charlotte layover."

"Well, Merry Christmas to you. Thanks for the call," Theresa said, again trying to sound sincere. "Oh . . . how long were you planning to stay?"

"Until Sunday evening. Now you know I've got to see you walk down that aisle all so beautiful. I wouldn't miss your wedding on Saturday for anything in this world."

Theresa couldn't believe it. Lena was actually coming down for her wedding. *How could my parents do this to me?* The most important day of her life, and now Lena was going to be there. At her wedding!

Theresa knew her mother and father were trying to do the right thing by inviting her. She just wished her parents had left that decision to her. Theresa had already planned to send Lena a set of photos—a videotape of the ceremony, even. *Why on earth would they invite her to come all the way from North Carolina just to be stared at? And they know people are going to stare, what with her messed up face and hands.*

Theresa was aware of her condition, and still *she* didn't deal with it well. *So how do they expect other people who have no idea to handle it? And for my wedding, at that!* Oh, and there were going to be plenty of people around to stare. Plenty.

Theresa could have managed her being there for Christmas. Fine. But her wedding? She couldn't believe Lena would be attending it.

Back when Theresa was young, she used to believe God hadn't been able to make up His mind what shade of black He wanted Lena to be. So He decided to make her mixed—dark in some places, light in others, with an unevenness that made her face and hands appear more like a bumpy road. Her scarred right eye sagged the way an old woman's skin tends to hang off her outstretched arms.

Theresa knew Lena couldn't help the way she looked; that it wasn't her fault. She'd heard about the fire Lena was in, all Lena had gone through, the pain she continued to suffer—even after so many years. *But, God! Did she have to make everybody else have to deal with it, too? To have to look at her when it was so difficult not to want to turn away? And now . . . at her wedding?*

Theresa learned a long time ago to keep her true feelings about Lena to herself. Most folks thought it was *she* who was wrong. And anyone who ever met Lena, seemed to instantly fall in love with her—hands, face, and all. Even Beatrice, her mother, or, as Lena liked to put it, "Richard's wife," whom Theresa was overprotective of, simply adored her. Theresa wanted to know where Lena got off still calling her father Richard, just because she knew him first. *He is a bishop now. She should—if for no other reason than respect—* Theresa thought, *call him Bishop.*

But Lena wasn't just coming for Christmas. She would definitely be there for Theresa's wedding too. And Theresa was sure her father and mother would insist on Lena being part of her wedding photos and the escorted-in ceremony.

"Let's get some pictures," her father would say to the photographer. "Lena, Theresa, come on now. Stand close, you two." He would then lean back on his heels and smile, as though he had created a new great wonder of the world. Then he would likely say, "Now, that's a beautiful picture!"

It wasn't that Theresa minded being nice to Lena (Lena had never done a thing to her). Her concern was that everybody would see her; they would stare at her, they would see them all together, and they would know. Know, that as ugly and messed up as Lena was, she was, in fact, her mother. Her *real* mother.

CHAPTER 7

Not by Power Nor by Might

George called Theresa right after she hung up with Lena.

"Theresa—"

"Where are you?! You haven't called. I get to church and I look like a complete idiot because I didn't even know you weren't going to be there!"

"Hey," he said, "calm down. I was calling to let you know I'm on my way home now."

"So why are you just now calling me? Why didn't you call this morning and tell me you weren't going to be here? The last time we talked, you were going to be here by Saturday night. It's Sunday night now, George. I'm sitting in church expecting to see you, and you're nowhere to be found."

"Theresa, I'll be home in about two-and-a-half hours. I'll call you when I get there."

"So, where are you now?"

"What?"

"I said, where are you now?"

George shook his head as he looked around the den area. "I'm at Johnnie Mae Taylor's house. But Theresa . . . it's not at all what you're thinking."

Theresa sighed long and hard. "That's interesting, George. Real interesting. Tell me, how could you *possibly* know what I'm thinking?"

"Theresa—"

"I'll talk with you later. Good-bye, George." She hung up.

George stepped into the kitchen. "Well, I suppose I'm out of here. I've got to get on down this road. Remember, if you need me, just call. You have my numbers at home, church, and my cellular, as well as my e-mail addresses at home and at church." George walked over and gave Mrs. Gates a quick, tight hug. "Don't you worry now, I believe everything's going to be fine from here on out."

Mrs. Gates smiled. "Thank you again, Pastor Landris. You've been a godsend, for sure. I'll keep your numbers handy but don't expect we'll be needing them. With all these numbers and addresses, you could have your own personal phone book."

"Will you please tell Johnnie Mae good-bye for me? And let her know I'm here if she needs anything . . . anything at all."

"Of course. She was *so* exhausted. I'm just glad you were able to talk her into coming home for a few hours. None of us have been able to get her to budge."

"Just happy I could help."

"You certainly have a way with my daughter. She can be stubborn sometimes. If she gives us any more trouble, I may need to call you," she said, teasingly.

Landris adjusted the collar of his overcoat as he walked outside to his car. He was also tired. Today had turned into a full day, beginning with the emergency page Johnnie Mae received at four in the morning from University Hospital about Solomon. They'd loaned her the pager specifically for that purpose.

Solomon had come out of his coma, but there were complications soon after he opened his eyes. Landris had taken Johnnie Mae to the hospital, but didn't want to leave without knowing what was going on with Solomon. Johnnie Mae told him he didn't need to stay, but he wasn't about to drop her off and leave her at the curb. She went in to see Solomon; Landris stayed in the waiting room.

"Hi there, beautiful," Solomon said as soon as he saw her face.

Johnnie Mae smiled, covering her mouth as she laughed out a cry. "Solomon. How are you feeling?"

"I believe I'll live and not die," he said. It was something that he and Johnnie Mae said when they weren't feeling so well about a thing, but were walking it by faith.

She brushed his face with the back of her hand. "It's so good to see you," she said. "You had me worried there for awhile."

"Princess Rose?" He was almost afraid to ask. "How's Princess Rose?"

"Oh, you should have heard her talking up a storm around one this morning."

He swallowed hard. "So she's okay? You're sure she's okay?"

Johnnie Mae wondered whether she should tell him, but she knew he would want to know the truth. "It was touch-and-go earlier, but the doctor says she's going to be fine. She had to have a blood transfusion after emergency surgery last night, but she's doing better already."

"She had to have blood?"

"Yes."

"They screened the blood, right?"

"Of course. Solomon," she smiled and held his hand, "guess who came all the way from Atlanta just to check on us?"

Solomon closed his eyes. "Who?" he said.

"George Landris. He's a minister . . . a pastor now. He heard about the accident, but Donald had it so the hospital wasn't giving out any information. So, he just drove to Birmingham to check on us."

"Johnnie Mae," Solomon said, "how are you doing? Are you okay?"

"Yeah . . . sure. I got banged around a bit, but I believe I'll live and not die."

He turned his head away from her. "I am *so* sorry, so very sorry. Can you ever forgive me for—"

Johnnie Mae squeezed his hand. "Solomon . . . don't. Let's not go there."

He turned and looked up at her. "I was wrong. We shouldn't have been arguing about something so silly. I love you, and you were right. I haven't been there for you like I should have. I didn't consider how you wanted more out of life and our marriage than I have been willing to give. I realize we should have gone on more trips together . . . to . . . dinner . . . dancing . . . an occasional movie. It shouldn't have been *just* what I wanted or didn't want to do. Marriage is a team sport—give-and-take. If I hadn't been so focused on making *my* point, being right that night, I would have seen the black ice. And none of this would have ever happened. . . ."

Johnnie Mae leaned down and kissed him on his lips. "Hush. Let's not talk about this now. It's in the past, okay? In the scheme of things, it's really not that important. What is important is for you to get well and to come home."

Dr. Adams came in. "Good morning, Mr. Taylor, Mrs. Taylor." He proceeded to tell them what was going on. Solomon's immediate medical problem was requiring them to introduce red blood cells into his system. Explaining the procedure, he told them it would be administered as soon as everything was set. "But otherwise, you're doing a remarkable job of recovery, Mr. Taylor."

"Dr. Adams," Solomon began, "when do you think I can get out of here?"

"Anxious, are you?" He laughed. "Well, we'll have to see how you continue to respond to treatment. But if you keep on the path you're on, it's possible you'll be out of here within a week. Maybe less, maybe more."

A nurse walked in. "Dr. Adams?"

"Yes."

"We're ready to start with Mr. Taylor."

Dr. Adams smiled. "That was fast," he said.

"Yes, Doctor. Blood type A negative was in ready supply for a change."

Solomon laughed. "So I'm A negative, huh? And all this time I thought I was *a positive* person," he joked.

"Well Mr. Taylor, whether you know it or not, type A negative blood is rather hard to come by. Not as hard as AB negative, but hard enough. During this time of year, it's something not having to wait to locate it," the nurse said.

Johnnie Mae backed up against the wall and rested her head on it. "Mrs. Taylor, are you okay?" Dr. Adams asked. "Maybe you should sit down."

She stood up straight and smiled. "I'm fine. Just a little tired, I guess."

"Johnnie Mae?" Solomon said. "Have you even been home since this began?"

"I'm fine, Solomon. I'm not leaving you. Especially now. I'm fine . . . really."

"No you're *not* fine," Solomon said. "Dr. Adams, how long is this blood procedure thing supposed to take?"

"About an hour, if things go as planned."

Solomon reached out for Johnnie Mae's hand. "I want you to go home and get some rest, do you understand me?" He squeezed her hand and smiled.

"Solomon—"

"Johnnie Mae, I'm not about to let you run yourself into the ground. You can go home, get a little rest, and come back." He looked toward the door. "Who's here with you now?"

"With me? Now?"

"Are you here by yourself?" Solomon asked. "Is your mother not here with you? Donald? Your sister, Marie?"

Johnnie Mae looked away, then back at him. "No. Mama volunteered to stay last night, but I made her go home. Solomon, I'm not leaving; I don't care what you say."

Johnnie Mae went to the waiting room while Solomon was taken for treatment.

"How is he?" Landris asked.

"I think . . . God has answered my prayers twice in a row now. They're doing something with his red blood cells. You know . . . it occurred to me while I was in there with the doctor, your blood may be doing more than you ever thought when you decided to give."

"What do you mean?"

"Solomon needed blood type A negative, too." She sat down and looked at her watch. "It's a quarter after seven. Shouldn't you have left already?"

"I called the church and told them I wouldn't make it in time today."

"You did what?"

"Look, I wasn't going to leave until I knew what was happening. It's okay."

"Landris—"

"It's okay. Maybe you'll let me take you home to get some rest later on."

Johnnie Mae rubbed her eyes. "I'll tell you like I just told Solomon: I'm not going anywhere. Not just yet."

"Johnnie Mae, you can try to be superwoman all you want. Your little girl and your husband both are going to really need you. You can't give what you don't have. You're not completely well physically, and you know it. Besides, you're pushing yourself way past your limit. You mess around, and they'll be assigning *you* a bed from exhaustion and God knows what else. Then you'll be no good to anyone. Understand?"

"But—"

"But nothing. Either you care enough about your family to take care of yourself, or you don't. There's no in-between. I'll be glad to hang around as long as you need. I'll take you home, bring you back here, *then* I can leave for Atlanta."

"Landris, you don't have to do that. My car is here; I can drive myself. I'll just go home—"

"But you won't. So, I'm going to be sure that you do. Johnnie Mae . . . you know me. And you know that I know *you*. I don't play games; I never did. Now when you're ready, I'll take you home so you can get yourself some real rest. Then you'll be ready for another round of giving. Okay?"

Solomon was back in his room about ten. At noon, after he had fallen asleep and Johnnie Mae felt it was okay to leave, Landris took her, first to see Princess Rose, then home.

Eight-thirty that night, George pulled into the driveway of his elaborate Cascade Hills home. There sat Theresa—waiting in her car.

"God," he whispered (a request more than in vain), "please. Not now. I am too tired to deal with this right now."

Theresa stepped out of her little red two-door BMW and walked toward his car. "We need to talk," she said.

"Theresa, can't it wait? I am really tired. Really tired. I'd like to get in the shower—"

"No, George. No. It can't wait."

CHAPTER 8

Fire Shut Up in My Bones

Inside the spacious foyer, a large crystal chandelier set the tone for the rest of the house. George really wanted to get out of the clothes he'd worn since last night, but Theresa started in on him before they got past his study.

No, she didn't understand why he had to be gone for three days. No, she didn't see why he had to go in the first place. No, she wasn't planning on acting this way every time he had to go check on or see about someone. Yes, she understood what life would be like married to a preacher—she'd seen it played out most of her life. Yes, she realized she was *probably* overreacting. Yes, she held she had a right to the way she felt—at least she was owning her feelings. Yes, he owed her a better explanation. No, she was not being insecure. Yes, this *was* the time to be discussing this. No, she didn't care that he was tired.

"And what kind of a relationship did you two have that would cause you to just leave like you did and go see about her?" Theresa said.

"Theresa, Johnnie Mae and I have worked together. We're close friends."

"Did you and she ever date?"

"She's a married woman, Theresa. She was married when we first met, and she's still married to the same man today. He's a nice guy, from what I have gathered in meeting him, and for the most part . . . they seem happy together."

Theresa let some of the wind out of her chest. "Then what did you mean the other day when you said you *loved* her?"

George leaned his head back against his burgundy executive swivel chair and closed his eyes briefly. "*When* did I ever tell you I loved her?"

"Thursday—just before you left. You said something to the effect of loving somebody you never had." She began pacing again.

He opened his eyes, sat up, and leaned forward. "Theresa, is this supposed to be a preview of the rest of our life together? Everything I think, say, or do is suspect for an argument?" He stood up. "Theresa, look . . . I'm really tired. Really. I told you what happened these past few days. I don't know what else to say."

"Do you love me?" Theresa said.

"Now what kind of a question is that to ask?"

"George. Do you love me? Yes or no?"

"Yes, Theresa. Yes!" He laughed. "I love you. Now can we—"

"Do you love me like you love Johnnie Mae Taylor?"

He had a strange look on his face. Shaking his head, he said, "*What* is going on with you, Theresa? Why—"

"George . . . do you . . . love me . . . like you love Johnnie Mae Taylor? And George? Do remember that when you give me your answer, God sees and knows your heart. Do think about *that*, Pastor Landris."

"Theresa, the love I have for you and the love I have for Johnnie Mae are totally different. To ask do I love you like I love someone else is not even a fair question to pose, to anyone actually. The love a parent has for a child is different from the love they have for their spouse or friends. You love B and Sapphire both, but I'd venture to say not in the exact same way."

"All right then, George. Let me ask it this way: Were Mrs. Taylor not married—"

"But she is."

"But were she *not* married right now, would you be the least bit interested in pursuing a relationship with her? Beyond being *close* friends?"

"Theresa, this is silly. And I really don't feel like playing this little game with you."

"George, answer my question! Before God as your witness, answer my question! *If* Johnnie Mae Taylor were not married . . . right now . . . today, would you have any interest, at all, in marrying her?" She waited, pain covering her face.

George walked over to Theresa and gazed into her eyes. He could feel her pain, and it hurt him.

"George . . . before God."

"Yes, Theresa," he said, barely above a whisper. "If she were not married, she would be the kind of woman I would be interested in having in my life. But—" he rushed to add, "she is married. So that settles that. And it is therefore, a non-issue."

Theresa turned and ran out of the room, grabbing her coat, which was draped over a French chair in the foyer.

"Theresa!" George said as he walked quickly, chasing after her. "Theresa, wait!" Then he heard the front door slam shut.

George called her apartment for hours, but there was no answer. He hated that she was hurt right now, and pondered whether he should go over. He wondered if the truth really did make people free, or was it a burden in disguise? It was eleven-thirty P.M. and she still wasn't answering the phone. Tomorrow was Christmas; they were supposed to visit with Bishop and Mrs. Jordan. Saturday, he was scheduled to be married. But at the moment, his life seemed really messed up.

On the positive side, Johnnie Mae was on her way to having her family back. So at least, he'd been a part of something that seemed to have turned out right. *But what had I done? Maybe all things did work together for good to those who love the Lord.* In this case though, he couldn't help but wonder . . . to what and whose good? And just where could Theresa be at this late hour?

Theresa decided to stop off at B's place when she left George. "How dare he! Who does he think he is?!" she yelled in a whisper at the steering wheel of her car as she sat outside B's apartment complex.

She hadn't known where else to go . . . who else to talk to. Her father and mother didn't need to know what was going on. *I shouldn't have gone over to George's with an attitude*, she thought. *How else did I expect him to react?*

She had considered driving over to Sapphire's, but she knew Sapphire would likely take George's side. She'd just make her feel like, not only was she wrong for being such a nag, but that she was really the bad guy in all this. *Who would want to marry a whiny, insecure person anyway?* Sapphire would say. *I'd rather be with someone who has it together, too. Can you blame the man for saying he'd be more interested in marrying someone who probably doesn't fall apart at the first sign of trouble? You forced him to say that. You knew he was tired; you shouldn't have pushed him.* That's what Sapphire would most likely say. So, Theresa decided on B.

B was probably the only one she could totally spill her guts to, who would understand completely where she was coming from. B already felt George was wrong in the first place for having left like he did. *Why did he have to go to Birmingham and mess everything up?* They were doing fine before Thursday. Fine. Now look at them. Here it was Christmas Eve, and they weren't at all the lovey-dovey couple she had hoped them to be. Instead of dreaming about tomorrows after the wedding on Saturday, she was camped outside of B's apartment, in the cold, debating whether or not she should bother her this late on Christmas Eve.

By the time Theresa rang B's doorbell, her face was puffy. She couldn't seem to sufficiently plug the hole where tears continued to find escape. Pressing the button again, the door suddenly opened with a jerk.

"Maurice?" Theresa said, startled. She sniffled, then dabbed at both her eyes. The last thing she needed was to give B's brother the satisfaction of seeing her broken. "Where's B? I need to talk to B."

"T . . . Theresa? What's wrong?" he said.

"I need to talk with B!" She stepped inside, brushing past him. He closed the door. "Could you just get her for me?" Theresa tried to sound like a woman in control.

"Baby, B is not here. But come, sit down. Can I get you something to drink?" He gently led her over to the paisley couch. She slowly eased down.

Usually, she wouldn't let Maurice touch her at all. But she couldn't think straight. She nodded about the drink.

"Something hot? Cold? Something to take the edge off the night, maybe?" he said, trying to read her face.

She half nodded, half shook her head, not hearing all he was really saying. She felt as though she would burst into tears at any given second.

He hurried back with a cup of hot chocolate and a box of tissues. "It's hot now, so be careful. I was making myself some when you rang the doorbell." He sat on the edge of the chair across from her and leaned forward. He could see she was about to fall apart. "Theresa, what's wrong?"

"I just need to talk to B—"

"B won't be back until around midnight. She and Junior went to visit his father. And knowing B, she probably won't be back until sometime tomorrow. You know she still has a soft spot for old Tyrone—despite how she dogs him. Junior is seventeen, old enough not to need his mama taking him to his father's. They'll be inseparable by tonight, and at each other's throats by the morning."

Theresa blew hard into the cup of cocoa, sipping as she half-listened. "I really . . . need . . . to talk to . . ." She began to cry again. Hard. The kind of crying done at a funeral of a loved one who has died too young or too soon or without sufficient warning. She fumbled to set the cup on the table.

"Baby . . . Theresa?" Maurice was quick to come over to the couch and hold her. "My Lord, *what* is wrong?" He rocked her until her heavings and moans became sniffles and groans. In between, she spilled out enough of her pain that he began to realize and understand: George Landris *might* not truly love her enough to be marrying her come Saturday. Yet, he didn't press her. He just kept her from falling . . . helped hold her up and keep it together.

He wondered, as she lay asleep on the couch (proof that there were times when people really cried themselves to sleep), how much different their lives would have been had that *one* day never occurred between them. That day she called—and still calls—rape.

Only he hadn't seen it that way. Not that way at all . . .

CHAPTER 9

Be Ye Not Unequally Yoked

Maurice had thought she wanted him . . . was ready to give herself to him.

"Why did you do this?" she cried, full of hurt and hate from her father's living room couch. "I told you I planned on being a virgin on my wedding night!" she said in between tears. "I told you that!" *Yes, she was crying that day, too.*

Maurice had believed the tears were more from it being her first time. He was twenty-four and experienced; she, six months shy of turning sweet sixteen.

He recalled how she kept trying to push him off. How she fought him and repeated for him to "stop!" She kept telling him she wanted to save herself for marriage. She pleaded for him not to do it. But eighteen years ago, virgins weren't exactly in fashion. He figured she was playing hard to get. No, not hard to get, more like testing him out . . . see if he really wanted her. And he did want her. She was beautiful and smart with personality. And he loved her . . . really loved her.

She was the reason he had started back going to church. Theresa was the preacher's daughter. Besides their huge age difference, Maurice knew her father would definitely object to his precious child being with a "heathen."

"Be ye not unequally yoked!" Bishop Jordan would declare from his reigning pedestal. And he meant that to include friends as well as mates.

Theresa and B were already best friends by then. So when Maurice became more active in church, it was no strange thing for him to hang out at the Jordans' house. If Bishop Jordan suspected that Maurice was interested in his daughter, he certainly never let on or objected. And each passing day, Maurice and Theresa only grew closer. They talked about practically anything and everything. Naturally, he thought she felt the same way about their relationship as he did. Otherwise, he never would have taken things as far as he did that day.

He tried to be gentle with her, telling her to "relax" several times. He never would have deliberately done anything to hurt her. He had to make her see that, to see how much he loved her. She wasn't just some mountain he had decided to conquer. He really did love her.

But she saw that day entirely differently. She said he raped her. "When someone says, 'No!' Maurice, they mean *no!* You had no right! No right to do that to me!"

And as far as he knew, she never told a soul about what happened that day—didn't want to get him in trouble, he figured. Even though she said he was wrong. She never even mentioned it to B, and Maurice knew she told B everything. They kept very few secrets from each other.

When she was in her mid-twenties, he tried to talk to her. He told her how sorry he was and asked her to forgive him. He wanted to, at least, still be friends.

"Sorry won't restore me!" she had said. "You raped me, Maurice. Not brutally like a stranger on the street—but rape, nonetheless."

"Theresa . . . I promise . . . I thought you wanted it, too. We had talked about being together. You and me . . . a couple. You said things that made me think you were ready—ready to take that next step."

"Maurice, even had I consented—which I didn't—I was fifteen! You were twenty-four. Twenty-four, Maurice! Legally, a man. Legally, I was still a minor. But I didn't want you to do that. I begged you to stop. Legally and physically, Maurice, you raped me! And I would appreciate it if you would just stay away from me! Don't talk to me, bother me, touch me. Just stay away from me!"

Now here she lay, if not more peaceful and beautiful than when he first saw her all those years ago. And even though she was marrying someone else in less than a week, he still loved her. But he knew she would never believe that, either.

B called around eleven to say they would be staying the night at Tyrone's house. *Surprise!* Maurice didn't tell her about Theresa being there. He knew he could take care of Theresa without B's help or causing her to worry. He didn't have any big plans for the night, so being here with Theresa was not a problem.

Having covered her already with one of B's new velour blankets, he made sure the fireplace roared with colors and warmth. He turned off the light, took vigil over her as he sat on the floor next to the couch, and watched the fire dance.

Theresa cried out. "No! Save me! Please, save me. Please . . ." He raised up and checked on her. She was still asleep, only dreaming. Adjusting the covers around her again, he looked at her and smiled, now viewing what he considered a dream.

CHAPTER 10

Arise, Shine for the Light Is Come

Theresa woke up wondering, at first, where she was. Looking around the room, she tried to recall all that had happened. *Why am I in this strange place that isn't my own bed?*

"My Queen," Maurice said as he strolled in with a smile. He was carrying a plate of food and a glass of orange juice. "Merry Christmas," he said as he set them on the glass table next to the sofa. "Did you sleep well?"

She slowly lifted the covers and took a quick peek. A grin crept over her face as she let out a short breath. She was fully clothed.

Maurice grinned too, knowing full well what she was doing. "You didn't have to worry. I was a perfect gentleman last night."

"Maurice—"

He picked up the plate and held it out to her. She took it, said a prayer over it, and began sampling a little of everything. "Did you cook all this yourself?" she said, looking at three strips of crisp bacon, eggs, grits, biscuits, and a cup of fresh mixed fruit.

"Yeah."

"I'm impressed. It's really good."

"Well, thank you, ma'am. Here at B's Bed and Breakfast, we aim to please," he teased.

"Oh, and Maurice?" she said licking the tines of the fork after shoving a forkful of grits into her mouth.

"Yes?" he said, grabbing a strip of her bacon and devouring it with two bites.

"In case you haven't heard—nobody's perfect."

They both laughed. "Touché," he said. "Touché."

An hour later, Theresa looked at her watch. "Oh my gosh! Is it ten-fifty already? I've got to get home and change. I'm supposed to be going to my folks' house for Christmas." She grabbed her things while slipping her feet inside her shoes. "George probably thinks I've lost my mind! I need to call him!" She went to the door, then stopped and turned back. "Maurice," she said, calmer and with a smile, "thanks."

"For what?"

"It's clichéd . . . but just for being there. I wasn't doing so well when I arrived last night. And I'll be the first to admit I wasn't thrilled to see you standing there. But—"

"Oooh, there's always a but," he said, smiling. "But this one sounds like it just may go more in my favor."

"*But*, I don't know what I would have done had you not let me get it all out." She turned the knob and opened the door. "Tell B that I'll call her later today—after I finish with the family thing." She smiled, then turned back again. "Oh, and Maurice, Merry Christmas."

He smiled, shook his head, and said, "Merry Christmas." She closed the door. He touched his lips, blew her a kiss, and whispered, "Merry Christmas, T."

Theresa came home to fifteen messages on her machine. George had left four last night and two this morning.

"Theresa, this is George. Look, I apologize for the way things went. Give me a call. It's ten o'clock. I'll be up awhile longer."

"Theresa, this is George again. I don't know where you are. I hope you're okay. If you get this message within the next thirty minutes, please give me a call. It's ten forty-five now."

"Theresa, I'm worried about you. It's eleven-thirty and I've not heard back from you yet. If you're there, please pick up and let me know you're all right."

"Theresa, listen . . . it's after midnight. I'm turning in now. I'm really tired. I'll call you in the morning."

There were messages from friends wishing her Merry Christmas, and a message from her mother and father, telling her to come over a little earlier than she had planned since they were having company. "We have a surprise for you!" they said in harmony. Like she didn't already know Lena was coming.

There was a message from B. "Merry Christmas, girl. You'll never guess where I'm calling from. Anyway, I should be home about two today, so I'll call you later. Wait till I tell you what Tyrone got me for Christmas. The man is crazy, I tell you. I don't know about him sometimes. And just where are you this time of the morning anyway? I hope you and Pastor Landris didn't start on your honeymoon early." She laughed. "I'll call you. Love ya, girl!"

"Theresa, where are you? Call me, *please*. I'm worried about you now. Let me know what time you want me to pick you up to go to your folks' house."

She played through the other messages, skipping those where people decided to sing their holiday greetings.

The very last message was from George. "Theresa, I'll be there at eleven-thirty to pick you up."

She looked at the time: it was eleven twenty-five. There was no way she would be ready by the time he arrived. "You'll just have to wait on *me* this time," she said to the answering machine.

The doorbell rang; she opened it.

"Theresa, where have you been?" George looked at her; she was still wearing the clothes she had on last night. "Did you even come home last night at all?"

"George, don't start. You were gone for three days. I believe I can be out of pocket for one night without having to answer to you."

"Theresa," he said, grabbing her wrist. She looked down at his hand; he let go. "I said I was sorry. I shouldn't have acted the way I did last night. You had every right to be angry. Can we *please* just start over?"

"Look, George. I shouldn't have acted the way I did, either. I knew you were tired. But I let my imagination get the best of me." She glanced at the clock on the wall. "My folks are expecting us earlier than originally planned. They have a 'surprise' for me." She used her fingers to physically quote the word "surprise."

George grinned. "A surprise, huh?"

"George, it's just Lena. She called last night—right before you did."

"Lena? Lena? I've heard that name before. She's a woman you guys have mentioned a few times in passing conversation. Lives in . . . South Carolina?"

"North." Theresa let out a sigh. "And she's a little more than *a* woman. George, I've not been totally up front with you about something. You see, Lena Patterson and my father once had . . . a thing for each other."

"Bishop Jordan? Well, that's interesting—that they still keep in touch and that your mother . . ." He thought about what he almost said and put a halt to his words.

"And that my mother is cool with it." She sat down and crossed her legs. "George, sit. There's something I haven't told you that I need to now." She sighed hard. "Lena Patterson and my father . . . my father and Lena . . . Lena . . ."

He looked at her and tried to figure out what could be so difficult to say.

"Okay, it's like this: *I* am the result of my father and Lena's *thing* for each other."

"What?"

"It's a bit complicated, and a story truthfully I don't enjoy thinking about, let alone having to repeat."

"But your mother . . . I mean Beatrice—"

"As far as I'm concerned Beatrice *is* my mother."

George leaned back against the chair. "Why didn't you tell me this before? I thought Bishop Jordan and Beatrice were your parents. Goodness!"

"They *are* my parents, George. I don't know Lena all that well. And physically having a child doesn't always make one a mother or a father. Richard Jordan is my biological father. And Beatrice is, for all purposes, my mother. Lena is someone I know basically by name. She's a nice lady, but that's about as much as I have or want to have to do with her. When I see her, I try to be polite. So . . . Lena is probably my father's surprise for today."

"Whoa, now that's a shocker. I can't believe you've never told me this."

"George, from the looks of things, seems we *both* have things we haven't *completely* shared with one another."

"But Theresa, having a mother that I didn't know about is different than—"

"Than what? Than a friend you love so much, you don't even bother to tell your own fiancée about?"

"So, I suppose you're saying I know about all of your old friends?"

"No, George. That's not what I'm saying. I'm just saying, sometimes there are people who mean more to us than others. And we know who those people are."

"Are you trying to tell me you have an old boyfriend I should know about?"

"Are you trying to tell me you and Miss Johnnie Mae have more going on than you've let on so far?"

He laughed. "What is it with you and Johnnie Mae? Why is it so hard for you to believe that I could care about someone without having something going on? Can't a man and a woman be close without there being some level of suspicion surrounding them or the nature of their relationship?"

"George, look. I don't know what you and Johnnie Mae Taylor have or had. And maybe I did overreact to your going there to see about her. And maybe I do need to evaluate my actions, because I know what a preacher's wife has to deal with." She looked at the clock on the wall again. "I'm sorry I jumped all over you last night. Okay? I mean, I knew you were tired, and I should have waited to discuss my feelings."

"It's all right. And I'm sorry I put you in a position where you had to feel that way in the first place."

She started toward her bedroom. "Well, I need to get ready. I know Daddy's going to be upset that he had to wait to 'surprise' me." She used her fingers to illustrate quotes again.

"Theresa?" George stood up and walked toward the bar. "Why are you not excited about your mother . . . I mean, about Lena being here? In fact, I'd say you appear a bit upset about it."

She laughed one short laugh. "Oh, just wait. You'll see. Soon enough." She then walked into her bedroom and closed the door.

George sat down and wondered. *What on earth could this Lena person have done that would make Theresa feel the way she does toward her? What?* He knew one thing, there had to be something—had to be!

CHAPTER 11

Mount Up with Wings as Eagles

Theresa stepped inside of her parents' one-level brick home. "Sapphire—wow, you're here already," she said. There was lots of noise and commotion as everyone began exchanging various holiday greetings and merriment.

"Theresa, you'll never guess who's here," Bishop Jordan said, smiling.

"Who, Daddy?" Theresa said it like she had no earthly idea.

Lena came around the corner. "Theresa, Merry Christmas," she said. "Come, give me a hug." She walked to Theresa with outstretched arms. "Look at you." She leaned back and smiled. "Just . . . look . . . at . . . you! So very beautiful."

"Thanks," Theresa said, trying to smile as she quickly pulled away from Lena's embrace. "Oh, I brought you something—for Christmas. It's in the bag . . . with George. George," she motioned for him to step forward, "I'd like you to meet Lena . . . Lena Patterson. Lena, this is my fiancé, Pastor George Landris."

George sat down the bundle of gifts and moved toward Lena. He tried to keep the smiling expression on his face, but he couldn't help but wonder how she had come to be so scarred. "It's so . . . good to meet you, Ms. Patterson."

"Oh," she said after hugging him tight and fanning her hand as though she were shooing away a gnat, "just call me Lena. Everyone else does."

"All right then . . . Lena." He managed to keep smiling. "And how was your trip?"

"It was a ride, that's all I can say. But I made it. Sort of like life. There are times when you have to take the bus although you'd rather have taken a plane. But in the end you get there; and after all, that was the goal, to get there."

"Now that's a good way to look at it," George said.

"Oh, Lena comes up with ideas that will make you stop and think all the time," Bishop Jordan said.

"Well, come on in, you guys," Beatrice said, "and get settled. Dinner is almost on the table. After everyone gets situated, we can get started." She wiped her hands on her terry-cloth apron tightly secured around her waist.

"Won't have to tell me twice!" Bishop Jordan said. "I've been smelling this good cooking all day, and I'm primed." He patted his stomach.

"Theresa," Lena said. "May I speak with you for a moment? In private, if you don't mind?"

"Sure, Lena. Just let me put these things down."

"You two can go in that bedroom there, if you like," Beatrice said. "Sapphire and I will just take all the menfolk with us."

Lena and Theresa stood in the bright yellow bedroom. Lena pulled out a box wrapped in beautiful purple foil-like paper. "I wanted you to have this. It's very old, very valuable. I thought since you would need something old for your wedding, maybe I could be the one to give it to you?" She held it out to Theresa. "Please, open it now."

"Lena, you didn't have to do that—"

"Open it . . . please."

Theresa took the box and tore off the wrapping. She was slow to open it. "Lena," she looked at her, "this is magnificent. I've never seen anything like it." She turned the necklace around in her hand. It was a huge—about ten carats—stone, a sparkling amethyst, housed inside an antique setting of sterling silver.

"It belonged to my grandmother. Something a lady gave to her . . . a woman she used to keep house for over twenty-something years. The woman said it was a family heirloom. An antique. Been in their family for generations. My grandmother passed it on to me, just before she crossed over Jordan. I've never worn it, though I thought I would on my own wedding day. But . . ." she looked down, then back up. "I kept it safe. I'd like for you to have it now. It's all I've got left really . . . of my past."

"Lena, I couldn't *possibly* accept this. You keep it." She held it back out to her.

"What? You don't like it?" Lena said, refusing to raise her hand to take it.

"No. I mean yes, I love it! I just couldn't take something like this from you. I mean . . . this belonged to your grandmother."

"And your great-grandmother. Or have you forgotten?"

Theresa bowed her head for a second as she looked at the necklace. She couldn't believe Lena was giving her this—the only thing left of her own past. And it was obviously very valuable. "Are you sure about this?"

"Of course I'm sure. I've waited a long time to be able to give this to you. There were days when I wondered if I'd make it . . . but I did. So, you're about to begin another phase of your life, and I want you to have something from me as a remembrance . . . a reminder."

"A reminder?" Theresa said.

"Yes. To remind you of how much I love and want the best for you. I've always loved you, even before you took breath. I always wanted you to have the best."

"But how can you still be so wonderful to me? I've not been at my best when it comes to you. You of *all* people know this."

"Child, it's easy when you love someone. When you truly love them. You don't think about yourself as much as about that other person. You go on living your life, and knowing that you've done something outside of yourself."

"Thank you, Lena. I'll cherish this always. I promise." She leaned over, about to kiss Lena on the cheek, when she turned away and gave her a hug instead.

"Oh, baby. I just hope you're happy." Lena looked at her as she glanced down at Theresa's wedding ring hand. "You are happy, aren't you?"

Theresa looked up. "Oh, of course. Of course!" She stood up. "I suppose we should go in with the rest of the family. The food smells delicious!"

It was during the time when they were sitting around talking that things began to unravel—after that glorious dinner, and the exchanging and opening of gifts. Theresa and Beatrice were off doing the mother-daughter thing; Sapphire had already gone home; and Bishop Jordan and George were in the den discussing the direction of churches—old church, new church ideas.

Of course, George was trying to get Bishop Jordan to see how young folks were tired of *playing* church . . . that they were serious about this God thing. Bishop Jordan took exception, like George was inferring the "old church folks" were actually *playing* church. George just wanted Bishop Jordan to see how "We've got to get away from traditionalism and realize God isn't tripping off what people are wearing, how their hair is done, whether or not they wear earrings or have on makeup. All that stuff is about style, and changes anyway."

"On the earring thing," Bishop Jordan asked, "is this about the men or the women? Because I've noticed plenty of young men sporting earrings here lately."

"What difference does it make if a guy wears earrings?"

"Do you wear them?"

"No, but that's beside the point. If I did, what would be wrong with that? When we get to heaven, I don't believe you'll be penalized or put in a separate section because you wore earrings—male or female."

"Well, I just don't understand why the young men today strive to look more like the women of yesterday. In fact, I don't understand why women today feel a need to cut their hair short and wear pants. Men now grow their hair long," he glanced at George's dreadlocks, "wear braids and plaits. It's confusing enough as it is. They say that Snoop Dogg fellow has his curled. It's getting to where you can't tell what's in front, by looking from behind anymore."

George began laughing. That was when he noticed Lena sitting off in a corner by herself. No one was talking to her. She just sat there, looking like it didn't bother her. Bishop Jordan saw her when he followed where George's eyes rested.

"Lena," Bishop Jordan said as he walked over to her. "Why are you sitting over here all by yourself?"

"Oh, no reason," she said. She continued to hold her own hands, alternating one with the other every few seconds.

Bishop Jordan and George both looked over at Theresa and Beatrice as they laughed and carried on. They hadn't noticed Lena was left out. More than likely, Lena had felt like she would be intruding. It was apparent they hadn't cared enough to see she had even moved so far out of their way.

Bishop Jordan said something to Beatrice, who suddenly realized she had forgotten Lena was still there. Theresa, on the other hand, acted as though she was glad Lena had allowed her time to spend with Beatrice—alone.

Everybody started fussing about, each one making a big deal about nothing, and how no one meant any harm. But it was Theresa who was saying some unkind things about Lena, like, "Probably used to being alone," and "Probably a habit for her to withdraw from the crowd anyway" and "Why were they making such a big deal about *her*?"

Bishop Jordan was the first to insist Theresa to "Apologize to Lena."

That was when Theresa seemed to really go off, saying things like, "Nobody was trying to mistreat Lena." "Who asked her to come in the first place?" "She's a nice person, but she rarely talks much anyway." "So what was the problem?"

"And now," Theresa yelled at her father, "she's even going to be here for my wedding, thanks to you two! So what does *she* have to complain about?"

"What did you just say?" Beatrice asked, stepping up to Theresa. "What did you just say?"

"I said, why does she have to be here for my wedding? You both know how I feel. You have to! I told you these past few months to let me handle this. But you went and invited her anyway!"

Bishop Jordan gently moved Beatrice out of the line of fire. "Young lady, you apologize! Right this second! Apologize!"

"Apologize? For what? I'm not a little girl anymore. I'm a grown woman! I don't have to do what *you* think is the right or the correct thing to do! Lena and I have nothing in common! *Nothing*. She knows and accepts this. So why—"

"Theresa!" George said, interrupting her. He looked at Lena and could see her hurt. "Stop it." He couldn't believe the way Theresa was acting. "That's enough."

"And *you*, *Pastor* Landris!" Theresa said. "You can't say one word to me. Not one! You go trampling off to Alabama to see about some woman I didn't even know you knew. What can *you* say to me, George? I'm tired of everybody trying to tell me how I should feel, how I should act. I'm tired of doing everything just to please other folks. This is my life, and I'm tired of wasting it trying to do what everybody else feels I should." She turned to Lena. "I don't mean to hurt you. I've never meant to hurt you. But you should have known I didn't want you here for my wedding. Of all things, not for my wedding."

Bishop Jordan grabbed Theresa by the shoulders. She snatched away from him, ran into another room, and slammed the door.

Lena stood up. "I knew this was a bad idea. I'm sorry to have put you all through this. Look, I'll be leaving tomorrow—"

"No, Lena. You're not leaving. You're going to stay here, and you're going to attend this wedding," Beatrice said.

"You don't understand. She's hurting right now. I don't want to be the one to add to her pain."

"Bishop, tell her she can't leave," Beatrice said.

"Lena, now you know you can't just always back down when it comes to Theresa. The world doesn't revolve around her. It's high time she knows that."

"Richard, it's okay. Just send me pictures of the wedding. That'll be fine."

"Bishop Jordan," Beatrice said, "I want you to go in there and tell Theresa everything! Everything, do you hear me? It's past the day she should have heard the truth."

Lena had the most frightened look on her face. "No. Beatrice . . . Richard. Please. No." She shook her head. "You can't do this."

"Why not?" Beatrice said. "We've done it your way, and look how it's turned out. Yes. Bishop needs to tell her the truth. And she needs to hear it now. Today. Right now. It should have been done."

"Please don't do this. Not yet. Not now. Just let her have her wedding in peace. I'll be fine," Lena said. "Really . . . I'll be fine. It's okay."

"No, it's not okay, Lena," Beatrice said. Then she turned to the bishop. "Bishop, if you don't tell Theresa, then I will."

"Beatrice, it's not your place to say anything," the bishop said.

"Not my place? What do you mean, not my place? I have as much say about all this as the two of you! I didn't raise that child to be like that. Grown or not, I'm not going to stand here and let her disrespect her own mother the way she continues to do. Not while I have breath. Not as long as I know the whole truth." Beatrice relaxed and spoke softer. "So, are you going in there? Or must I?"

Bishop sighed. "I'll do it."

"Richard, please. I beg you," Lena said. "Not yet. Beatrice, just give her a little more time. Let her be upset right now, but let her at least have her perfect wedding. Weddings are special. They're supposed to be. They shouldn't have clouds hanging over them. Brides are supposed to be beautiful on their wedding day. Not miserable because some old woman decided she had to show up. I can understand how she feels. I really do—"

"But it doesn't make it right," George said. "I don't know what you guys are referring to, but I do know that Theresa has no place acting like she just did."

"Bishop, are you going to talk with her . . . or do I?" Beatrice said. "Lena, I hear you, but Theresa needs to know. Now, before this goes any further!"

Lena sat down quickly as she clutched at her heart. "I don't want that child being hurt no more than she has to be. Life is cruel enough at times; why must we heap on more when it's not necessary? I'll be fine. Really, I will."

"I'll speak with her," the bishop said to Beatrice before turning to Lena. "I don't know what all I'll tell her just yet, but I'll make her see where she's wrong about you being here, Lena." He patted Lena's shoulder.

Theresa knows Lena is her mother, George thought. *So what doesn't she know that they feel she needs to be told right now?*

Lena began to rock. Her mind traveled back thirty years ago, to the time she classified as her season of being "chosen in the furnace of affliction"—not the actual day of the fire but the week after, at the hospital. *Had I made a mistake telling that nurse how to contact Richard? No, Richard had been a good father. A great father—that promise, to love and take good care of Theresa, he had definitely kept.*

But thirty years later, things weren't at all the way Lena had hoped or ever imagined they would be. And all Lena could do at this moment was rock and pray—pray that all would be well.

Beatrice kept busy in the kitchen, finishing up mounds of dirty dishes. The bishop stood outside the door Theresa had chosen to use to separate herself from them, wondering what, then how much, he would truly reveal to his only daughter, his precious Theresa.

George sat, unable to question—let alone answer—what had actually happened here. Nor could or would he attempt to speculate on just what might happen next.

CHAPTER 12

Honor Thy Father and Thy Mother

Bishop Jordan knocked on the door.

"It's open," Theresa said dryly. She was sitting in the middle of the bed, looking at pictures and other things she'd found inside an old shoe box.

"Theresa, we need to talk," her father said.

"I know, Daddy. I was wrong. That was un-Christian-like, and I plan to apologize. I don't know what gets into me sometimes. I get angry. My mouth flies open. And before I know it, I've said things I can't take back or make vanish into the air I've polluted."

"Theresa, an apology may not be able to undo the damage you've heaped upon Lena. She's your mother, but you make her feel like—"

"Dirt not even good enough to eat," she said. "I know, Daddy. I don't mean to, but I look at her and I just can't help myself. People act like I'm the bad guy, but kids do that to their parents all the time. They're either too fat or too skinny. Too dark or too light. Too short or too tall. In church if they sing, they're too loud or, even worse, plain off-key. A car they drive that might run fine but is *just* not right—whether it's too loud, too raggedy, too ugly, or out-of-style—causes you to be ashamed. In my particular case, my mother happens to have a severely scarred body—"

"Theresa, that's not her fault."

"I know that! But why didn't she get plastic surgery or something?"

"Back when this happened, plastic surgery was mostly for the wealthy. Lena's still trying to come out from under all the bills she incurred from the hospital. She won't let anyone help her . . . tells me to use the money for you."

"Daddy, I know she's a nice person. And truly, I don't mean to hurt her. Look, I'll do whatever I need to do to get her to stay for the wedding. But I want you to know, I'm only doing this for you and Beatrice." She threw a picture off to the side as she continued shuffling through the old photographs.

"Theresa, there's something I want to tell you. Something you ought to know about Lena—"

"Daddy, is this you?" She held up an old photograph.

He took the picture. "Where did you find this?" His voice sounded accusing.

"In this shoe box. There are tons of pictures in here. Nobody I recognize, though. Except that one looks like a younger version of you."

"I was seventeen then, I believe."

"And who is that gorgeous woman you have your arms around?" She grinned. "Looks like a model; definitely not Beatrice. She's gorgeous!"

He continued to stare at the photo, not really hearing what Theresa said or was saying. "Uh-huh," he said.

"Now *that's* a woman you should have kept. You two really looked like you were in love; not that I'm not glad you married Beatrice. So what happened? Why didn't the two of you end up together? The woman in that picture?"

"She turned me down. Several times, I asked her to marry me. The first time, she had said yes. We were making plans; then she changed her mind. The next six times I asked, she said no."

"Six times? That must have been hard. For you, that is."

"Yes, it was."

"Daddy . . ." She paused a second. "Did you ever get over her? Completely?"

He looked at Theresa. "Why do you ask?"

"Just curious. I was wondering if a person truly loves someone, no matter how long ago it was, does he ever get over her?"

"Theresa, if love were that easy to turn on and off, there would be many happy souls in this world. Sometimes, you don't ever get over them. You just adjust and move on." He sighed. "Listen, there's something important I need to talk with you about. Theresa—"

Just then, a horn blew outside. "Ooops! That's for me." She jumped up. "I'm sure it's B coming to get me."

"Why would B be coming here to get you now?"

Theresa thought about what she should tell him. Actually, she had called B because she was sick of all them awhile ago. As soon as she left them standing there accusing her of being insensitive, she called B and told her to get over there as quickly as she could. She knew it wouldn't have done any good to ask George to take her home—not then. He would have seen she was angry and leaving for the wrong reason. He would have had no part of it. Calling B, she could make it look like B was the one who needed her. Everybody knew B.

"Oh Daddy, you know how B is. Makes no difference to her if we're having plans that she might be interrupting. When she wants to talk about something, she wants to talk." Theresa didn't feel like she had totally lied. B did call this morning and said she wanted to talk.

"Theresa, but *we* really need to talk—"

"Okay, Daddy. Later. I don't want to keep B waiting. And I already know she's not coming inside."

"Then you are planning to come back here later, aren't you? You know Lena's here, and she would like to spend some time with you."

Theresa was at the doorway now. "I plan to. If anything changes, I'll call and let you know." She ran back over to her father, who was still holding that photo of himself, and kissed him on the cheek. He always had to bend down a little for her to hit his cheek just right. "See ya later, Daddy."

"Tell B Merry Christmas for me."

"Sure thing." Theresa walked into the other room and told everyone she was going over to visit with B for a little while.

Beatrice started to say something, but she figured the bishop must have finished his talk with her. *Theresa sure seemed to be taking it well,* she thought.

"Theresa," George yelled after her, "are you coming back, or did you want me to come get you at B's?"

"Don't worry about me. I'll either get B to bring me back here, or get her to drop me off at home." And with that, she closed the front door.

When Theresa reached B's car, she stopped before she got inside. "Maurice? What are you doing here?"

"Hope you don't mind, pretty lady. But B asked if I'd do her a huge favor and pick you up. She even offered to let me drive her *fancy* car." He said the word "fancy" as though he were being sarcastic. "Seems something important came up just as she was on her way out the door to come get you. A call she had to take. I told her I *suppose* I could do this *one* thing for her. But that she owed me—big time." He kept both hands on the steering wheel. "So are you coming . . . or staying? You're letting all the heat out and the cold in."

She got in the car. "Let's go," she said. She didn't want anyone to look out the window and notice it was Maurice and not B behind the wheel.

"Your wish is my command," he said, smiling.

"Maurice, did you—"

"Tell B about you coming over last night?"

"Yeah."

"Nope."

"Thanks. I don't want her worried."

"No problem," he said and winked at her. "I know how to keep a secret, too."

CHAPTER 13

A Balm in Gilead

Beatrice and George sat in the sunroom while the bishop and Lena were in another room looking at photo albums and talking. Beatrice wanted to give them some time, seeing how Theresa had just acted up so, and how the bishop hadn't told Theresa what he went in to say. Beatrice had a glass of eggnog. "A special kind with an added punch," Sapphire had said when she made it earlier. The more Beatrice talked, the more comfortable she felt telling George things that popped into her mind. She talked about people marrying people they don't really love or while they're in love with someone else. George wondered why she was telling him all this.

"The bishop cheated on me once, I think," she said. "Technically, you might say, I cheated on him. Once. But the bishop has always missed having his complete heart. One missing piece." She drank more eggnog.

"Mrs. Jordan—"

"He still loves her, you know," Beatrice said, not looking at George.

"Who?" George said.

"The bishop. He still loves Lena."

George looked at her as she stared into the nothingness beyond the sunroom windows. It was like she was in a trance . . . or watching a movie that was only being shown inside her head. "Well Mrs. Jordan, I'm sure on some level—"

"Not on some level," Beatrice said. "He really, truly loves her." She turned and looked at him. "And this is not just the eggnog talking, either. But it's okay. I've known it since the first day I met him. Women sense these things, you know. Whether we acknowledge it as the truth or not. Oh, it used to bother me—especially when we first were married. But now, I've reconciled myself to it."

"How? Why?"

"I realized, in his own way, he loves me, too. Wouldn't ever do anything on purpose to hurt me. Everything he does now, though, is only a denial to his true feelings. Being with Lena would bring his heart back together and complete him. I know this. Yet, he denies himself. He keeps trying to do the *right* thing—what he believes is the *correct* thing to do."

"Correct?"

"By society . . . people. They say you shouldn't leave one for another. Once you have committed or made a promise, you should honor that promise. No matter what. Even if it means you'll lead a joyless life for the rest of your life. It doesn't matter whether you're happy or not, you must do the correct thing. *You made your bed, now lie in it.* Who cares if you dread waking up in the morning? So what if you're facing a day without excitement or passion? *Go out and make it a terrific day anyway!* Then," she turned the glass up again, "there's the extra pressure that comes with being a preacher. No longer a man . . . but now a *man of God.*"

"Extra?"

"Yeah. Extra. People treat you as though you're no longer a human being, but more like a human done. Like you're some kind of *little* god. Oh, they'd never admit it; but the signs are there. They hold you to a different standard than even they are willing to walk. '*But you're of God,*' they say. And they put you on a pedestal . . . although I know some who put themselves there."

"Oh, I understand that. But ministers of God are supposed to be an example to the flock. It's important that we walk the standards set by God so that we don't cause another to stumble who might be watching or following us."

"Yeah. And *should* you slip, there are people waiting. 'I knew it! I told you!' they'll say. Like they get pleasure in seeing God's chosen ones fall. They're just waiting to oust you. '*Fall from your pedestal! Fall! We like seeing giants fall!*' But they forget, people are human beings being used by God—not God himself. You don't get extra credit because God called you to a work. In truth, we're all called for a specific work. In God's eyes, is one person's calling better than another's?"

George sat back, relaxing his body. He'd become tense from the first moment she began speaking. Now, he saw she was sincere in her talk. She just needed to get some things off her chest. "I hear you, Mrs. Jordan. And I for one know it's a tremendous pressure being called. Even greater pressure to be chosen. The scriptures say, "For many are called, but few are chosen." People accuse God's people of so much, when all many of us are trying to do . . . is to do our best."

"My husband is a good man. He truly believes in his mission. Wants to always do the right thing. But there are things people expect out of you. You shouldn't always do these things because *they* think they're right. He married me originally not because he really wanted to spend the rest of his life with me. He did it because a group of people didn't believe a minister—a man of God—should be ministering to them without a wife. It was the church he was called to pastor that decided he should get married. Like he was some kid in a candy store, and he might go wild with all those candy and sweets in church if he didn't have something sweet at home."

"I'm familiar with that one, too," George said, smiling and recalling his own church folk trying to push him into marriage before he'd heard from God about it.

Beatrice looked at him and then went back to her place again. "The bishop also had his daughter . . . Theresa. Here he was, this handsome young man, all the women thought he was something, and many of them—both old and young—were interested in the young preacher man. There were also those who didn't believe a man should be raising a child alone. Of course, this was years back—when people didn't think fathers were good for anything except to work and bring home the money. Women have been raising children by themselves for years, and there hasn't been an outcry about that. But people back then didn't believe a man was equipped to raise a child, and especially not a little girl."

She sat back against the chair and took the last gulp of her eggnog. "Anyway, the bishop was under a lot of pressure. A *lot* of pressure. Lena, at the time, was fighting for her life on a day-by-day basis. From all those burns, third degree, I believe they said."

"She was burned?"

"Yes, in a fire about thirty years ago. Bishop was waiting on her to get better so they could be a family like they'd always planned. Lena didn't have any family to speak of, so it was just Theresa and the bishop really. Her mother had her when she was fourteen. I don't think she ever knew who her father was. And like so many, her grandmother raised her. She died right after Lena turned sixteen. She and the bishop had been together since he was fourteen, she thirteen. They had planned on marrying when he graduated college." Beatrice let her head fall back against the chair.

"Somehow, Lena and the bishop couldn't wait to *be* together. I don't know all the details, but she ended up getting pregnant just before the bishop left for college at Fayetteville State University in Fayetteville, North Carolina. He even had a scholarship. Well, Lena didn't want him to know about her being pregnant. She figured if he knew, he'd forego college altogether, get a job so he could be responsible and take care of his family. Lena was bound and determined not to let him do that."

"So he went to college not knowing Lena was pregnant?"

"Yep," Beatrice said. She looked at him. "Something to drink?"

"No thanks, I'm fine."

"Well, I'd like a refill. The eggnog is exceptionally good this year." She had trouble pronouncing the word "exceptionally." "I must compliment Sapphire the next time I talk with her."

She was sitting forward when George jumped up and took her glass. "I'll get it," he said. It didn't take long for him to go and come back. "Here you are."

"Thank you. Now," she said, taking a sip and acting as though it had hit an originally missed spot, "where was I? Oh yes. College. That's where he and I eventually met. I thought he was the most handsome thing; he could have stepped out of any upscale magazine. Certainly should have been on the cover, if not the centerfold. On campus, he was something. I was a junior, studying to be a teacher; he was a sophomore, interested in counseling. I knew I wanted him the moment I laid eyes on him. But he stayed off to himself. He was smart, active in extracurricular activities, but he didn't seem attracted to anyone on our campus." She laughed. "I even gave him a Christmas gift early on to woo him my way—an expensive lighter."

George laughed. It was funny hearing someone like Mrs. Jordan talking about days that sounded as though they could have easily happened in this day and time.

"You're laughing because we're old now, aren't you? You know, people aren't born old. Shoot, it takes some living to get to this place in life. Live long enough, and people will laugh at you someday."

George didn't consider himself a kid at forty. "I pray I do have long life."

She took another swallow of eggnog. "You see, George, once a man has given his heart to another, it's hard to get it back. Don't get me wrong, now. The bishop is a good man. A good husband. An exceptional father. He's been pretty faithful to his mission and to me. It's just, he's human. He feels pain just like anybody else—gets lonely, needs to feel loved. God never promised us life would be a bed of roses. But the bishop still has some dark places in his life right now that he needs to shine the light on. Search things out. He and Lena," Beatrice pointed in their direction, "are in there right now trying to find some kind of happy medium. Lena is a good woman. A good woman. Better than I would have been in her position. Now if you want to hear a story, she has one to tell."

"I don't understand—"

"What? How I can believe the bishop loves her, but sit so calmly out here without worrying about what they're doing or talking about in there? Alone?"

"Yes," George said, "as a matter of fact."

"Like I said . . . really, they both have places that need revisiting. Some folks' scars are on the outside and visible. Others have their scars hidden from public view or on the inside. Yet, scars are scars. Lena's are visible for all the world to see. But the bishop's . . . Theresa's . . . heck, mine . . . maybe even yours," she looked at George and smiled, "they're more hidden or on the inside. But the question was asked before I even thought about it: Is there a balm in Gilead? They say there is a balm. To heal the soul. I certainly hope they're right."

"Mrs. Jordan? Are you going to be all right?"

"Of course, George. But I believe there are some things you yourself need to search in your heart. Like what Theresa said about you going to see some woman in Alabama. You need to think about that. 'I do,' can turn out to be a long, long time." She stood up. "Well, I suppose we should go interrupt Lena and the bishop now. Don't want them thinking we've gone and thrown them away."

George couldn't help but wonder what Bishop Jordan and Lena Patterson had been discussing. When Lena walked into the sunroom, she was crying and holding what appeared to be a newspaper pinned with her hand to her heart.

"Beatrice, you'll not believe what we found," the bishop said.

"What?"

"The article."

"What article, Bishop?"

"The article. About the fire."

Beatrice looked a little annoyed. "Bishop Richard Jordan, what article are you talking about?"

"You know . . . about Lena? The newspaper article? The fire?" Bishop said.

"The one he promised to give back to me some day." Lena added. "I thought he hadn't kept it. But he did. Just like he said. And here's the proof."

Beatrice went over to take a look. "Oh this? I remember this. I found it in one of the bishop's old Bibles some years ago. I wondered why he saved it. Truth be told, I almost threw it away. Instead, I put it and some other things in a shoe box. I meant to ask you about that stuff, Bishop. Must have slipped my mind."

"I've been searching for this piece of paper for ages, it seems," the bishop said. "I told you, Lena. I believed. I did keep it. I just couldn't remember where I had put it, what with trying to get Theresa released into my custody from foster care after you had signed for me to do so. After no one could tell me anything—none of the hospitals had you listed as a patient—I finally found you. In just one day, it was as if you never existed. I had come back to rubble and couldn't find you anywhere."

He looked over at the article. "I first put that article in my coat pocket with plans to ensure it was safe. Then I decided to have it framed, just to prove how much I believed. I stuck it in my Bible. With so much happening, I guess I ended up forgetting exactly where I had put it. It wasn't long afterward I was called into the ministry. Bought myself a new Bible—retired that old one. But here it is—that article. Yellow as all get-out, but it's right here."

Lena was crying. Beatrice went over and gave Lena a hug. "Lena, don't cry. It's all right." She handed her a fistful of tissues. "My goodness, who would think an old piece of paper could cause such a commotion!"

"Guess what else we found? Well, Theresa found it really," the bishop said.

"What?" Beatrice took the photo he held stretched out to her. "Who is this you're standing next to?" she said to the bishop while handing the picture over to George.

George drew back his head. "Wow! What a fox. I mean, she's gorgeous. And this would be you, Bishop Jordan? A fedora. Look at you . . . leaning . . . just styling."

"Yeah. I was about seventeen."

"You were a handsome something," Beatrice said. "But that woman next to you sure makes you work hard just to look good. Who is she? An old girlfriend?"

Bishop laughed. "Yeah. You could say that. That fox. That gorgeous woman standing beside me. That's Lena. She was about sixteen then. This is possibly the only photo left of her before . . ." He stopped himself from finishing his sentence.

"You can say it, Richard," Lena said, although her eyes said more. "Before the fire disfigured me."

"No one is saying you're not still beautiful, Lena," Richard said.

"I know that, Richard. I've accepted myself. I know who I am. And if other people can't deal with me, then it's just their loss."

"Well in my book, Ms. Patterson, you're one beautiful woman right now. That goes for you too, Mrs. Jordan."

"I'll drink to that!" Richard said as he headed for the eggnog.

"Bishop, I wouldn't drink any more of that if I were you," George said. "I think Sapphire went a little heavier on the nog than the egg."

"Oh, I know that. What do you think, I was born yesterday?" He laughed.

Lena and Richard spoke briefly when no one else was around. "Thank you, Richard. Thank you for believing. And thank you . . . for keeping your promises."

Richard smiled. "Lena—in all honesty—there are some promises that go even beyond myself."

"Promises, beyond Jordan?" Lena said. "Oh, I like that! Promises . . . beyond . . . Jordan." She nodded and smiled. "Oh, yeah . . . I like that. And that much, Richard, whether you realize it or not, you did do. You absolutely did do. You went far beyond the promises you made to me that day, when all I had left . . . was my faith."

"Lena, what are we gonna do about Theresa?"

"Richard, I'm not sure. At this point, I'm really not sure."

CHAPTER 14

Fret Not Thyself Because of Evil Doers

B was still on the phone when Theresa arrived. She made gestures to let Theresa know it shouldn't be too much longer before she would be finished.

Maurice sat forward across from Theresa, his fingers forming a nice little triangle. "Looks like we're back where we first began," he finally said.

Theresa smiled. It felt strange yet familiar to sit and have a decent conversation with Maurice—just like they used to a long time ago.

"Can I get you anything?" he said.

"What you got?"

"Well, since I know you've already eaten, how about some dessert?"

Theresa frowned and shook her head. "Probably shouldn't. I've still got a wedding dress to fit into on Saturday."

He laughed and looked down at his hands. "Yeah. That's right." He looked around the room, over at B, then back at Theresa again. "How about something to drink?"

"Sounds good."

"Apple cider? With a stick of cinnamon maybe?"

Theresa laughed. "Apple cider with cinnamon? Come on, is that the best you can do for Christmas? Even my folks had eggnog. Spiked, of course, but that was because they let Sapphire make it this time. But still . . ."

"Okay, I've got a bottle of Arbor Mist put back. It's not *too* too alcoholic, and it has a good taste with a tiny kick. How does that sound?"

She nodded. "But not too much for me. I'm not a drinker at all."

"Sure." He got up and went to the kitchen.

B hung up the phone. "Hey, girl! Merry Christmas," she said, coming over and hugging Theresa. "Sorry I couldn't come get you, but Tyrone had something he *had* to say, and he didn't want to *hear* about me calling him back. I hope you're not too upset with me for sending Maurice. But it was either him or your having to wait, who even knew how long, for me to get there."

"It was all good."

"So what's up with the crew at your folks' house? You sounded a little ruffled when you called."

"Oh, it's calmed down some now. But they were getting on my *last* nerve. I had to get out of there before I ended up really going off on somebody! One can only take so much at one time. I don't care how holy you try to be."

B sat on the sofa next to Theresa. She brushed a flower in the pattern of the paisley sofa. "So what were they ragging you about? The wedding, I bet. All the major bucks they're having to shell out to pull off that monstrosity?"

"Not exactly. You see, Lena was there. She's coming to my wedding—"

"Lena? She's that woman who used to come visit y'all from time to time when you were little, right? The one who was all the time trying to act like she was your 'play-mother.' "

Theresa stopped for a second to think whether she should tell B everything or not. The truth. No one outside of her family knew that Lena was not her "play-," but real mother. Theresa met B the year after she moved to Atlanta the second time she officially went to live with her father. Theresa was eight then.

Theresa had stayed to herself most of the time . . . one thing she did learn from living with Lena. It wasn't until Theresa was eleven that she started talking to other people in the neighborhood and at school a little more. By the time she was twelve, she and Bellona were best friends.

Theresa recalled the day her father had taken her back to live with Lena. She had just turned six. It was July 4, the summer before she was to start first grade. She didn't know Lena. Naturally she was frightened when they first met. But her mother and father told her it was okay . . . that Lena was *actually* her mother. It was hard for little Theresa to understand how a total stranger could be her mother, just like that. Beatrice was the person she'd grown to call mother since she could remember.

And her parents didn't do a great job explaining it, either. They just said that Lena had been sick for awhile and now she was better. They told her that Lena loved and missed her very much and that she would take care of Theresa "just like before."

Theresa didn't want to stay with Lena . . . she told her daddy as much. But he told her Lena loved her and she had to give her "mother" a chance. She could still visit with them during the summer. They would certainly come visit her every opportunity they could during the other times. They stayed with her over the weekend, but left Sunday night to go back home—without her. And although Theresa cried, they still refused to take her with them. She had to be a big girl, for their sake. Everything would be fine. "We promise," they said. So for them, she tried—tried not to cry, tried to make them proud. But she couldn't help it.

Lena wanted Theresa to be happy. They did things together like have grand tea parties. They played all kinds of card, board-, and other types of old-fashioned games. Lena would read to her all the time. And Theresa loved their reading time together. She grew to love books!

Theresa started school, and all the children adored her. She made lots of friends. Lots. She was beautiful—everyone told her so. Life was settling in fine.

Then, in the second grade, Lena received a notice about an urgent need for room mothers. There just weren't enough parents available, and the teachers were in dire straits. It would be hard, but Lena signed up and agreed to help out. And that was when Theresa's troubles began.

The teacher was taken aback when Lena walked in that day. Richard had always been the one to carry Theresa for orientation—no teacher had met Lena face-to-face. The students in Theresa's class acted terrified. Two days later, the teacher sent a note home to Lena: "Thanks, but your services are not needed after all. We have more than enough help now."

Following Lena's visit, Theresa was teased and taunted by schoolmates and the neighborhood children alike. Sometimes, they even tried to fight her.

They went so far as to create a song just for her: "Monster's child, come out and play. Little Monster's child, where's your ugly mama at today?"

Lena hadn't realized how bad things had gotten for Theresa until it was too late. She had no idea of the rage that had built up inside of her daughter.

"I hate you!" Theresa said. "Hate you! I want to go live with my daddy. Why are you making me stay here? I don't want to live with you!" She cried and cried.

"Baby, you can't let people get next to you. You've got to be strong. It doesn't matter what people say. It's what *you* believe, that's what matters. God will—"

"I don't care what you say. I want to go home! This is not my home. Why are you making me stay here with you? You're just mean and evil! Just like everybody says! Talking about God. I'm leaving this place the first chance—"

"Theresa, baby. Look at me—"

"No, I don't want to look at you! You're ugly! Ugly, ugly, ugly! Please, please. Just let me go home to my family. I'll be good. I promise."

"Theresa, this is not about your being good. And I am your family—"

"No you're not! You're not my mother! I want to go home! Please, just let me go home! I want my daddy! I want Beatrice! I want my *real* mother!" she cried. "I hate you! I hate you, you hear? I can't wait to get away from you, with your ugly face and your ugly hands! Why don't you go back where you came from? I wish I'd never met you! Why did you have to come into my life anyway?"

And that was what the eight-year-old had said to her mother to make her, finally, relent. She agreed to let Richard and Beatrice take her back to Atlanta to live.

"Just until she's calmed down," they had said. Beatrice was pregnant at the time, her third time expecting. The other two times had ended in miscarriages. She and Richard both believed that Theresa would do better if she had some time away "for a little while." Richard could talk to her . . . get her to understand how much Lena truly loved her and what she had gone through—just for her.

Beatrice lost the third baby almost six months into the pregnancy. Then, the two following that one. Deciding the pain of loss weighed too much, she called it quits. She and Richard had managed to get Theresa to settle down, but she never wanted to visit with Lena in North Carolina. Lena didn't push it, just decided she'd come to them whenever she could to spend time with Theresa.

Theresa was much nicer to Lena once she didn't live with her anymore. But it was only because she believed she *had* to. She was fully aware that if her father wasn't convinced she was bonding with

Lena, she could easily be sent back to live with Lena—forever. So, Theresa learned to play the game within the rules the grown-ups had set. Lena quit pressing Theresa about coming "home," and she didn't have to deal with the humiliation that always seemed to come with being "Lena's daughter"—at least not in public.

When people Theresa knew saw her with Lena, she would tell them Lena was her mother *only* if Lena made it difficult for her to get around it. Afterward, in private, she would explain how Lena was really like a "play-mother" . . . someone her parents wanted her to play with to make her happy. They only had to look at Lena and see the poor thing needed *some* joy in her life. They all understood, and she made great efforts to keep each from the other. That way, she didn't have to deal with explaining Lena at all. The older she got, the less time she made for Lena, her calls, and her little visits.

Richard told Lena, "You have to understand. It's a teen thing, a phase all teenagers go through."

Only thing, Theresa's phase was still happening. She still didn't make time for Lena. She, B, and Sapphire were best friends, and she hadn't told either of them the truth about Lena. When she had arrived at her parents' and saw Sapphire settled and friendly with everyone, she was afraid someone might have slipped already and said something. Fortunately, no one had. Sapphire was long gone before the major blowup.

Now Theresa was sitting in B's great room, debating whether she should tell her the whole truth or keep things as they were.

"Theresa," Maurice said, as he held out a beautiful crystal flute glass to her, "your drink, madam."

"Theresa!" B's scream almost caused Theresa to jump and waste the drink. "I can't believe you're actually drinking something, with sparkling bubbles, other than Sprite!" She looked at Maurice. "Brother, I'd like one too since you're being so generous with your stuff. You know, Maurice hardly ever shares his Arbor Mist with anyone," she said to Theresa. "Still trying to get on Theresa's good side, big brother, I see." She smiled and stuck out her tongue at him.

Maurice smiled and shook his head as he strode back into the kitchen.

"Now. What were you about to say? About Lena?" B said.

"Oh, let's not talk about her. I came here to get away from all that. Tell me about Tyrone and your visit." Theresa sipped the crystal flute of strawberry-colored Arbor Mist. She'd never had it before, but thought it was pretty good.

"Okay. Now, you do remember my name theory, right?"

Theresa rolled her eyes and smiled. "Yes, yes, *yes!*"

B looked at her cockeyed, then sucked her teeth. "Well, there's a little catch I've discovered. There are times when you can look at a name, and find another meaning that you may have completely overlooked."

"Like?"

"Like Tyrone. There's the word 'tie' in there. The word 'one.' And the word 'on.'" She leaned over and whispered in Theresa's ear. "And he really *tied one on* last night and this morning, if you know what I mean."

Theresa pushed her away from her in a teasing-like fashion. "Girl, stop that! You are so nasty." She giggled like a teenager.

"Girl, I'm too serious. Well, he called me, just when I was coming to get you actually. Said he *had* to talk to me. Said I really *rang* his *bell*. He was calling to find out . . . 'for whom the bell tolls.' That's the title of a book, you know."

"Yeah, I'm familiar with that book. I—unlike some people—actually *read* it."

"Well then, see? Bell . . . Bellona. Bell? For whom the bell tolls? Get it?"

Theresa laughed. "You know, you two really deserve each other."

"You think? Interesting that you would say that. He wants us to get back together. Claims he's never happier than when he's with me."

"Yeah, I bet. So, you believe him?"

"After this morning? Yeah. You would have too, had you been there."

Maurice came in and set a drink down for B. She picked it up without looking, like she knew exactly where it was, and turned it up. Maurice sat across from them, watching a show on TV. He continued to sneak peeks at Theresa. She could feel his gaze on her. He would casually glance up, and then she'd catch him clearly staring at her. It made her so nervous, she finished off the Arbor Mist faster than she had ever intended.

Maurice took her glass and came back a few minutes later with a refill. She had no idea he was planning to do that or she would have stopped him. But she ended up drinking it all anyway. His staring made her that nervous.

When George called to see if Theresa was still there, B told him she was. Theresa didn't want to talk to him because she was really having fun playing along with the game show *Who Wants To Be A Millionaire*. She knew he was looking to come get her, and she wasn't ready to leave yet.

"Tell him you'll bring me home so not to worry about me," she whispered, mouthing the words to B.

B told him, although he didn't sound too pleased. It was already after six. B had drunk *way* too much to drive anybody home. So around eight, Maurice offered to drop Theresa off at her place. B looked a little surprised that Theresa didn't put up much of a fight about it. But she also knew Theresa would let the devil himself drive if her choice was between him and a potential drunk driver—something to do with a college friend who had been killed by a drunk driver.

"Maurice, you can take my car if you want," B said with a slight slur.

"That's okay. I'll use my own. That way I can go home afterward."

"Oh . . . so you're not coming back?" B said it like she was about to cry.

He leaned down and kissed her on the forehead. "No, sister dearest. It's about time I fly back to my own nest now."

Maurice smiled at Theresa, who surprisingly smiled back. "Ready to roll?" he said.

"Sure." Theresa was glad she hadn't drunk as much as B apparently had. "Is she going to be all right here like that?" she said in a whisper.

"Oh yeah. B does this from time to time. She's probably worn out more from being with Tyrone than from the alcohol anyway. Arbor Mist is not as bad as some things I've seen her consume."

Maurice opened the door and locked it behind him as he allowed Theresa to walk in front of him. They got to his car.

"This is your car?" Theresa asked.

"Yep."

"I didn't know you drove a 3000 GT."

"Theresa, there are a lot of things you don't know about me." He winked.

They got inside the all-white car and Theresa sunk down into the seat and closed her eyes.

"Better fasten your seat belt," Maurice said. "I wouldn't want anything to happen to you." She smiled, then opened her eyes when she felt his body slightly brush against hers as she heard the seat buckle click.

"Let's roll," he said. "Got to get you home."

Theresa glanced over at him as he shifted gears. There was something different about him. Or maybe, it was just her seeing him through the eyes of Arbor Mist. In any case, he'd been really wonderful for an entire twenty-four hours.

Maybe he's not so bad after all, she thought. She closed her eyes again and decided to just enjoy the ride for a change.

CHAPTER 15

As a Thief in the Night

"Thanks for bringing me home," Theresa said.

Maurice rushed to open the car door for her. "No problem," he said.

Theresa laughed as she struggled to get out. He took her hand. "Wow," she said, getting to her feet, "a girl could get used to being treated like this."

"I hope so. A woman such as yourself should be treated as no less than a queen." He bowed at his waist, his right arm across his stomach and left arm behind his back.

"Maurice, stop that," she said. Then she giggled. "Well, I guess I'll get upstairs now." She looked upward toward her apartment.

"I'll walk you to your door."

"Oh, that's not necessary."

"I know. I want to." He smiled and held onto the car door as she cleared its path so he could close it. When they got to her apartment, he took her keys. "May I?" He waited, holding the door key in midair, for her to answer.

She nodded. He opened her apartment door, flipped on the light switch, and took a quick look around.

Theresa stepped inside; he stepped back out. "Maurice," she

said, "again thank you for everything. You've been . . . great. And I mean that."

"You sound surprised."

"Well, you know how I've felt about you these past years."

"It's okay. I'm sure I deserved it, if you felt that way. But Theresa . . . people can and do change. I just hope one day you and I might . . . begin again? A fresh slate, if that's what it takes." He stroked his neatly trimmed goatee against his smooth, light-brown chin. "Later, My Queen." He smiled and turned to leave.

"Maurice?" she said. He stopped and turned back around. "Why don't you . . . come in for a minute? I've not been the best company today, but you've been great through it all. I can cut you a slice of my famous red velvet cake."

"Like I said, it was nothing. Just glad I was around to help and glad you let me, for a change. You know, Theresa, there was a time when you and I could talk about anything. I've never stopped being there for you. And whether you know it or not, I would never do anything to hurt you. Not ever again."

She pushed the door open; he strolled casually through. Closing the door, she rested her head against it for a second, took a deep breath, then hung her coat inside the hall closet. He laid his leather jacket across the back of a chair.

They talked for hours. And it seemed to her it was just the way it had been when she was in high school some eighteen years earlier. She laughed, cried, shared how she'd felt the past few days with George leaving like he did, and how all she'd ever wanted in life was to feel loved—really, truly, loved. She even told Maurice how she'd questioned whether George might be gay, having heard him talk while asleep. "About a month ago. He fell asleep on my couch . . . ended up sleep talking," she said.

"Gay?" Maurice's face lit up with a satisfied grin.

"Yeah. You see, he kept calling out to Johnny. Saying something like, 'Johnny, my heart' or 'Johnny, my love.' " She laughed at the thought now.

"Johnny, huh? Wow . . . and you *still* want to marry this guy?" Maurice teased.

"Well to be honest, I was a bit nervous up until I learned this past week that the Johnny he was probably calling for was this woman named Johnnie Mae Taylor. The woman he just went to see about."

"Johnnie's a woman, huh?" He continued to smile.

"Yeah. So that turned out to be a relief."

"Even with him saying, 'My love'?" he mocked.

"Even with that," she said. "I've never mentioned it to him, though."

She told Maurice how she had remained celibate for the past ten years following that wild spell she went through after what he'd done to her that day. "It's simply amazing how one incident can send a person completely in the opposite direction of where they were originally trying to go," she said.

Maurice apologized again. He turned on the radio to V-103; they were playing old-school music. The two of them continued to talk when suddenly, *their* song came on: *It's Been A Long Time* by The New Birth.

Oh, the memories, sweet memories. Quietly, he took the phone off the hook, and they began to dance—slow. Eyes . . . breath. Gently, they danced into her bedroom, he laid her down on the bed . . . kissing her again and again and again . . . so much care . . . so much passion. And for the second time in her life, Maurice claimed her "virginity" for himself. Only this time, she didn't say, "No." And this time, he didn't have to tell her, "Relax."

Maurice left early the next morning. Theresa couldn't believe what she had allowed to happen between them. But at the moment, she was really feeling something for Maurice that was difficult to explain. She had made him breakfast, served it to him in bed as she sported a short white negligee with a long, sheer, white robe. He kissed her long and hard before braving the cold of the early morning. He had to be to work in thirty minutes; she was on vacation.

As Maurice walked down the long steps that curved in direction midway, he almost bumped into a man coming up from the opposite direction.

"Morning," the man said.

Maurice looked and realized it was Pastor George Landris. "Morning."

George stopped and turned around. "Excuse me . . . but you look familiar. Where do I know you from?"

Maurice made an effort to look like he was really thinking about it. "You're the pastor of Wings of Grace Faith Ministry Church, aren't you?"

"Yes."

"That may be where. I've attended your church a couple of times," Maurice said. He didn't bother to mention that he was also B's brother.

George smiled. "That's probably it. Well, have a blessed day."

"Oh," Maurice said, "it already is. It . . . already . . . is!" He smiled.

George reached the top of the stairs and rang Theresa's doorbell. Not sure if something was wrong, he rang it again, then knocked.

Theresa rushed to the door almost smiling. "So, what did you forget?" she said as she flung open the door without bothering to ask who it was or checking the peephole.

George stood with a confused look on his face. He looked down at her, dressed in that sexy outfit, and knew he should turn away. Except he was too busy wondering, *why* she was dressed like that? *Why* she had opened the door without checking to see who was there? And *who* had she assumed was on the other side of the door when she so excitedly answered it?

"What did I forget? Or you?" he said, holding up two bags of gifts she left over to her parents' house. "Sorry to have come by so early, but I left several messages last night that you never returned.

Then your line was busy forever. I thought something might be wrong." He looked at her again. "Apparently, I was mistaken. Seems you're just fine."

She tried to cover up better, realizing for the first time, what had truly happened last night and this morning between her and Maurice. "The phone . . . I must have accidentally knocked it off the hook or something. I was just about to jump in the shower." She looked at the gifts he still held. "Would you like to come in?"

He sat the two bags on the floor, off to the side and just inside the doorway. "No, I . . . only came by to check on you. And to bring you those. I suppose we'll talk later." He turned and started walking away, processing too many thoughts now.

"George?"

He stopped but didn't turn around. "We'll talk. Later," he said, then quickly jogged down the steps. *Something's not right*, he thought and felt in his spirit. *What am I saying? From the looks of it . . . a lot of things aren't right!*

CHAPTER 16

Judge Not, that Ye May Not Be Judged

"Johnnie Mae," Mrs. Gates said to her daughter, "can we talk?"

"Sure, Mama." Johnnie Mae was washing off a head of lettuce.

Her mother sat down at the kitchen island counter. "I know this is probably none of my business, but I need to ask. You and that Pastor Landris. What *exactly* is going on between you two?"

Johnnie Mae laughed what could have been easily mistaken as a nervous kind of laugh. "Going on?" she said. "Nothing, Mama. Why do you ask?"

"Just a feeling I get when the two of you are together. It's not natural. I mean, it *is* natural but not natural for two people claiming only to be friends."

Johnnie Mae looked at her mother. "Now you're starting to sound like you've been talking to either Honey or Sister. Sister, most likely, since she—"

"No, I've not discussed this with either of them. This comes from what I've observed. A man driving all the way from another state to check on a friend—"

"It was just from Atlanta. Atlanta's really not that far. In fact, some people who work there have been known to commute from here to there on weekends."

"Johnnie Mae, like I said at the start, it's probably none of my business. I'd much rather you tell me that, than try and yank my chain about it."

Johnnie Mae sighed hard. "Mama—"

"It was him who sent you three dozen roses back when Princess Rose was born. I thought something about it then, but didn't say anything. Now he shows up, turns out Princess Rose needs blood that's not so common and, miraculously, someone donates blood matching her type. Then, when Solomon comes out of his coma, who is there with you but your friend—Pastor Landris. Something's not fitting quite right with me. Like I said, if it's none of my business . . . please feel free to say so."

"Mama, Landris and I . . . have a special relationship. It's hard to explain." She sighed again. "But when I've needed someone to be there . . . I mean *really* be there, Landris somehow always manages to show up. It's like we're on the same wavelength or something. Like our souls have somehow been knitted together. I don't know how to put it into words."

"Johnnie Mae, I'm not quite certain how to ask," her mother said. "I'm not even sure I want to really know the answer. But it's been playing with my mind awhile, and I figure I just need to ask. Who's the father of Princess Rose?"

Johnnie Mae stopped chopping the lettuce for the seven-layer salad she was making and merely gaped at her mother. "What?" she said with a frown.

"It doesn't make me any never mind one way or the other. But I just want to know. Not trying to start nothing, and you know whatever you say will remain between us. I feel like there's something more to you and Pastor Landris. Now I'm not saying it's obvious to anyone else, but I wasn't *born* old. I've seen plenty in my day. And I know what real love looks like. Of course I see it between you and Solomon, so I'm not trying to insinuate anything. It's just—"

"Mama, Landris . . . I—" She covered her mouth, holding in a cry. "It's hard not being able to talk to anyone or say anything about it. I've learned to keep my thoughts inside. You know I love Solomon with all my heart. But Landris . . ." Johnnie Mae looked at the ceiling and tears began to flow. ". . . Landris fills me."

Her mother came over and hugged her close. "Feels you? What do you mean by, feels you?" she said. "Like, knows what you feel?"

Johnnie Mae lifted her head and looked into her mother's eyes. She couldn't believe, of all people, she was telling this to her mother. Her mother! She had to laugh at the thought of it. "No, Mama. He *fills* me. Not by touch, not by spirit. He f-i-l-l-s me. The empty pockets of my life . . . the parts that seem to rattle around . . . threatening to make so much noise—he fills. He . . . *fills* . . . me."

Her mother held her tighter as she continued to cry. "Shhh, shhh. Don't. I'm sorry. So sorry. I shouldn't have pressed you. Whether that's his child or not, it doesn't make any difference to me. I just wasn't getting you and Pastor Landris. The way he can talk you into doing things nobody else can, including Solomon, if you don't mind my saying it. Like the other day when he convinced you to come home and rest. And the way he planned to stay around and carry you back to the hospital if I hadn't come to your house looking for you."

"See, Mama. That's what I mean. I don't know why he can do what he does. But it's like, I know he truly cares. And Mama? Princess Rose's father . . ."

"Yes, baby."

"Princess Rose *is* Solomon's child. As close as Landris and I have been, and I mean there have been times and situations when it's a wonder we didn't, but he and I have never gone past the boundary—too far, at least. And Mama," she turned and looked at her, "it's not that we didn't want to a few times. I hate to admit that, especially to you. But it's true. How can a person love someone as much as I know I love Solomon, and yet have strong feelings for another?"

"You *love* Pastor Landris?"

"Mama, I don't want to admit it. I don't fully understand it myself. But it's so . . . hard. I was glad when Landris moved away two years ago. But it's like our relationship goes beyond sex. Our love surpasses what's merely physical."

Her mother laughed. "Looks like I should have kept my nose out of your business on this one. I don't know if I can handle this." She shook her head.

"Landris donated blood for Princess Rose the other day. And if he hadn't been here, I don't know what we would have done. The doctor said he would have managed, but I could see it all over his face that night. He didn't want to have to deal with that particular complication. And she might have died."

"So Pastor Landris's blood matched Princess Rose's?"

"Yes."

"And you're sure he's not her father? Not even a remote chance?"

"Mama, there is *no* chance. But wouldn't you know that when Solomon needed red blood cells from that same blood type, I do believe it was Landris's blood they used." She smiled. "Landris's donation may have helped save them both. You see what I mean? It's like Landris and I are connected on a higher plane. He knows how I feel about my family. But what are the odds of his blood matching both my child's and my husband's? And then for him to show up just when I seem to need him most?"

"Lord have mercy. Child, you've had a lot locked inside you. I'm kind of glad I asked now. It's not good for one to carry such a heavy load in their heart as you apparently have been doing."

"Mama? Do you think I'm an awful person?"

She laughed. "For what? For loving somebody?"

"Yeah, while I'm committed to love someone else."

"Baby, my place is not to judge. I figure, God gave us the capacity to love for a reason. As long as you keep things in their proper places, who can say what's right or wrong? I know when it comes to matters of the heart, that's a hard thing to regulate. No matter who you might be."

Johnnie Mae hugged her mother. "Thank you," she said with a whisper.

"Oh, child. Let's finish up this seven-layer salad so it can set overnight in the refrigerator like it needs to. Now, you're sure the doctor said it was okay for Solomon to have this on Wednesday?"

"Yes, Mama. I'm sure. And you know I want Solomon to be happy. He missed having a real Christmas dinner yesterday. But he asked for this salad."

"Oh yeah, you've spoiled him. It's no wonder he keeps begging the doctor to let him come home Saturday. He knows where he'll get the best care."

"Princess Rose will be home Thursday and Solomon may be here by Saturday afternoon. Things are really starting to look up." Johnnie Mae leaned over and kissed her mother on the cheek.

"And what was that for?"

"Just for being you," she said. "My mother . . . and a true friend."

CHAPTER 17

The Tongue of the Learned

Theresa knew she needed to talk with George. She didn't know what he was thinking, but he wasn't acting like his usual self. Not since he'd come to the door Tuesday morning, barely missing Maurice as he left. She didn't know how she had managed to get herself in this mess. Here she was getting married at the end of the week, and she ends up in bed with Maurice. *How could I jeopardize my future so stupidly?* Then to open the door like that . . . expecting that Maurice had just forgotten something. She recalled the look on George's face. *He knew something wasn't right—had to.*

There was so much still left to handle before the wedding Saturday, and Theresa was stressing herself, trying to take care of the finishing touches. She was glad she'd decided to take off from work this week. The wedding director was working wide-open as well, but there still was too much to be done. It was going to be difficult to squeeze in any time to sit down with George, but she knew she had to. George himself had a full schedule with various church-related business. For one, several members were sick or in the hospital. Although there was a ministry dedicated to seeing about them, George always made time to stop by to see them at least once, if at all possible, especially with the elderly, who might have little or no family in town to speak of.

During the holiday season, he knew it was a notably difficult time for widowers, widows, and people who had recently lost loved ones. Since he would be honeymooning the following week, he had particularly made a point to schedule any available time to visit with them. So, Theresa knew that Tuesday and Wednesday wouldn't be a good time for them to talk—not the way they would need. Wednesday night was Bible study and it would be late by the time everything wrapped up there.

"George, could you possibly come over Thursday night around seven? We really need to talk," she said over the phone Wednesday afternoon.

"Yeah. Sure. I agree. We *do* need to talk. You know, I've been praying and thinking a lot these past few days. There are some things you and I need to discuss."

That was one reason Theresa hadn't been in a rush to sit down with George. She knew he would want to talk about how she had acted at her parents' on Christmas day. Fortunately, Beatrice and Bishop Jordan had talked Lena into staying for the wedding. But Theresa hadn't done what she said she would, which was to apologize to Lena and ask her to stay. She didn't do that until late that Tuesday afternoon. She knew George wasn't going to just let her off the hook about that day as easily as her father had. Her parents were equally caught up in finishing their part for the wedding, so they didn't have the time or energy to really fuss about it.

But George would. And it seemed one disaster after another had occurred. First, the way she reacted about him going, then staying, in Birmingham for what she believed was just too long. Then there were her feelings and actions regarding Lena. And last, Tuesday morning when George had decided early to come over. She'd known he wouldn't call her early; he always took great pains not to wake her. The last thing she would have ever expected was for him to show up at her door early. And of all times, the one morning she just *happened* to be doing something she had no business doing.

After the wedding on Saturday, she would be able to put these problems behind her. Life would settle down, and she could begin looking forward to the future again. The congregation was working on a huge expansion to the church building, and then there was the Community Development Center project. She figured all of this would keep George busy and out of her hair, for a little while anyway. And since she and George had made the decision to start their family right away, she believed she might even get pregnant on their honeymoon. Seven days and nights in Hawaii . . . what a perfect place to conceive a love child!

She only needed to find out where George's head was now. Right now. The last thing she needed was him having an attitude on their wedding day. The rehearsal dinner was scheduled for six on Friday evening. The wedding party would be at the church Saturday morning no later than eleven to get ready for the ceremony. She wasn't going to chance anyone being late or getting stuck trying to get there, so rooms would be set up for the attendants to get dressed.

B would be there with her trusty curling iron, pulling double duty as the resident hairstylist and one of two maids of honor (Sapphire was the other). B had already made it well known to the ten bridesmaids, five junior bridesmaids, two flower girls, and a couple of the groomsmen, "I'm only doing touch-ups of what had *better* be a style before you arrive."

Maurice had called Theresa on Tuesday afternoon to tell her how much he enjoyed their time together. She had been quick to let him know what happened between them had been a mistake and would never happen again. She could tell how much her words stung him at first, but she couldn't chance him getting the wrong idea. "It was something that happened; let's just forget about it and move on. Okay?"

He had said, "Sure, no problem." But she could tell he had expected a much different reception than the one he received. "Ain't no thang but a chicken wang," he said. She knew he understood.

Theresa paced as she waited for seven o'clock. Having rehearsed what she would say to George when he got there, she would be able to tell what was going on in his head by the way he responded. She wore his favorite color: red. It was the color she believed had gotten him to notice her the first time they met.

She'd been a member of her father's church when she heard talk about this minister who was doing great things in a mighty way to get the message of God's love and power across to the people. He wore dreadlocks, which in itself was something you didn't see every day on a minister. Upon hearing him speak, it was like the angel Gabriel took a deep breath and blew it out through his trumpet.

Her father didn't understand what all the ruckus was about. But it seemed that young and old alike were attending this church. They would have to build a grander building just to keep up with its growing congregation. Bishop Jordan didn't believe erecting all these huge sanctuaries was part of what God originally commissioned the church to do. They were supposed to be spreading the gospel, not trying to see who could have the largest and most spectacular building. It seemed like every time he turned around, someone was building up something other than the name of Jesus.

But Theresa was looking for something deeper than what she had been receiving in her life. She knew the stories of Abraham, Moses, Noah, Daniel, Ruth, and the three Hebrew boys. What she, and others it appeared, wanted and needed was something that would effect a positive change in their lives today. It was great how the Hebrew boys were delivered out of the fiery furnace, but what about being delivered from the heat of a lousy eight-to-five job? It was wonderful that Daniel walked out of that lion's den, but what about walking out of the den of the hypocrites waiting around the corner for you—even in your own church? That's what so many were searching for: answers. Like how, for instance, to rise above those floods of ordinary bills.

Pastor George Landris shared how the Word of God could be applied in a mighty way in their lives everyday. All they needed to do was search the scriptures dealing with their specific desires, stand on God's divine written promises, and then be delivered from or into.

And *that* was what the new preacher, with the unconventional ways, was teaching. That was why people were flocking in like birds flying south for the winter to this church. They were hearing word about the Word of God taking place within what was clearly a thriving congregation of spirit, mind, body, and soul.

The day Theresa felt he noticed her, she'd worn a red two-piece suit, having stood in that long line just to shake this mighty pastor's hand after service.

"That was a wonderful message, Pastor Landris," she said. "This was my second time visiting, and I plan to come back again."

"Well, thank you, Sister—"

"Jordan. Theresa Jordan," she said. "My father is Bishop Jordan."

He smiled. "Yes, I'm familiar with Bishop Jordan. But then, who's not? A powerful man of God himself. I'm so glad you came, and do come back again."

To her, she believed he held her hand longer than was necessary, emphasized the words *so* and *do* more than the others. She thought she saw him taking note of her tailor-fitted suit. The next time, she hoped, she wouldn't have to remind him who she was.

"Sister Theresa. So *good* to see you back again," he had said. "I was wondering if I might have a word with you after I finish here?" There was still a long line of people waiting to shake his hand.

Theresa sat on the pew in her green suit and waited for the line to end. When it did, Pastor Landris walked back to her with a smile. "Sister Theresa. I'm not too sure of the correct protocol for this. First off, might I ask if you're married or seriously involved already in a relationship?"

Theresa batted her eyes and pretended to blush. "Why no, Pastor. I'm about as free as the black butterfly."

"And as lovely, if you don't mind me saying." Then he was quiet.

"Pastor? Was there something you wanted to ask?"

"Yes. I was wondering if you might be interested in going to dinner one evening."

She smiled. "With you?" she said. "Why, of c—"

"No. Actually with my associate there. Up front." He nodded at a short guy standing near the carpeted steps. The guy waved. George smiled, then turned back to Theresa. "He's sort of shy. I told him I'd ask for him," George said with a serious look.

"You're kidding, right?"

"No. I'm quite serious. And so is he—Minister Huntley."

Theresa leaned forward. "Pastor Landris, I'll tell you what. When *you're* interested in dinner, let me know." She handed him her business card. "And tell your *associate* there . . . thanks, but no thanks." She stood up and walked out.

The next two Sundays, she stayed away from Wings of Grace Faith Ministry Church. But when she did return, she wore another red outfit. She shook his hand, and this time, she made sure she was the last person in line. "Pastor Landris," she said with a nod.

"Sister Theresa." He nodded back. "Dinner today?" he said.

"With you?" She smiled. "My pleasure."

She figured he liked red. They dated for six months. He was always a gentleman. It became obvious to her, though, there were times when he was uncomfortable around her. The church had around two thousand members then. Out of the blue it seemed, he asked her to marry him. She figured he couldn't stand the temptation of being around her any longer. "It's better to marry than to burn," her father would preach.

Theresa had no idea at the time the top folks at the church were pushing Pastor Landris to find a good wife—to get himself a helpmate.

"It just doesn't bode well for a pastor of this many people . . . a good majority of them women, too, to still be single. Do you have any idea what kind of trouble you're inviting?" Deacon Woods had said. "Pastor Landris, surely there is someone out there for you. You know the Bible clearly tells us that 'Marriage is an honorable thing.' Proverbs 18:22 assures us, 'Whoso findeth a wife, findeth a good thing and obtaineth favor of the Lord'."

"I don't see where my marital or lack of marital status poses any negatives upon my ministry," Pastor Landris said. "When God leads me in that direction—"

"Pastor, I know you've only been at this pastoring thing for a short while," Mother King said. "I'm just not sure you know what you can come up against when you have a church full of women who are looking at you like you're the last rib at the best barbecue in town. I know. I've seen it too many times. My late husband was a pastor. You'll have enough on your hands fighting off the ones who could care less that you belong to someone else at all. And believe me, you'll run into plenty of those kind before it's over. It seems there's nothing more magnetic than a man with power."

"She's right," Deacon Perkins said. "I've seen some poor *and* ugly preachers who still have women chasing them. There's something powerfully attractive about a preacher to some women. A man who loves God *and* is in charge. A man in authority. It's like a mountain just begging to be climbed."

"I appreciate all of your concerns, but I've not heard a word from God on this. Not when or whom I should marry," Pastor Landris said. "And until then—"

"Well Pastor, we'll be praying that both you and God speed things up a bit. Apparently you don't know there's a group plotting to take you down, so to speak," Mother King said. "In my opinion, you already have enough to deal with. Personally, I believe it would be good if you had some help. A good woman. A God-fearing woman. Someone who can handle the pressures that come along with the office of Pastor's Wife."

Pastor Landris had laughed at the silliness of it all. His hands were full already, pacifying his mother who never missed a time asking, "*When* are you going to get married and give me some grandchildren? I'm not getting any younger, you know! And neither are you." But then he began noticing just how many women were calling him for things he *knew* didn't require his attention. Too many (single and some married) women were bringing him food—homemade desserts—and were openly flirting. That's when he fervently prayed and seriously considered the wisdom and counsel of the elders.

"For the sake of the church, Pastor," Deacon Thomas had said, "pray about a wife. It's just not good for man to be alone. Jehovah-Jireh will provide."

Three months later, he asked Theresa to become his wife. It seemed they got along well. They had a lot they both enjoyed doing together. She appeared to care about the things pertaining to his ministry and the Wings of Grace Faith Ministry Church congregation.

He didn't believe he had decided to marry her because some church members (and his mother) felt it was past time. Still, even with his having prayed about marriage and for a godly woman, he could not help but wonder: Had he moved too fast? Had he truly heard from God? Or had he missed what God had said to him about it altogether?

A preacher once told him, "Sometimes, even we miss it. We don't mean to, and it's not a comfort to wonder, especially when you pastor so many who count on you to always hear God's voice. But whether folks admit it, believe it or not, it does, on occasion, happen. No one's perfect. Just repent, and listen better."

Just then George heard the words, "free will" drop in his spirit. Had he heard God, but Theresa had changed? She was, indeed, free to choose her own will, her own path in life. George knew, God's will or not, that God never *forces* anyone to do anything. He could, but He doesn't. He knew God's desire is that everyone might be saved. But even that crucial decision is a thing each individual must choose to accept.

George's talk with Beatrice on Christmas had opened his eyes to the true cost of doing what's considered right, when it may not necessarily be the truly right thing to do. And although he had never been married (he only allowed Johnnie Mae to believe he was when they first met because he was convinced it would make her feel more comfortable around him), he knew marriage was not something to be taken lightly.

Theresa waited impatiently in her red chiffon tight-fitting dress for George to arrive. She was convinced that, tonight, she could smooth things out between them.

George was just about to leave for Theresa's apartment—determined to learn, once and for all, where they stood on issues that mattered to them both before any permanent "I do's" were exchanged between them.

CHAPTER 18

Lift Up Your Heads, O Ye Gates

George had just closed the garage door when the phone began to ring inside his house. He was trying to decide whether he should answer it since he had told Theresa he'd be there by seven and he was already going to be late. They needed to talk, but he wasn't sure what would be resolved. There were so many questions now that needed to be answered, mainly: Why had she changed so?

The more he thought about it, the more he wondered what he was getting himself into by marrying Theresa. She was not the woman he had first believed; she'd seemed so innocent, godly, sincere. But how could a woman like he believed she was be so heartless to someone like Lena? Her own mother?

He thought Lena was great. He'd been caught slightly off-guard when he first saw her. One would have thought Theresa would have told him about Lena's scars from the fire. Instead, she had left him with only a "You'll see."

He didn't mean to make Lena uncomfortable when they first greeted, but she'd handled his reaction well. Later that evening, after Theresa left without any warning to visit with B, he and Lena had talked. That was when he again saw the amazing strength of a woman—the length and depth a mother will go for her child. He wished Theresa had been there to hear all Lena had said. And the more she talked, the more of the true beauty he had seen in this miraculous woman. From all she had told him, he could see she shouldn't have still been here. But she wasn't going to lay down and die. She refused to give up.

Not sure how Lena felt about it, George didn't ask her much about the actual fire. But he could tell Lena had learned to live in the time she had been granted on this earth. Even when she couldn't get a decent job (people always had a good excuse not to hire her, it seemed), she cleaned other people's houses. That was how she had taken care of Theresa and herself.

"That was before Theresa decided she didn't want to live with me anymore," Lena had said. Now she owned a cleaning service with ten people on her staff.

Lena didn't seem bitter about the way Theresa and others had treated her. Even being a minister, George couldn't help but wonder how she could be so forgiving. He believed he was staring true love in the face, and saw how love had refused to back down. He told Lena as much.

She smiled. "Son, you just have to sing with the voice you've been given. There's no need for me to try to sing with your voice. Life wasn't set up to work that way."

In addition to the situation with Lena, Theresa didn't seem to be the type to stick around for a conversation she didn't care for or for one that wasn't going her way. She would simply hang up or walk out if she didn't like the direction of the discussion. That was what she had done when he called her from Birmingham that day, and when she came over to his house on Sunday night, and when things had gotten a little heated at her parents' house on Christmas. *How did she expect to resolve conflict if she didn't want to put any effort into the communication process?*

He decided to answer the phone, just in case it was Theresa. As soon as he reached it, the phone stopped ringing. His caller ID read, "Unknown."

Walking back to the garage, he then heard his cell phone ring in the car. Ironically, he had left it on when he was out visiting with the sick earlier. Not many people had that number. He was quick to reach it before it rolled over.

"Hello," George said.

"Pastor Landris?" an older woman said.

George didn't recognize her voice. "Yes," he said.

"This is Mrs. Gates . . . in Birmingham . . . Johnnie Mae's mother."

His voice grew steady and stronger. "Yes, Mrs. Gates. How are you?"

"Not so good." Her voice trembled. "I'm so sorry to bother you. But I had to call and let you know, Pastor Landris. Something terrible has happened."

George's heart began to pound faster. "What is it, Mrs. Gates? Please tell me."

He sensed she was trying to keep from breaking down as she spoke. He wanted her to speak faster, but he knew all he could do was wait on her to bring forth the words.

"It's Johnnie Mae, Pastor Landris. I didn't want to bother you like this, but I knew I had to call. It's Johnnie Mae. My baby is—" Suddenly the phone went dead.

"Hello! Hello! Mrs. Gates? Mrs. Gates? Hello!" He began pressing buttons. The battery had gone totally out. He rushed out of his car and into the house. The phone in there was now ringing; he made a dash to answer it.

"Mrs. Gates?" he said.

"No George, it's me. Theresa."

He was breathing hard now. "Theresa?"

"What's wrong with you? Why are you breathing like that?"

"I just got a call from Mrs. Gates—"

"Who's Mrs. Gates?"

He hesitated a second. "Johnnie Mae's mother," he said, still attempting to catch his breath. He rubbed his mouth . . . looked around the kitchen. He had to get in touch with Mrs. Gates. *But from where had she called? And where did he put her phone number? He'd gotten both her and Johnnie Mae's number when he was there. But where—*

"George? George?! Did you hear what I said?"

"What?" he said, with just a tad too much of a snap.

"I said why haven't you left yet? I'm here waiting. I was hoping you'd be early. I really want to see you." Her voice was slightly flirtatious.

"Yeah, yeah. I know." He tried to calm himself. "I was going to the car when the phone rang. Then my cell phone rang, but the battery died in the middle of what she was telling me."

"Who?"

"Mrs. Gates! I just told you she called."

"Well, call her when you get back home. Look, I really need to see you, George. I miss you."

"Theresa . . . look. Mrs. Gates was saying something about Johnnie Mae, and she was really upset. I want to find out what's going on before I leave here."

"What?" Her frustration became apparent in her voice. "Look, George. Now, I've tried to be understanding, but I'm getting a little tired of Johnnie Mae Taylor seeming to always come before me. George? Do you hear me?"

George rubbed his chin and tried to relax himself. "Theresa, I said I was coming. I just want to contact Mrs. Gates and find out what's wrong. Believe me, she wouldn't have called unless it was important. Do you understand that?"

"I'm not a child, George. I *understand* quite well. But I asked you to come to talk tonight because I thought *we* were important. There are some things I feel we need to discuss, considering we're scheduled to rehearse a wedding tomorrow night for a ceremony due to take place this Saturday." She said the words as though she were taking great pains not to upset herself.

"Okay, Theresa. I'll leave now. And we'll talk. Then maybe you can enlighten me on what's up with you. Because at this point, I'm not sure I know who you really are myself. Or maybe . . . I never really knew."

"What?" she said.

"Look, I'll be there shortly," George said.

As soon as George hung up, he thought about where he had put those phone numbers. Hopefully, he could locate Mrs. Gates and find out what had happened. The phone rang just as he was pulling the paper with the phone numbers out of his wallet.

"Pastor Landris, this is Mrs. Gates again. Seems we were cut off," she said.

"Mrs. Gates. Please tell me . . . what's going on?"

"It's Johnnie Mae . . ." An intercom page filled the background and drowned her out as she spoke. "So is there any way you could possibly come to Birmingham? I wouldn't bother you, but I don't know what else to do. Pastor Landris, we're at University. I know it's late . . . and I'll understand if you can't come." She began to cry. "I just didn't know what else to do. I'm in the MICU waiting room. They won't let me in there with her. Pastor Landris, I don't know what to do."

"Mrs. Gates . . . listen. I'll be there. But could you *please* tell me," he spoke slowly, afraid of what he had *not* heard her say, "what . . . exactly . . . has . . . happened?"

"Pastor . . . oh, God," she began to cry harder, "I just told you . . . oh, my Johnnie Mae . . . my baby. I don't know what to do. Solomon was due to come home on Saturday, but now . . . Johnnie Mae . . . my baby!"

George could see he wasn't getting anywhere with her. "Mrs. Gates, is there anybody there with you I could speak with?"

"No, it's just me. I'm here by myself right now. I was with Johnnie Mae when all of this happened. Some of the others are on their way. I really didn't want to call and bother you . . . but I truly didn't know what else I could do."

"All right, Mrs. Gates. Is it possible for me to speak with Johnnie Mae?"

"My Lord, haven't you heard a word I've been saying? No, it's not possible for you to talk with her! Oh, my baby," she cried. "What are we gonna do?"

"Mrs. Gates . . . I have a meeting I'm late for already, but I'll get there as soon as I can. I promise."

"Thank you. Thank you, Pastor Landris. Good-bye. Oh, Lord . . ." she said as she was hanging up the phone, "we need you to help us through . . ."

George was confused. He had no idea what was going on, but Mrs. Gates obviously wasn't taking it well, whatever it was. Theresa was waiting for him so they could "talk." He knew enough from the last time: going to Birmingham without taking care of Theresa first would be a major problem. He also knew it would be difficult to concentrate on anything Theresa would be saying while he was wondering what had happened in Birmingham.

And just why had Mrs. Gates called him, instead of Johnnie Mae?

CHAPTER 19

The Lord Hath Anointed Me to Preach

George hurried to Theresa's apartment.

"So you finally made it, I see," Theresa said as she flung open the door. "You're only fifteen minutes late. But I guess, better late than never."

"Theresa," George said, "I told you I was on my way. Mrs. Gates called again. I don't know what's wrong, but she's in a bad way."

Theresa spun around. "That's tough, George! But it's not really your problem. You see, I'm starting to get concerned about us. I'm in a bad way, too, right now. So what's more important? Making sure things are all right with me, or your attempt to be everything to everybody else? I'm about to become your wife, Pastor Landris."

"Theresa, don't you think you're being a bit unreasonable?"

"*I'm* being unreasonable? I've had to wait two days . . . two," she held up her fingers, "just to talk with my own fiancé."

"That's not true," he said softly. "You and I have talked every day this week."

"We haven't *talked*. We've exchanged greetings, held pleasantries. But we've not actually *talked*. For instance, have you picked up your tux yet?"

"I'm doing that tomorrow," George said.

"See, I didn't know that. What time does your mother's plane get in?"

He rubbed his chin. "Theresa, she'll be here around one. What's all this about? I thought we had *important* things to discuss."

"What's the matter? Can't wait to finish up with me so you can go check on your precious little friend in Alabama?" Theresa asked. He didn't answer.

"Why are you marrying me, anyway? You don't seem to care enough to spend time with me. I don't get it! If you'd make half as much of an effort to see about me as you have with other people just these last few days, we *might* not even be having this ridiculous conversation." Theresa flopped down on the couch.

"Is that what this is about? You don't feel like I give you enough attention? Is that it, Theresa? I go see about the sick and the ones who have lost loved ones, and you're upset because you feel I've taken time away from you?"

"Oh, sure. Make me out to be the bad guy. I am so tired of people taking what I do wrong just because I care enough not to let people step all on me."

"Is that the way you see it? Like people are out to get you? That they're deliberately trying to run over you?"

"See! See what I mean? Now if I was the good little person who was being all supportive of you and your ministry, everything would be just fine now. But because I demand you treat me with respect, you act like I'm being selfish."

George sighed as he sat next to Theresa. "Look, I know you're under a lot of pressure right now yourself. It's not easy being with me. I know that. But you must know me well enough to know I wouldn't do anything to hurt you. Not on purpose anyway. I'm generally a straightforward person. Always have been. Johnnie Mae is my friend. Unfortunately, I don't just push my friends off to the side because it's inconvenient." He took Theresa's hand. "Those people at church, I made a covenant with them to be their pastor. Like a shepherd watching over sheep. I take what I do seriously. People are skeptical enough of preachers these days, Theresa. I'm working hard to make a real difference."

"But you're like the kid trying to throw a slew of beached starfish back into the ocean. There are just too many and only so many you can do anything about." She looked into his eyes. "I don't want to make it hard for you, George. I don't want you regretting the day you ever laid eyes on me. But George Landris, hear me on this: You can't throw all the starfish back into the ocean by yourself. It's just too large a job."

He tapped her on the nose. "Theresa, I may not be able to throw them all back into the ocean, but maybe I'll encourage others to come along the beach and help me. If enough of us work together, maybe we can make some kind of difference. And as the story goes, even if I'm there throwing all by myself, at least I'll have made a difference to some. Do you understand that at all? I want to make a difference. That's what I've been called to do—teach, preach, and make a difference."

"George, I hear you. And I'm trying to understand. But all I know right now is that I'm the one feeling like I've been beached. And nobody seems to care enough to help get me back into the ocean."

"Theresa, you're not as bad off as some. There are some who will literally perish if somebody doesn't reach them. And soon. You are so loved; you must have some idea of how special you truly are."

She laughed a little. "Yeah? But what about you? Am I loved by you, George? My husband-to-be?" She took her hand out of his and stood up. "You can barely wait to finish up here with me so you can go check on your precious Johnnie Mae. And you don't even realize I can see it. It's all in your eyes." She looked away, then back at him. "So what were you going to do this time, George? Did you promise them you'd come to Birmingham? Again?"

George couldn't believe she knew that. "Theresa, I don't know what's wrong there. But I do know, it's not good. Johnnie Mae's mother would *never* have called me unless it was something awful. She wasn't even able to tell me what happened or at least repeat it after a loud page drowned her out—"

"Then go, George. It won't matter what I say anyway. You're going to do what you believe, regardless of how I feel about it."

George looked at his watch. It was seven-fifty already. He stood up. "Theresa, I'll be back later tonight or by early morning. I'll get there, see what's up, then come right back. Mrs. Gates was falling apart on the phone. She asked me to come. It must be important."

Theresa looked up at him. "Are you sure about this, George? Remember the last time? The last time it took you three days to find your way back. Three days this time, and you'll miss your own wedding. But you want to know what I'm thinking?" She didn't wait for him to answer. "I'm thinking . . . maybe our getting married isn't such a great idea after all. I'm thinking, maybe if you leave now . . . you don't need to worry about rushing back. Because I won't be here waiting this time."

"Theresa—"

"Go on, George. Call me when you can." She turned her back to him.

"So are you saying you don't want to get married now? You want to call the wedding off?"

She turned and looked him up and down. "I'm saying if you leave now, don't worry about coming back to me. Because I won't be here waiting. Not this time. And that church full of folks expected to arrive for a wedding this Saturday? Well, you'll just have to be the one to explain to them how your *job* and other matters come before everything else. Because George, I refuse to be second to anyone. I don't have to be, and I won't! And *that's* what I want *you* to understand."

She curled up into a ball on the couch—red dress and all—and closed her eyes, refusing to shed even one tear this time. Silence would be her friend. And if George Landris left her now, then so be it.

But she would not watch him walk out of the door. She would not!

CHAPTER 20

They Shall Walk and Not Faint

George sat at the end of the couch as Theresa lay sleeping. But he could only think about what was going on with Johnnie Mae. Mrs. Gates should have told him more. Theresa slept until five after midnight. When she opened her eyes, she began to smile, reaching out for George.

"You stayed," she said, almost in a whisper. "George. You stayed." She tried to cuddle up to him as he continued to gently keep her at arm's length.

"Theresa, wake up. Wake up so you can go get in your bed. I need to go home, but I didn't want to leave you like that."

"Hold me," she said.

"Come on now. Get up and go get ready for bed."

"You get me ready for bed," she said in a sexy voice.

He kept trying to keep her arms away from around his neck. "Theresa, come on now."

"George, it's only what? One day? We'll be married on Saturday. What difference will a day or two make?"

He stood up and tried to stand her up. "You're just sleepy. You don't know what you're saying."

"I do know what I'm saying. I want you, George. Who would know?"

"*We* would know. And God. So come on, now. I need to get on home. We both have a lot to do tomorrow. Well, technically, it's Friday already."

"See what I mean? It's Friday. We'll be husband and wife tomorrow. Saturday. What's one day? You know I love you. I'm sorry I got mad with you earlier. I just want you to love me. I only want to be loved. That's all I've ever wanted: to be loved."

"You *are* loved, Theresa. Now, be good, and go get ready for bed."

Theresa began to pretend like she was pouting. Then she smiled as George pushed and guided her into her bedroom, sitting her on the edge of her bed. "Help me take my clothes off," she said. "Please, George."

"Theresa, don't."

"What's the matter?" she said. "Am I not good enough for you to make love to?"

He laughed. "Well, I'm marrying you. That should answer your question."

She sat up straight. "So, I'm supposed to be glad because you're marrying me?" Her voice was suddenly sober. "Like you're doing me some kind of favor? Is that it?"

George shook his head, tired of this particular drama from her. "Look, Theresa. Enough already. This hasn't exactly been a picnic for me either. Now, you can take your clothes off and get under the covers, or you can sleep in them. Either way, I'm out of here." And with that, he walked out of her bedroom, snatched up his coat, and left.

Theresa fell back on the bed. It didn't matter that he was upset with her now. The point was, he had stayed instead of going to Birmingham to see about his phony, needy, manipulative Johnnie Mae. *She probably put her mother up to making that call anyway.* But he had stayed . . . and that counted for something!

* * *

When George got home, there was a message on his answering machine.

"Pastor Landris, this is Donald Gates. I'm Johnnie Mae's brother. My mother said she called you earlier. I just wanted you to know if you haven't already left, don't worry about it. It's about eleven here. We're on our way down to the coroner's in about thirty minutes. Just trying to get through all this. It was totally unexpected, and we're all pretty much in a state of shock. My mother asked me to thank you, and to ask you to please continue to pray for the family."

"What?" George said to the machine. "What happened?" He was so confused, and he still had no idea what had happened. He looked at the time; it was twelve-twenty, eleven-twenty in Alabama. Without thinking about it, he got in his car, and before he knew anything, he was on I-20 West going toward Birmingham. It was amazing how much quicker he was able to reach the University Hospital during that time of morning.

George walked in to what felt like a deserted building, searching waiting rooms and other areas. When he got directions to the coroner's, no one was there. As he went back to leave, he saw Mrs. Gates was standing near the exit door gazing into space.

"Mrs. Gates?" he said, rushing quietly over to her. It took a few seconds for him to break through her seemingly self-induced trance.

"Pastor Landris," she said, still crying. "I told Donald to call and tell you not to worry about coming. I suppose he must have missed catching you."

He hugged her. "What happened, Mrs. Gates? Please . . . tell me. What happened?"

"Gone," she said. "Just like that. Just gone." She shook her head. "No warning. No good-bye. No nothing. Just gone. Johnnie Mae . . . Lord, my poor baby. I pray the Lord will give us all strength to make it through this. Please Heavenly Father, help us make it through."

CHAPTER 21

Sent to Bind Up the Brokenhearted

Pastor Landris called Deacon Thomas around seven Friday morning. The good deacon was such an early riser that Landris knew he would not be asleep.

Sadness laced his voice. "Deac, this is Pastor Landris. Something unexpected came up. Again. My mother's plane is due to arrive at 1:10 this afternoon. I *should* be back in town by then, but I don't want to chance it. I've been up all night, and need to close my eyes for a minute. Could I trouble you to pick her up for me?"

"Of course, Pastor. Which airline?"

"Delta. Flight three sixteen."

Deacon Thomas chuckled. "Like John 3:16: 'For God so loved the world that He gave His only begotten son. That whosoever believeth on Him should not perish, but shall have everlasting life,'" he said. "Oh yeah, I can remember that one easy enough. No trouble. I'll be there waiting on her."

"Thanks, Deac. I've always been able to count on you—pinch or not."

"Well, contrary to what many believe, the deacons are not here to run the church, but to help the overseer in making things run better."

"And you've certainly done that," Pastor Landris said.

"Oh!" Deacon Thomas said as though he'd gotten stuck with a pin. "Would you like me to make one of those signs and hold it up in the deplane area? I don't know what your mama looks like, and she sure won't know me from Adam."

Pastor Landris smiled. His mother would definitely get a kick out of that. "Yeah, that will be nice. But I'll call and let her know you'll be the one picking her up instead of me."

"Tell her, I'll be the one holding up her name. Is it Sister Landris?"

"No. It's LeBoeuf. She remarried a few years after my father died."

"Good goobly-woobly! And just how do you spell that?! Hold on a minute, let me get a pencil and write this down. La-boof, you say?" he said, making sure he was pronouncing it correctly.

Pastor Landris laughed and spelled it. "Thanks so much, Deac. I'll see you—"

"Pastor? Where do you want me to take her if you're not back by then?"

"Oh, I'll be home for sure by that time. I'll just see you at my house."

"All right." Deacon Thomas cleared his throat. "Pastor? You all right? You don't sound much like yourself today."

Pastor Landris rubbed his forehead, then wiped his face with his hand. "Everything's going to be all right, Deac. But thanks for caring so about me."

"The rehearsal dinner's at six tonight, right?"

Pastor Landris hesitated. *The rehearsal dinner . . . his tux . . . the wedding tomorrow.* "The dinner? Yeah, it *is* at six."

Deacon Thomas frowned at the phone. "Pastor, I still feel like I'll be crashing if I come. Seeing as I'm not really part of the wedding. I don't know why you insist on my coming."

"I want you there because you're like family to me now. I told you that. But Deac—"

"Well, I don't have any other plans, and truthfully, I'm looking forward to all the festivities. Since my wife passed away four years ago, I pretty much keep to myself. This affair is the buzz of the town. I feel like a big shot just getting invited to the wedding. Then to be welcomed to the rehearsal dinner like this, and that invitation-only shindig down at the center—"

"Deac, listen . . ." Pastor Landris thought for a second. He needed to pick up his tux today. No, he would not ask him to do that. "Look Deac, I've got to run. I need to call my mother before she gets out of there, headed for the airport. I'll see you when I get home."

George considered calling Theresa. *But how would I explain my being in Birmingham?* And knowing her, she would ask. They needed to talk before tonight's dinner, but Theresa was taking everything entirely too personally lately. And now, they were set to be married tomorrow. He knew in his heart what he was feeling, but there was no way he would feel right calling off the wedding. There was just too much money already spent. Things were already set.

People would be arriving at the church tomorrow expecting a wedding. Then there would be the people who would believe he had gone back on a commitment. *But does it make sense to forge ahead with something you know doesn't feel right, just because it's inconvenient if you change it?* That's what he wondered.

He sat down in the big blue swivel rocker next to the phone in the den at Johnnie Mae's home for a minute. The next thing he knew, he was waking up to the smell of something delicious frying in the kitchen. Glancing at the clock on the wall, he sat straight up. It was three-fifteen in the afternoon! And this was Birmingham, which made it four-fifteen in Atlanta. "Oh my goodness!" he whispered to himself. *A two-hour drive in going home traffic on a Friday could easily turn into three or four hours.*

"Well, good afternoon," Mrs. Gates said, obviously exhausted.

"Mrs. Gates." He tried to smile and shake off the sleep.

"Hope you got at least some rest. I saw you there so peaceful. Didn't want to disturb you."

Pastor Landris wished she had, but he didn't tell her that. He knew she had a lot to deal with already. "I've got to hurry on down this road," he said, getting to his feet and stretching.

"Pastor Landris . . . I want to thank you again for all you did for my daughter and our family, especially through this whole ordeal. I know if she were able to right now, she'd be telling you this herself, letting you know how much she truly appreciated everything."

"Mrs. Gates—"

"Oh, you don't have to explain nothing to me. You're a good pastor . . . from all I can tell. Her own pastor never even came to the hospital to see about any of them. Oh, he sent his first-line generals. Even called once, I believe. You don't find too many pastors nowadays who will go see about people when they're hurting the most. I understand congregations are larger now. That it's physically impossible to be everywhere yourself. But people in the church are somewhat like your children. And if you can't do for all, you shouldn't do for one. Cause you'll always make the ones who didn't get personal attention believe you don't care as much about them. Then you have a mess on your hands."

"It is hard to visit *all* the sick at home and in the hospital, especially when you have so much to do. And you can almost forget it if you have a family, too. Then there are the normal things life requires of you. Like a little sleep maybe, now and then."

"Well, I can't speak for how you are at your church in Georgia, but just from what I've seen about you . . . the way you even took the time this morning to comfort that woman who had just learned she'd lost her seventeen-year-old son to a senseless gunshot wound."

"Mrs. Gates, there are a lot of brokenhearted people out there. They're hurting like people wouldn't believe. Many of them learn to cope or mask it, but most folks have no idea what it feels like to hurt and not know how to make it any better."

"If there were only a bandage to bind up the broken heart." She shook her head. "At least while it's still trying to mend and heal."

"Why Mrs. Gates, there *is* a bandage. It's called love. The agape kind of love. Unconditional love. Love that doesn't judge. Love that doesn't condemn. Love that wraps around the hurt and holds it."

"Don't get me wrong; I don't have anything against big churches. I just love my small church. Too many of these places today seem too busy building McDonald's franchise–sized churches. Feeding lambs like they were chickens."

"Chickens?"

"Yeah. Chickens. A long time ago people would let their chickens roam the yard. Back when folks had chickens, that is. When it was time to feed them, they'd say, 'Here, chick, chick, chick.' Like they were speaking to one chicken in particular. Like there was one chicken being singled out. Who'd suspect you weren't caring about any one more than the other." She sat down in the rocker. "Then they'd reach down in the feed sack," she took her hand and scooped it up, "and throw feed up in the air. It would scatter. The flock of chickens would then crowd and gather, pecking here and there before going about their business of clucking, scratching, and, hopefully, laying some eggs later."

Pastor Landris had on his coat. "Mrs. Gates, it's a challenge when you pastor a large congregation, I'll say that. And you learn quick you can't be everything to everybody. God may have called us to supernatural work, but we still have these natural bodies to work in and with. It serves no one's purpose if we should die before our part of the work is completed."

She smiled. "I'm sure, and I know you speak the truth. The only thing I'm saying is you should never be the cause of some members feeling you have preferences. Don't make one lamb feel like they're better or worse than another. That's what I'm saying."

"Sounds like a fair thing—all or none."

"At least then nobody can accuse you of being biased or showing favoritism. Nothing can cause division in a church quicker than somebody feeling like you've mistreated them or someone they love. Maybe that's why I'm not feeling so great about Johnnie Mae's pastor. The Lord will just have to forgive me. But I know for a fact her pastor has his favorites. But then, Johnnie Mae never was a suck-up."

"I'll keep that point in mind, Mrs. Gates."

"Like I said, I appreciate you for all you've done. My pastor will be along later tonight. But then, I make it a point to stick with a church where someone at least notices if a sheep has gone astray. How on earth you gonna leave the ninety-nine to go after the one, if you don't even know he's missing?"

Pastor Landris glanced at his watch. "Mrs. Gates, if you need me, call."

"Yes, I will." She shook her head and began to cry again. "It's just something. And I know there's going to be a full house here tonight. The phone was ringing so much earlier, I ended up taking it completely off the hook. Everybody's hearing the news, and nobody can or wants to believe that it could possibly be true."

"I know. It's hard for me to believe, and I was here."

"And of all things, a stroke. Blood pressure shot up. Just like that. Then that blood clot, in the brain of all places. It was just too much." She looked upward.

Pastor Landris hugged her. "Mrs. Gates, we know that God is able."

She pulled away, found her tissue in her shift pocket, and wiped her eyes. "I know. But my poor baby. What are we gonna do?"

She looked in the direction of Johnnie Mae's bedroom. "She's in there still, don't even know she exists in this world. The doctors were worried she was going to have a stroke or something herself, the way she was carrying on. They gave her a sedative. And to think, we had just gotten to the hospital when that whole floor seemed to go into a total uproar. People running around, pushing machines and contraptions. Yelling orders. We had no idea at the time it was about Solomon." She shook her head. "He was supposed to come home tomorrow, you know. Was laughing and joking with everybody just the morning before. Always treated me like I was his mother and not some out-law."

She laughed. "That's what we'd say sometimes: in-laws, not out-laws. They wouldn't let me and Johnnie Mae go in. Said they were pumping him with heparin, trying to get his blood pressure down in a hurry. I couldn't get her away from the door. I'm telling you men, you need to go to the doctors more and keep a check on your blood pressure. High blood pressure may be deaf, but it's not dumb. There ain't no signs, so no way you'll be able to tell it by how you feel. I got high blood pressure myself; have to take Ziac once a day. I was feeling fine too, but the doctor said it was a good thing I kept my regular check-ups. My blood pressure had shot up so high, he said I could have had a stroke at any moment."

Pastor Landris knew he needed to leave, but felt it would have been insensitive to go now. This was the second time she had talked about what happened. He knew she was telling it again more for her sanity than that she'd forgotten she had already told him.

"We couldn't do nothing but stand out there and wait. They wouldn't let nobody in there. Wouldn't even let Johnnie Mae in. And she begged them. 'Please! Please! That's my husband!' When they told her he was gone, she all but lost it. Right there. Passed out. They had to get her on a table to revive her. She woke up screaming and hollering at the top of her lungs. I had seen it coming. When they first were in there working on Solomon. That was when I called you. I didn't know what was going to happen, but I could see her losing it. I tried to keep her together; I just didn't know what to do. My own daughter, and I didn't know what to do. I was scared. I thought of you for some reason. I don't know, maybe I knew something tragic was coming. Knew I would need someone who could help me, help her. And you did. After we came from the coroner's, if you hadn't been there, I don't know when I would have gotten her to leave that place."

"Mrs. Gates, I'm truly sorry."

She looked at him. "I just want to thank you. I had no right to call you, but it's hard for a parent to just sit and watch their child hurt and not be able to make it better." She hugged him. "Now you go. I know you have your own life to live. I don't want to hold you any longer with all my babbling. Hope I've not kept you from anything important." She started toward the kitchen. "I'm sure you're hungry now. Let me pack you some chicken to carry down the road with you," she said. "And don't worry; I'll be quick about it."

George thought about all that had happened on his drive home. It was six o'clock in Atlanta by the time he passed the Anniston exits. He reached for his cell phone to call the church and let Theresa know he was on his way. He pressed the power button—nothing. He tried again before he remembered he hadn't taken the time to recharge the battery yet. Theresa had told him a few months back he should get a DC plug to use in the car, or at least activate the car phone already installed in his Mercedes. At that moment, he was thinking he wished he had listened to her.

Trying to decide whether he should stop and call or keep driving—praying that he wouldn't be too late arriving—wisdom suggested he stop.

"George? Where are you?" Theresa said.

"Running late. I should be there in about an hour."

"George. Your mother's here. With Deacon Thomas. No one's heard hide nor hair from you all day. Except of course, Deacon Thomas . . . who, as usual, isn't full of any *useful* information to share."

"Theresa, I'm on my way—"

"Fine, George. But George . . . I still want to know: Where are you?"

CHAPTER 22

Behold the Bridegroom Cometh

No one knew what was going on at the rehearsal dinner. George got there right at seven-thirty. People could tell something wasn't quite right, but no one had any answers. They had already rehearsed the wedding without Pastor Landris because some of the attendants had prior commitments limiting them from staying any longer than eight. Theresa wasn't sure if or when George would arrive, so they decided to proceed without him. Monique, the wedding director, said she could easily fill Pastor Landris in on his part later.

Theresa didn't have two words to say to George during the whole dinner. He kept telling her he really needed to speak with her "in private." There was something important they needed to discuss. But every time he came near her to open his mouth, she just walked away.

George's mother was there—laughing and carrying on with Deacon Thomas. George noticed how well they were connecting. He figured his mother must have told the deacon that she was a widow for her second time now. She didn't seem too upset with George for him not being there to pick her up from the airport. Or that, apparently, she and Deacon Thomas had sat waiting outside his house for over an hour before Deacon Thomas suggested she was more than welcome to wait over at his place, quaint as it was.

After almost everyone left, George went to Theresa.

"We really need to talk," he said, cornering her.

"About *what*?" She cocked her head to one side.

"This wedding tomorrow."

"Let's see now. A wedding? Tomorrow? Hmmm, now that's news to me."

"What are you talking about, Theresa?"

"Where were you all day today? Did you even pick up your tux?"

"Theresa—"

"George, don't give me this crap! You think I'm stupid? So, where were you?"

"Look—"

"You went to see her, didn't you? The day before our wedding, and you had to go see her!"

"Theresa, please. Lower your voice."

"What? You don't want anybody to know? Know how you, the good reverend who just happened to have made a vow to me . . ." She held up her ring. "Remember this, George? You asked *me* to be your wife! Last night, what did I tell you?"

"Theresa—"

"What . . . did . . . I . . . tell you?"

He took her by the arm and pulled her into the hallway. "You and I need to talk," he said between practically clenched teeth. "Why don't you get your things so we can go somewhere private and discuss this?"

"Who do you think you are? You don't tell me what to do! I'm not one of your servants you can order around! I don't bow down to you, George Landris!"

"Theresa, I'm not trying to order you around. I told you, we need to talk."

"About what?"

"About us. About you. About why your own mother wasn't here at the rehearsal dinner."

"My mother *was* here," she said, twisting her mouth like she was sucking on something sour.

"I'm talking about Lena, Theresa. Lena."

"And what's it to you? You keep making a big deal of it, like she was *your* mother or something. Oh, and speaking of your mother, I still don't think she likes me all that much. But she seems pretty into the old Deacon in there. Old Deacon Thomas, who acts like he's too good for any of the good old sisters around here. Yet, he can buzz all day long around a flower he can't even pronounce the name of: LeBoeuf."

"Theresa, what *is* it with you? I don't understand you. If anyone had told me this is how you act, I—"

"Act? What do you mean by 'act'?"

"Theresa, look. Let's either go to your place or mine. And talk."

She walked away. "I'm going home. Do whatever you like."

"Then I'll be over—"

"Whatever!" she said as she threw her hand in the air and kept walking.

"George?" his mother said. "What's going on out here?"

"Nothing, Mom." He smiled at her, then kissed her on the cheek. "We've not had any time to visit, have we?"

George's mother looked down the hall where Theresa had just disappeared. "That there Theresa? Are you *sure* about this?"

"Mom, to be honest, the only thing I'm sure about at this point is how much I'm *not* sure about at this point." He put his arm around her. "You're looking so good. Your trip to the Caribbean seems to have agreed with you."

"And I had such a great time. Thank you for sending me. I wanted to stay a little longer, but you know I had to get back to get ready for my baby boy's wedding. George?" She smiled and traced the crooked curl that lay to the side of her head. "You know it's never too late to do the right thing."

George shook his head. "It's not *doing* the right thing sometimes. It's doing it without hurting other people in the process. You know, Mom? Most people, even Christians, have a hard time with telling or hearing the truth. Oh, we think we have our reasons, whether it's not to hurt someone's feelings, or because it's not convenient . . ."

"You mean like when I asked you earlier if you liked my hair?" She patted the back of her head. "And you said, 'Of course.'"

"Mom, your hair looks . . . okay."

"The truth."

"I think you'd look better if you would quit dying it. There are just some colors older . . . mature women use that tend to make them look too hard."

"Even though it would be just *too*, too gray?"

"The truth, Mom? Gray looks good on a sophisticated woman. It's delicate. You're trying so hard to stay young, but you have to realize that youth is from the inside out. However, if you like blond hair, then who am I to say?"

"Now see," she said, "that didn't hurt so bad." She laughed. "Oh—and I hate your dreadlocks, always have. But then, hey, whatever floats your boat! Ebbs the web."

He laughed and kissed her again. "So let me carry you to the house. Get you situated. Then I really need to go talk with Theresa. Before it's too . . . late."

"Tell you what. If you want to go on now, then give me the key to your house, the access code for your alarm system, and I'll just get Bernard to take me."

"Bernard?"

"Yes, *Bernard*," she said smiling. She leaned over and whispered. "You've got to admit, he's a cute little chocolate fudge pop."

"Mom!" he said and frowned, but with respect.

"What? It's the truth. Now why don't you go practice a little of it yourself!" She flicked her hand to scoot him away. "Go on. You two seem to have a lot to talk about. And there's a wedding scheduled for tomorrow. The last thing you need is to come dragging in looking like you've been beaten with an ugly stick."

"Are you sure you'll be all right?" He gave her a key and the alarm code.

"Go," she said smiling. "Oh, and son . . . I heard somewhere that the truth will make you free."

George rang the doorbell. There was no answer. He rang the doorbell again. Still no answer. He then knocked on the door. "Theresa. It's me . . . George. Theresa." He pounded on the door this time. "Come on. I know you're in there. We need to talk!"

CHAPTER 23

As the Bridegroom Rejoiceth Over the Bride . . .

". . . so shall thy God rejoice over thee," Pastor Landris said from the pulpit-like platform. He was dressed in white: a white Avalon long Raffinati tux coat, white and gold Andrew Fezza Platinum Collection herringbone vest, and white with gold colored pants. Five groomsmen and five bridesmaids stood on the lower step: men on the right, women on thc left, while the flower girl and ring bearer stood beside each other in the middle.

"That was taken from Isaiah 62:5. We see where Isaiah 62 begins: 'For Zion's sake, will I not hold my peace, and for Jerusalem's sake I will not rest, until the righteousness thereof go forth as brightness, and the salvation thereof as a lamp . . . that burneth.'"

George looked up from the Bible that rested on the acrylic podium of a praying hand overlaid with a gold cross. "You see, there are times when you just can't hold your peace for Zion's sake. Sometimes you'll find you will not rest until the righteousness goes forth. We see salvation here as a lamp. And you know a lamp's purpose is to help us find the way. There are many walking around in darkness now, because *somebody's* not holding up the light! Oh, y'all don't hear me!" He cocked his head to the side and scanned the crowd.

"The second verse of Isaiah 62 says: '. . . And the Gentiles shall see thy righteousness, and all kings thy glory: and thou shalt—*not might, shall*—and thou shalt be called by a new name, which the mouth of the Lord shall name.' The third verse goes on to say: 'Thou shalt be a crown of glory in the hand of the Lord, and a royal diadem in the hand of the Lord.' Now I looked up the word 'diadem' in the *Merriam Webster's Collegiate Dictionary*. It defines diadem as 'a crown; a royal headband; something that adorns like a crown.' You see, we should be a crown, but not just any crown. We know there's the Miss America crown. And of course, there's a title crown that we refer to as representing a championship in a sport. Then there's a royal crown, and I'm not talking about the hair grease or that Crown Royal drink either. Diadem is a royal or imperial headdress. A cap of sovereignty.

"God tells us we are the *head* and not the *tail!* We are *above* only, and not *beneath!* We're blessed in the *city*; we're blessed in the *field*. The world should be able to see, that not only are we blessed *coming in . . .*"

"Say it, Pastor."

". . . but that we're blessed *going out!* He wants to use us as a crown for His glory. Isaiah the fourth verse says: 'Thou shalt no more be termed Forsaken; neither shall thy land anymore be termed Desolate.' Now I hope that you already know, Forsaken and Desolate are not something you want associated to your name. Then if you skip on down to verse five, it reads again: 'For as a young man marrieth a virgin, so shall thy sons marry thee: and as the bridegroom rejoiceth over the bride, so shall thy God rejoice over thee.'

"Now if you'll turn briefly to Matthew, chapter 25, beginning at the first verse, it reads as follows: 'Then shall the kingdom of heaven be likened unto ten virgins, which took their lamps, and went forth to meet the bridegroom. And five were wise, and five were foolish. They that were foolish took their lamps, and took no oil with them: But the wise took oil in their vessels with their lamps. While the bridegroom tarried, they all slumbered and slept. And at midnight there was a cry made, Behold, the bridegroom cometh; go ye out to meet him.'

"The seventh verse: 'Then all those virgins arose, and trimmed their lamps. And the foolish said unto the wise, Give us of your oil; for our lamps are gone out. But the wise answered, saying, Not so; lest there be not enough for us and you; but go ye rather to them that sell, and buy for yourselves. And while they went to buy, the bridegroom came; and they that were ready went in with him to the marriage: and the door was shut.' The eleventh verse: 'Afterward came also the other virgins, saying, Lord, Lord, open to us. But he answered and said, Verily I say unto you, I know you not. Watch therefore, for ye know neither the day nor the hour wherein the Son of Man cometh.'"

Pastor Landris looked up and out into the congregation that almost filled the church. "I realize," he said, his voice booming over the sanctuary, "some of you came here today for a wedding. You got all dressed up. May or may not have purchased yourself something new. Might have brought a gift here with you for the bride and groom. Well, I stand before you today to tell you: Church, the bridegroom cometh! And I want you to know, that He's coming back for His bride. And if you brought any other gift for the couple-to-be other than a pure heart, you might as well take it on back and get yourself a refund.

"Today, saints of God, we came to proclaim for those of you who didn't know, those who know but have forgotten, and those who are too foolish to believe or have otherwise come up short; we want *you* to know: Behold . . . the bridegroom cometh!"

"All right," voices sang out all over the sanctuary.

"You see, the Bible clearly tells us that we know not the hour nor the day. But that's really not the concern. Because we do know this much—and how do we know, Pastor, you might ask? We know—as the song proclaims—because the Bible tells us so. We *do* know that He's coming back again. The bridegroom is coming for His bride:

the church. No, not this building. We can build all the buildings we want. But Jesus is coming back for a people. Coming for His virgin bride.

"You see . . . years ago when people married, they would have *saved* themselves for that one special person they would someday pledge their eternal love to. To give them something that no one else has *ever* had.

"But now, society advocates that it's okay to test-drive before you buy. It's all right to try a slice before you commit to purchase the whole pie." Pastor Landris paused as he looked out among eyes staring back at him.

"My, my," some said and others followed with "Go on and say it!" "Preach, Reverend!" "Tell it like it is, Pastor!"

"There was a time in my life when I felt the same way. But then God spoke to my heart, and He saved me. He told me my name was no longer Forsaken or Desolate. I was no longer Sinner, because Jesus had died for all that I should be held accountable for. He told me that in the test of life, I had flunked. Oh, yes, I did. I flunked! And you flunked! Your mama flunked!

"That's right," he nodded, "I'm talking about your mama. We all *flunked* the test. Would not be able to pass to the next level. But then Jesus said to the Father, 'Father, let me take the test. And whatever I make on that test, give my grade to them. Then charge their score to my account. And whatever the price . . . whatever the cost . . . I'll pay it. Do with me, in their stead.' Oh, I hear some of you Bible scholars saying, 'That's not in the Bible!' But let me tell you this: On the third day, Jesus rose with *all* power! His grade—an 'A.' A charge to keep. Amazing grace. Alpha and Omega . . . the beginning and the end. And because Jesus lives—I live!"

Pastor Landris began to walk around as he spoke. "Isaiah the prophet said in chapter six, 'In the year that king Uzziah died, I saw also the Lord sitting upon a throne, high and lifted up, and his train filled the temple. Above it stood the seraphim: each one had six wings; with twain he covered his face, and with twain he covered his feet, and with twain he did fly. And one cried unto another, and said, Holy, holy, holy, is the Lord of hosts: the whole earth is full of his glory.' Then if you'll skip on down to the fifth verse, it reads:

" 'Then said I, Woe is me! for I am undone; because I am a man of unclean lips, and I dwell in the midst of a people of unclean lips: for mine eyes have seen the King, the Lord of hosts. Then flew one of the seraphim unto me, having a live coal in his hand, which he had taken with the tongs from off the altar: And he laid it upon my mouth, and said, Lo, this hath touched thy lips; and thine iniquity is taken away, and thy sin purged. Also I heard the voice of the Lord saying, Whom shall I send, and who will go for us? Then said I, Here am I; send me.' "

Pastor Landris stood in front of the flower girl and ring bearer and smiled before looking back into the audience. "When Jesus comes, He wants His bride to be special. Beautiful. Waiting for Him, and only Him. His bride will walk down that aisle pure, and with her heart toward Him. Because I can tell you with assurance, the bridegroom already has His heart on His bride. Jesus made us a promise. Said He was going to prepare a place. And He's not talking about some little starter house either. The mansions He has prepared will put these houses we call mansions down here to shame! Imagine—gates made of pearl, shiny streets paved with gold. Waiting for His bride. And church, the Lord is not slack concerning His promises."

"Hallelujah! Thank you, Lord," people began to shout out.

"God made us promises. Anything he's ever asked of us comes with promise. 'Delight yourself in Him, and He will give you the desires of your heart.' That's something with promise. 'They that wait upon the Lord, He will renew their strength. They shall mount up with wings as eagles.' Something with promise. People have often talked about crossing old chilly Jordan. But God has promised blessings well *beyond* Jordan. Ask yourself today: Have I crossed over Jordan yet? Or am I still on the other side looking—contemplating it?

"Joshua 18:3 asks: 'How long are ye slack to go to possess the land, which the Lord God of your fathers hath given you?' God has promises *beyond* Jordan! He desires that we walk in these promises. Being in good health and prospering is *not* a bad thing. For God tells us in Third John, verse two: 'Beloved, I wish above all things that thou mayest prosper and be in health, even as thy soul prospereth.' God is urging us: Go and possess the land I have *already* given you!

"Isaiah says, 'he is,' not was, 'despised and rejected of men; a man of sorrows, and acquainted with grief. Surely he has borne our griefs, and carried our sorrows. He was wounded for our transgressions, he was bruised for our iniquities: the chastisement of our peace was upon him; and with his stripes we *are* healed! Because he has poured out his soul unto death: and he was numbered with the transgressors; and he bare the sin of many, and made intercession for the transgressors.'

"My sisters and brothers . . . Jesus took our failing grade before we were even born, *He* paid the price, *He* bore our sickness, our poverty, and all the curses of the law. He is saying to us today: There's no need for you to bear what I already bore. Think about it—what sense does doing that make? Because I assure you: When you get to the checkout counter, you'll find the debt has already been *paid . . . in . . . full.*

"I'd like to conclude this wedding ceremony with the words I began with. Behold! The bridegroom cometh! And what God has joined together, let no man put asunder. Be blessed in the Lord and the power of His might. Oh, and saints of God, you don't have to wait until the battle is over. You can shout now!"

The church erupted into shouts and praise. People were standing to their feet. The organist began playing shouting music. The entire congregation was on fire. Pastor Landris opened the doors to the church as everyone sang, *Now Behold the Lamb* by Kirk Franklin and The Family. Seventy-three people came forward to be saved. And if you had looked close enough, you would have seen one tear streaming down Pastor Landris's face. He looked to the hills and nodded to the Lord. And the presence of the Lord filled the temple.

After the ceremony concluded, everyone went to the fellowship hall for the reception. There was so much food and elaborate settings: everything that a first class wedding should have, and be. Everything, that is, except a bride with her groom. For Theresa Marie Jordan was nowhere to be found.

A woman ran to catch Pastor Landris as he walked toward his office. "Oh, Pastor! Pastor!" she said, huffing from the effort it had taken her to catch up with him.

"Yes?" He turned, not surprised. "Sister . . . Murray."

She looked sincere. "I was just wondering. I mean I feel so bad for both you *and* Sister Theresa. But what should we tell people? You know they're going to ask."

"Tell people?" He frowned at her as he brushed down his mustache.

"Yes," she said, blushing somewhat. "Tell people. About the wedding. Why there wasn't one today between you and Sister Jordan, as was announced?"

"Sister Murray, if you *must*, you can tell them there wasn't a wedding because there just wasn't one."

"But—"

"Good day," he said.

"But, but—"

"Good day," he said, firmer as he turned and walked away with a solid stride.

CHAPTER 24

Who Hath Believed Our Report?

It had been a month since the special wedding service that had taken place Saturday, December thirtieth, but it was still being talked about everywhere. The people who were in attendance claimed they had never experienced anything like it. Naturally, there was much talk and speculation about what had actually happened with the scheduled wedding. The truth was that few people really knew the truth.

"Well, I heard the good reverend and the little bride-to-be got into this big argument at the church during the rehearsal. And she hauled off and slapped the mess out of him! Right there in front of everybody."

"Oh, that's not true. I heard he didn't even show up for the rehearsal or the dinner, and she called it off right then and there. But he still strolled in there on Saturday afternoon expecting her to stroll down that aisle. Then when he got all embarrassed, he got up in front of the church and bawled like a baby."

"Where'd you hear that? You know you can't believe everything you hear. I was there, and I'm gonna tell the truth. That man preached like I've never heard a preacher preach before. He was dancing, folks were walking all on top of the pews, doing back flips, shouting all over the place."

"I heard about three hundred people went up to get saved."

"It wasn't three hundred nothing. It was a hundred and fifty."

"Well my sister-in-law has a cousin who has a friend who gets her hair done where the bride-to-have-been goes. So I got it on *good* authority, it was he who called off the wedding because he was in love with some other woman—somebody famous. A movie star out in Hollywood. Halle something or other."

"You know, I heard something similar to that, too. Must mean there's some truth to that one, then."

"Somebody said Miss Movie Star came to the church the other week. Sat right in the congregation. Uh-huh. Say his ex-fiancée sat there looking all sick to her stomach. I heard they got into it. A real live catfight right there in the House of the Lord."

"I'd have been sick too if my husband had left me. Couldn't be Halle, though; she's with Eric . . . the singer."

"But they weren't married, so what's the big deal?"

"They were close enough, that's what!"

"But guess who I heard ended up footing the bill for the extravagant 'wedding' that never happened?"

Everybody leaned closer. "Who?"

"Some say the church. Since he did end up performing a service that *technically* benefited the church."

"See! See! Now, that's just why I don't give my money in church. What's a wedding, canceled at that, got to do with the likes of the kingdom of God? Crooks, I tell you. Plain . . . old . . . crooks!"

"Well, all those folks did give their lives to Christ; that should mean something."

"I don't think the church paid for it, though."

"They probably did. You know they do whatever he wants. Be making fools out of folks. That's *exactly* why I don't put nothing in *nobody's* church."

"And that's *exactly* why your tail ain't being blessed, either! You receive what you give. You give nothing, you get nothing. And nothing from nothing leaves—"

"Woman, you don't know *nothing* about me!"

"I know you barely making it. Now, I do give my tithes. I don't have nothing to do with what they do after that. But I'm gonna do what I'm supposed to do. Not gonna let anybody be a reason to cut off my blessings. Whatever they do that's not right, they're gonna have to answer to God for it. Not me."

"Well, I wonder what the real story is behind what happened that day. Frankly, after listening to the five of you, I don't know whose report to believe."

"I know I don't trust none of those preachers! Human or not, I don't want to hear it. And people say Pastor Landris is trying to be what God has *called* him to be. I can't wait until he falls just like the rest of 'em. I'm so sick of these high-and-mighty folks strutting around . . . trying to make the rest of us feel like peons."

"Pastor Landris is not like that—"

"We'll see. You mark my words. Something's going to come out real soon. Then the good reverend will have the light shining on him. We'll see just how clean his little corner really is swept. Oh, I usually know these things. Got myself a gift. Something's going to come to light before this year is gone good. You'll see. Then we'll all see, just how righteous the good reverend *really* is."

"Well, Cleophus, I happen to love his teaching."

"So, Marilyn, you're just like those other folks can't nobody understand. It doesn't matter what the preacher gets caught doing, you'll still be right there in his corner."

"Forgiveness, Cleophus, comes with promise. And yes, too many of us scream 'crucify' when we should be standing and praying."

"Well, I don't want to hear nothing about some preacher's excuse of being human. If you're of God, then act like it. Don't tell me you were a man before you were called. That old man ought to be buried now. Don't resurrect him."

"And the woman?"

"Man . . . woman, same thing. If you're of God, then represent. Re-pre-sent!"

And so it went. Still, those who knew the whole story never had much to say to those who didn't.

CHAPTER 25

Behold the Lord's Hand Is Not Shortened . . .

"How do so many things seem to get so messed up so quickly?" Sapphire said. She and Theresa were lying across Theresa's king-sized bed talking about one of Sapphire's cases: a twelve-year-old girl who refused to speak anymore. The little girl, named Tamika, had been referred to her since she was the best licensed professional counselor around when it came to dealing with black folks who didn't believe black folks needed to see a "head doctor."

"I don't know. Grown folks expect there to be problems in their lives. But kids shouldn't have to deal with stuff they have no control over," Theresa said.

"Well, this little girl has truly had a lot to deal with to be so young. She's lived two lives already. I can't discuss her case, but it's so unfair how children can be so mistreated by their peers, then by adults who are supposed to be there to protect them . . ."

"How do you mean, protect them? Parents can't be everywhere at once."

"Like to make sure no one's doing things to them then threatening them to not tell. If parents would talk to their children as early as seven or eight, let them know if anyone ever tells them not to tell something they don't feel good about, that *that* probably *is* the time they should tell it. Family members included. We'd save a lot of children from a lot of heartache, not counting messed-up minds."

"I know."

"I had someone once try something with me when I was young. Funny thing was, I really thought we were in love. Didn't realize at the time, you weren't supposed to grow up and marry your own kinfolk."

"You're kidding. You? Miss Cool-headed Sapphire?"

"Growing up, you tend to develop feelings that go beyond curiosity. I had a cousin—" Sapphire suddenly stopped.

"What's wrong?" Theresa asked, flipping over onto her back.

"I was just wondering whether I should tell this or not. I've never mentioned it to anybody. Only two people in the world ever knew about it." She looked over at Theresa. "The other one is dead now."

"You must feel like you want to talk about it, or else you wouldn't have brought it up. So tell me."

"I don't know. Haven't you ever had something you didn't know if you should ever share with another soul? There's just something about a secret where you can only be certain it remains one, if nobody knows it except one person—yourself."

Theresa looked up at the ceiling fan. "I'll tell you what: If you really want to share it with me, I'll share something with you that I haven't told anyone. Because to be honest, I need to talk as well."

"*You* have secrets no one knows?" Sapphire teased.

"Of course. Oh, you're trying to be funny now."

"Okay," Sapphire said. "Maybe this might even end up being therapeutic for me to tell after so many years." She flipped over and gazed at the ceiling fan also. "Well, like I was saying, I had this cousin that I absolutely loved to death. It's sometimes hard to manage your feelings when you're young, I suppose."

"Young, my foot. I can't manage mine and I'm thirty-three. You see what happened between me and George."

"Yeah. Well, this one time my cousin came to visit us. It was my father's younger sister's child. We always played together and we talked about everything. I always hated when it was time for him to go back home. I was twelve that particular year; he was thirteen. They were leaving the next day. He and I had been talking about what it would be like to be married to someone you really cared about who really cared about you. Just talking, you know."

"I'm familiar with *that* conversation."

"Early in the morning . . . before the sun rose, I woke up and he was on top of me. At the time, I really didn't know what he was trying to do. Instinctively, I began to fight him off." Sapphire flipped back over onto her stomach and placed her chin on her fist. "But the kicker was, I didn't want to scream or do anything that might wake anyone. I didn't want him to get in trouble. When I figured out what he was trying to do, I just fought him that much harder. He must have decided it was a bad idea, so he stopped."

"Wow. That sounded close."

"Oh, it was. And I vowed never to speak to him again. He knew I was upset, even though I knew he wasn't doing it to harm me. He wasn't that type of person. But I still was mad at him. He was my cousin! All I could do was try to stop him without getting him in trouble. I never told, although he never threatened me or asked me not to tell. Never."

"At least you were able to stop him," Theresa said, recalling her own experience with Maurice those many years ago.

"He did try to apologize. But the next year when he came to visit, I avoided him completely. Everybody knew something was different, but fortunately, people attribute change to growing up or out of something. The following year, he was killed in a car accident. A drunk driver crossed the lane. He was in the back of the van. Nobody even thought the accident affected him, being so far back. Turns out, he died instantly. His parents couldn't believe he was dead. They thought for sure he might have been faking or something. It was horrible."

"I don't care for drunk drivers myself. It's scary when you consider somebody in an altered, drunken state, wielding a weapon as large as a two-ton vehicle." Theresa looked at Sapphire. "So you never forgave him?"

"I forgave him; he just never knew it. But you see, I really did love him. And had we not been kin, he would have made a wonderful boyfriend. Matters of the heart are so complicated. But yet, we expect children to be able to sort out what most grown folks can't."

Theresa stood up. "Feelings are not that easy to turn off just because someone wants you to or because they've changed their heart toward you." She walked to a chair across the room and sat down. "If it's difficult for adults, what can we expect it to be like for children who have yet to develop their skills and tools for life?"

"You're talking about George, right?"

"Some of George. Some of something else entirely. So you've *never* told anyone about what your cousin tried to do?"

"Not until today. I guess I never wanted anyone to think badly of him. I have still, in my own way, been trying to protect him."

"In spite of what he almost did to you?"

"Theresa, I never really thought about it in terms of me. I didn't see what he attempted to do that day as mean or evil. I know he really loved me. He just got confused. He didn't realize there were boundaries that shouldn't be crossed. Love can make you do foolish things. It makes you wonder how you could have, in your right mind, gone as far to the edge. Going over it, at times. Like, what makes someone keep loving someone who continues to hurt them?"

"Or worse—loving someone who just plain doesn't want you and has made that fact *abundantly* clear."

"Love can make people crazy sometimes. And most folks don't even see how close they are to the edge until it's too late."

Theresa stared off into space, twisting her fingers on one hand between the fingers of the other. "I'm pregnant," she said without any prior warning.

Sapphire sat straight up. "What did you just say?"

"I'm pregnant. Pregnant."

"Oh my Lord! Are you sure?"

"Yes, I'm sure. I went to the doctor because I didn't believe those four separate, positive EPT results could possibly be right."

"How far?"

"The doctor says eight weeks, but since I know exactly what day it was, I'd say I'm closer to six."

"How can you know the exact day?" Sapphire asked, getting to her feet.

"Because I only did it one time. Well, more than one time the day I did it—"

"Oh man, Theresa. That's messed up. Now *that's* a secret."

"Won't be for much longer, though. I'm already gaining weight. I've got a little pouch showing." She pressed her shirt down across her bulging stomach.

"Like a kangaroo," Sapphire said with a smile. "So who all knows this?"

"Just you. And my doctor, of course."

"Serious? You mean, you haven't even told B?"

"No."

"That's right. As mad as she is at Pastor Landris already, that's the last thing she needs to hear. Looks like he didn't just leave you at the altar—"

"He didn't leave me at the altar! I was the one who called it off. I was so upset when I thought he had gone to Birmingham to see Johnnie Mae Taylor, I told him where he could go and how fast he should take in getting there."

"Girl, you were so wrong—"

"Sapphire, I heard you the first time. I don't need a repeat lecture. I allowed my mouth to rule, and in the process, I learned I spoke too soon. After I practically blessed him out, I felt like a fool when I learned her husband had died and how she had literally fallen apart. I tried to apologize, but he wasn't 'impressed.' "

"Can you blame him for not hearing you? You showed your behind. You should have known he would think twice about saying 'I do' to you then."

"Well, if you ask me, he was all too eager to call the wedding off when I suggested it. I wouldn't doubt if he had planned to do it first already anyway."

"You'll never know now, Miss Quick-Tongue-Draw."

"B still thinks *he* was wrong. She thinks he and Miss Johnnie Mae had a little somethin-somethin going on just the same. Keeping it holy, my foot."

"From what you're telling me tonight, sounds like Pastor Landris is not the good Bible-abiding person he claims and encourages us to be. Pregnant?"

"Sapphire, there's something I need to tell you about this baby." Theresa sat back down at the foot of the bed.

"Before you tell me that, I've really got to use your little girl's room. Hold that thought. I'll be right back."

When Sapphire returned, she sat next to Theresa. "Now. What were you about to say?"

Theresa looked at her and smiled. "Never mind." She decided against telling Sapphire she was mistaken about who the father of her baby was.

"Theresa?"

"I'm planning to keep this baby," Theresa said.

"Well, what did George say?"

"About?"

"About the baby. I'm sure you've told him." She looked at her. "You *have* told him, haven't you?" She scrunched down and looked into Theresa's face. "You haven't told him, have you?"

Theresa shook her head. "Sapphire, listen. There's something—"

"You need to tell him, girl. That's some jacked-up stuff, just knowing that he preaches against adultery and fornication, but apparently he wasn't practicing what he preaches. Or maybe you two just got carried away that time, which is understandable. I mean, you *were* about to be married. If things had gone as planned, it wouldn't have been a problem, I don't suppose. No one would have had a clue *when* it happened. But you *didn't* get married. And now, it's a problem."

"Sapphire, you don't understand—"

"What's not to understand? You need to tell him. This is going to affect him just as much as it does you. And when the people at church get a whiff of this, you know rotten eggs are going to hit the fan. That's some stinky, messed-up stuff. Who knows, maybe the two of you can work things out and—"

"Sapphire, will you please stop! George doesn't want me, don't you get it! There are things about me he's not willing to put up with. That pretty much sums up what he told me that night we officially broke up."

"Like what?"

Theresa thought about the night she and George talked—the Friday before the wedding, when he came over after the rehearsal dinner. She heard him ring the doorbell and knock, but she didn't want to hear what he had to say. Then he started yelling how they needed to talk, and he wasn't leaving until she opened the door. So she opened the door and decided to get it over with. He'd told her he had problems with her actions and didn't think she had the heart he first believed her to have. In his spirit, he felt that something just wasn't right. Then there was the Lena thing; he couldn't seem to get past that *at all*. Nothing about who he thought she was, was still fitting with who she was now.

Lena. One good thing she was thankful for in this whole situation. Now, no one had to know the truth about Lena. But George couldn't understand why she felt the way she did. He wanted to know what on earth Lena could have done to cause her to feel the way she did. Did Lena abuse her? Had Lena allowed someone else to hurt or abuse her?

"What did Lena do that was so awful?" he asked again.

"She embarrasses me!" And as soon as the words erupted, she

heard how juvenile she sounded. *It was okay for a child to feel that way, but I am an adult. I should be able to think more rationally now*, she thought.

"What?" he had said. "You don't like her because she embarrasses you? My God—I really do feel sorry for you. Do you have any idea how Lena got burned?"

Theresa didn't open her mouth to say anything more. She wanted him to leave her alone, to let her think. And she knew, before midnight, there would not be a wedding for her and Pastor George Landris. It was too late to cancel much of anything; they would be charged for everything regardless. She had no idea what George would do; she decided to let him arrive at the church on Saturday and inform everybody. Of course, she told her parents, B, Sapphire, and the attendants. Most of the bridesmaids were mad because they had bought dresses and shoes for a wedding that wouldn't be happening.

It was only that night after the wedding should have taken place, that she heard from some people who had gone to the church, unknowingly, what Pastor Landris had done. From what she gathered, some of the bridesmaids . . . *her* supposed-to-be-loyal friends, and one of the flower girls, had participated. After hearing what Pastor Landis wanted to do, and considering things were already paid for, they wanted to take part. It went over so well, they say churches all over were planning to conduct a ceremony just like it.

She had heard people were accusing Pastor Landris of charging the church for the expense. Some people, behind his back of course, were ragging him about it. Theresa knew for a fact George had paid for it with his own money. Whether the church gave him a love-offering afterward, she didn't know. But almost every dime she and her parents had spent (except for her wedding dress), he had reimbursed them for.

Her father insisted he didn't have to pay for the whole thing. Theresa had been honest enough to tell them they had "mutually, kind of, called it off."

"Mutually, kind of? How do you *mutually, kind of?*" her father asked.

Beatrice was the one who calmed him down about it. Saying stuff like, "Bishop, we should just be glad they had the courage to do what they felt was right on this end of marriage, regardless of the inconvenience to others or the expense. Too many people walk down the aisle knowing they should stop the wedding right then and there, and walk away before they've gotten in too deep."

Theresa wondered, *Who cared about other people's inconvenience? Did they not realize the humiliation and embarrassment I would face if people thought I had been dumped at the altar? But no one ever seemed to see things from my point of view—only their own.*

"Theresa, I'm waiting. What is it about you that the two of you couldn't work out if you really tried? Really wanted to?" Sapphire said.

"I'm spoiled, selfish, self-centered, whiny . . ." Theresa looked at Sapphire. "Stop me anytime now."

Sapphire looked at her and laughed. "You're a nut. That's what you are. And soon you're going to be a mother nut."

"Yeah, that's what it looks like."

"Theresa. You need to tell George. This is not something that only affects you. He's going to have his hands full when they barbecue him at church. There are already plenty of people mad because he didn't keep his commitment to marry you. They are going to put him on the grill and sear him on both sides when you start showing. Because *everybody* will know the real truth then. Let's see him get himself out of this one."

"Dang, girl. You sound like B the way you said that. That's something I'd expect from her, not you."

"Well you know me. I'm only on the side of right. If you're wrong, I'm not going to go along with you just because you're my heart. I love and respect Pastor Landris, but I'm not going to sit here and uphold him in his wrongdoing. I won't call for them to crucify him, but he's going to have to come correct. How's he going to tell the young men at the church not to do what he apparently has done? That's just too two-faced. Everybody makes mistakes, but don't beat me upside my head about what I'm doing, when you're out there doing the same thing or something just as bad. I'm not going to lie; I would love to pull an all-nighter with old fine Maurice—"

"Maurice?"

"Yes—B's brother. That brother is too fine, too smooth, and forty-two. Just within my pre-approved age range—not too old, not too young."

"I didn't know you liked Maurice," Theresa said with a nervous, worried look.

"That's because it's apparent you hate his guts. I don't know what the deal is with you two, maybe you think his rap is tired. That 'My Queen' thing has played out a bit, but . . ." she shivered her whole body, "I love it when he says it!"

"Just out of curiosity, Sapphire. Have you and Maurice ever . . .? You know . . ."

"What? Been together?"

"Well, that. Been out? Kissed, even?"

"I'll tell you a little secret about me and Maurice," she said, putting her mouth closer to Theresa's ear as she whispered. "Maurice—"

The doorbell rang. Theresa looked at Sapphire. "Go on," she said.

"Your doorbell's ringing."

"I know, but finish."

Sapphire looked at her watch. "Oh my, look at the time! I should have been gone." She stood up. "Do you want me to get the door on my way out?"

Theresa didn't care about the door. She wanted to hear what

Sapphire was about to say. Instead, Sapphire hugged her and rushed to get the door. It was B.

"Sapphire, I didn't know you were here," B said.

"I was in the neighborhood. Thought I'd stop by and check on my girl."

B leaned over and whispered. "How is she? Really?"

"She's going to be all right," Sapphire said as she slipped on her jacket. "Theresa, B's here!" she yelled. "She's back there . . . locked up in her room," she whispered.

"Good," B said. "I brought a half-gallon of rocky road ice cream—my prescribed therapy. I'll just get us a couple of spoons, and she and I can get to work."

CHAPTER 26

Verily I Say Unto You, No Prophet Is Accepted in His Own Country

"Johnnie Mae, how are you?" Landris said.

"I believe I'll live and not . . ." Johnnie Mae stopped. "I'm okay," she said.

"You had us worried there for a while. Your mother especially."

"Yeah, I know. I hated putting Mama through all that. She didn't need it, that's for sure. I just couldn't help it. It was such a shock. Solomon was doing so well. He was looking to come home that Saturday and . . ." She sighed. "Look, let me tell you why I called. You know I have a new book out? My publisher's been really great these past two months, but they're really pushing me to get out there, and do some signings and radio and TV interviews to get the word going again."

"Are you ready to get out there and do this just yet?"

"Landris, I've got to do something to quit thinking so much. I'm going crazy in this house! In fact, there are so many memories here, I probably need to get away for a while just to give my mind a break."

"Well you know I told you, you are always welcomed at my place if you ever need a safe hideout."

She laughed. "I know, and I really appreciate you. I truly do."

"My other offer still stands as well."

"Landris. Please don't."

"Johnnie Mae, you know how I feel about you. You've known for a long time. I can't help it that I can't turn my feelings off. I don't mean any disrespect to what you're going through right now . . . having lost your husband. I just want you to know, I fell in love with you the first day I saw you. That was wrong, and a lot has changed during those years. For one thing, who would have ever thought I would have become a minister? But I still have feelings."

"Landris—"

"Hear me out. I never wished any ill to fall upon Solomon. Never. That much you must know."

"Landris, I know that."

"I love you, Johnnie Mae. For some reason, I always have. I pray one day you might actually consider becoming my wife. I'm willing to wait until you feel it's the right time for you. That is, if you'll have me."

"But I can't say if or when that might ever be."

"I understand that. And I'm not trying to pressure you into anything. I just want you to know where I stand. The truth. The way I feel toward you, it is definitely better to marry than to burn. And I don't intend to give any place to the devil. You know?"

"I hear you."

"One more thing, Johnnie Mae. I'm sure Solomon would have been the first to have wanted you to go on living even though he's no longer here." Landris sighed hard. "Okay. So that's the last I have to say on *that*. And I promise, I won't bring it up again. Now, you were saying about your publisher?"

"They have me scheduled for a few bookstores in Atlanta. Shrine of the Black Madonna and Two Friends Bookstore, both off Ralph David Abernathy Boulevard. Then there's another Two Friends Bookstore off Cascade Road?"

"Yeah, I'm familiar with that one. It's close to where I live."

"Oh, okay. Anyway, they have me set with some Borders, Barnes & Noble, Books-A-Million, and Waldens there and around the country. I'm trying to set my schedule since it looks like when I hit the road, I'll be out of pocket several weeks. While I'm in Atlanta, I was thinking maybe you and I could visit for a while."

"That would be great. In fact, maybe we can schedule something here at the church for you, if you're still available. I'm sure there are lots of folks who read your books. And they'd get a thrill hearing you speak—"

"Speak? Landris, I don't know about all that."

"Johnnie Mae. I've seen you deliver a presentation. Remember that time with Mr. Bijur . . . with A Upper Hand, Inc.? It should be *An* Upper Hand. But anyway, Mr. Bijur ended up offering you a vice-president's job. I just know the people here will love you!"

"Speaking? I don't know. I've been mostly low key the past two-and-a-half years."

"Then it's time for you to get back out there. Say yes. Unless you don't feel up to it just yet?"

"It's not that." She made a moaning sound. "Okay."

"So let me know when you're looking to be here—"

"I have it already. March eighth, ninth, and tenth," she said.

"Great. Then let's look at having you here on Sunday, March eleventh, if that's okay with you. I'll give this information to a Sister Miles; she's over our women's fellowship. She'll set everything up for you here."

"All right. Then I'll just add Sunday, the eleventh to my calendar . . . at your church. Thanks, Landris."

"Now when you come to Atlanta, you know you don't need to worry about getting a hotel. Oh, and you are bringing Princess Rose with you, aren't you?"

"No. Mama's keeping her for me. She's been begging to spend some time with her little 'Rose of Jericho' as she calls her. This way,

I won't have problems trying to get a sitter while I'm signing and such."

"Like I was saying, you don't need to worry about getting a hotel. I have plenty of room here, and you're more than welcome—"

"Landris, you know I'm not going to stay there with you." She laughed.

"Why not? If it's because of my being here, I could stay with Deacon Thomas—give you the house . . ."

She laughed again. "Think about it. If anybody gets even a whiff of my staying at your house—with or without you there—it would spread like wildfire."

"Johnnie Mae, you know me. Do you really think I care what other people think?"

"Landris, in your position, you had better. People make up enough lies on other folks as it is. There's no reason for you to give somebody something to work with. And what did you just say about not giving place to the devil?"

"Okay. I hear what you're saying, and I know you're right. Although I can't see how anyone could possibly know what's going on in my house."

"I'll just get a hotel room like always. I don't mind. Really."

"You *will* let me take you to dinner while you're here? I mean, it's all right if we *eat* together in public?"

She started laughing. "Now you're just being silly."

"Yeah, but it's good to hear you laugh."

She stopped. "Landris?" Johnnie Mae said. "Thank you. For everything. For always somehow being there when I really need a friend. For being so understanding. For not pressuring me about *things*. For lending me your shoulders to lean on . . ."

"Hey, you are first and foremost these days, my friend."

"And you . . . mine. Oh, and thanks for offering to roll out the carpet for me when I come to town. People have been so great since my books hit the reading turf."

"So what's going on in Birmingham?"

"You mean besides WENN radio changing its format to become V-105.9? The V standing for Variety, of course."

"Yeah, besides that." He laughed. "I can't believe that was the first thing that came to your mind when I asked that question."

"It's just, I love having competition. Personally, I was glad to see them come back so strong. Everybody's been talking about it since they debuted their new format on Dr. King's birthday holiday. They even played excerpts from his speeches periodically throughout the day for weeks. It's a great way to teach the kids, and some adults, about our history."

"When I asked what was going on in Birmingham, I was meaning as far as your book was concerned."

"Oh. Let's just put it this way: They say a prophet is not known in his own country. The main newspaper here has yet to do a big story on me. They keep saying they're trying to see what they want to do with me. I've stopped worrying about it. A few of the TV stations just plain ignore me, but if a visiting author comes to the city, they jump to have them on. But that's okay. When I'm mega, I'll remember this. I've had a few news organizations who've been really great. I was part of the Words Escape Me Summit. And Alice Gordon—Alice just got this major deal. You've seen her show before?"

"Yeah. She's fabulous! You can tell she really cares about what she's doing. A major deal, huh?"

"Yeah. And Fredia Lucas, out of Tuscaloosa with WTUG, I've been on her show. She's good. There are others like O.B. the 'Masta' Brewer of 98.7 KISS. We did a little philosophy and psychology thing once. And I'll be doing *Alabama Bound!* again this year at the end of April at the Downtown library. That's become a major event."

"Well, I'll see what I can line up here. I'm a *little* connected. And there are plenty of outlets I believe we can get you on . . . if you feel up to it."

"Sure. I'll inform my publicist of all her work you're doing. I'll check with you before I head that way. Landris . . . how's everything with you? Really?"

"So-so."

"And that means?"

"I've been throwing myself into my work here at the church. We have the Community Development Center project, and it's really shaping up. People will have access to all kinds of things: indoor basketball, volleyball and tennis courts, computers, tutors, exercise facilities, and performing arts and movie theaters. Leander Sales, a film editor in residence at North Carolina School of the Arts in Winston-Salem—a talented brother—has volunteered to do a few workshops when we're ready. Leander has done editing for Spike Lee. Charles McClennahan of North Carolina, one of only a few black beekeepers in America, has agreed to come share some marvelous presentations for both the kids and adults. I'm excited."

"That's great. Now, how are you personally?"

He laughed. "You mean since the thing with me and Theresa?"

"Thing, huh? That's what you call it? I think it's called a break-up."

"Theresa and I haven't spoken since that day. There's a little tension in the church because a lot of the members don't know what really happened. There are plenty of rumors floating around. I'm not saying anything. I figure it's nobody's business but mine and Theresa's. I refuse to add kerosene to the fire."

"But Theresa's okay with the way things ended between you two. Right?"

"I don't know about okay, but she seems to be coping. For the most part, she still attends church here. And I am still her pastor. If she needs anything, I will treat her with the love and respect I try to do with all the members of the church."

"Glad to hear that. Well Landris, I've got to run. I'll be talking with you."

"Johnnie Mae?"

"Yes."

"Take care of yourself. Okay?" To which he heard her smile break through.

"I will," she said.

"Promise?"

"Promise."

CHAPTER 27

Lift Up a Standard for the People

"Pastor Landris, you have an appointment today that wasn't originally on the schedule," Jocelyn said. It was Tuesday, February twenty-seventh.

Pastor Landris took the red folder she held out to him. "And who might that be?"

"Theresa Jordan. She says it's important. I thought under the circumstances . . ."

Pastor Landris smiled, dropping his head slightly as he read the typed paper he now held. "That's quite all right. What time did you put her down for?"

"Four. She asked if she could come after your last appointment. I figured you might not mind staying longer . . . since it was her."

"You figured right, Jocelyn. Thank you. You do excellent work." He signed the letter at the bottom and handed it and the folder back to her. She smiled.

"Oh, and Jocelyn. Don't feel obliged to stay past your normal four o'clock leaving time. I'll see Ms. Jordan in myself."

"It wouldn't be a problem," she said.

"But not necessary."

She smiled again. "Sure."

At ten till four, Theresa arrived and sat on the couch outside the office.

"Pastor Landris is expecting you. He should be finished with his meeting any minute now," Jocelyn said.

"I'm early, so it's fine."

"May I get you something to drink? Coffee? Water?"

"A cup of water would be nice."

Jocelyn got up and came back with a paper cup of water. Theresa didn't really want any water, but she figured it would give both of them something to do to pass the time.

George came out with two men who looked like they were contractors or builders. He was laughing and telling them how pleased he was so far with the way the Community Development Center was coming along. He looked at Theresa and nodded slightly.

When everyone was gone, including Jocelyn, who seemed to find everything in the world to keep her there later than four, George invited Theresa in. She sat down quickly.

"Thank you for seeing me on such short notice," she said.

"No problem. But you didn't have to make an appointment to talk with me."

"I wasn't sure. We didn't exactly separate with a clean break, as the boxing referee would say."

George smiled. "Yeah, I guess you could say that." He looked at her. "You're looking well. Can I get you anything?"

She laughed. "No, I just drank some water before you came out."

"I can get you something out of the machine if you'd like something stronger than water."

She smiled. "No thanks. I'm trying to cut back on caffeine these days."

They sat for a minute in silence.

"So, how have you been?" George said.

"Let's just say, maybe I'd be a great contender for the next cast of the show *Survivor*."

More silence.

He leaned back against the front of his desk. "So . . ."

She laughed, then looked down at her hand where she still wore the two-carat diamond he had bought her. She had offered to give it back to him, but he had told her to keep it. "I suppose you want to know why I'm here?"

He smiled. "I admit, it has occurred to me a time or two since I learned you were coming."

"I want to talk to you."

"Okay."

"As my pastor."

"No problem. But Theresa, I don't understand."

"I have something I need to talk with you about, but I don't want this to be a conversation based on our past, but based on your being my pastor."

"Like I said, go ahead."

"First, do you discuss what people tell you in confidence?"

"Theresa—"

"I just need to know for sure before I begin."

He walked around to his chair and sat down. "Theresa, whatever you and I discuss will stay right here."

"No matter what?"

He leaned back in the chair. "Whether you know it or not, I take my work seriously."

"Okay," she said, relaxing. "I have a slight dilemma that has come up. I've known about it for a few weeks now, but I've not been able to get up the nerve to come talk with you."

He leaned forward. "Theresa, what is it?"

"I'm pregnant."

He fell back against the chair. "You're what?"

"Expecting. I'll be thirteen weeks this Friday."

He glanced at the calendar on his desk. "March the second? Thirteen weeks?"

"Yes."

"Wow, Theresa. That's about the last thing I expected to hear you say."

"I'm sure."

He paused for a minute, as though he were performing a quick calculation in his mind. "Theresa, if you're a little over three months—"

"Yes, George. I got pregnant while you and I were still together."

He started rubbing his head, then his chin and around his mouth, making several quick passes. "Wow!"

"Is that all you can say?"

"What else do you want?"

"I don't know."

"Whoa. Man," he said. "Theresa, since you and I were never together in that way, that can only mean—"

She looked down. "I never meant for it to happen, George. It just did. I suppose you could say I got caught up in the moment. The song was playing, memories filled me. I was upset with you about your having left like you did—"

"When did it happen?"

"What?"

He sighed. "When did you sleep with someone else? When?"

She stood up and walked over to the window behind his desk. "George, I never meant to hurt you. You must believe that."

He placed his face in the palms of both hands and rubbed it with them. "Theresa, when?"

"Christmas Day, technically. Somewhere thereabout."

"Christmas Day? But how . . . ?" He thought a minute. *That was the day she left her folks' house to go over to B's. I had called and left messages that night. The next morning, I had gone over there—early. That was the day she came to the door dressed in that white sexy outfit.* "The day you came to the door and said, 'What did you forget?' You were talking to him, weren't you?" He recalled the guy he had passed on the stairs as he went up to her apartment.

She went and sat back down. "George—"

"Theresa . . . I can't believe this."

"George, you had gone to see about Johnnie Mae. I didn't know what was really going on between you two. I never told you this, but a month or so before the accident, I heard you call out 'Johnnie, my heart' or 'Johnnie, my love' in your sleep. I didn't know at the time who Johnnie was, but then when you ran off to see about Johnnie Mae Taylor, I put it together."

"But Theresa, I told you what I was doing. Why? How could you . . . ?"

"Look . . . I didn't come here for this. I'm sorry if this hurts you—"

"The guy leaving your apartment, I presume, when I came over to your place that morning—was it him? Is he the one?"

"George, this has nothing to do with what I came here to tell you."

"Was . . . it . . . him?" he said with a little more force.

"Yes! Now are you satisfied?"

"My goodness. He and I spoke briefly; he said he had visited the church."

Theresa stared hard at George. "When did you talk to him?"

"When he was leaving. That morning. I asked him about from where I knew him. He said he'd been to the church a few times."

"Listen, George. Can I please just speak my piece and be on my way?"

He continued shaking his head. "We almost got married, and you'd slept with someone else? The same week as our wedding, no less?" This was not going the way of his normal sessions. Usually, he was not so closely involved.

"George, I'm sorry! Okay? What more can I say? But here's where we are now. I told Sapphire about a month ago; she knows everything—"

"Including who the father is?"

Theresa looked down at her hands again, then back up into his now glistening eyes. "No. It's kind of complicated. Remember now,

I'm telling you all this strictly as my pastor. And just so you'll know, I've not shared who the father is with another living soul. I'm pregnant by . . . Maurice Greene. Maurice is B's brother."

"B's brother? You're talking about your friend B? And she doesn't know?"

"Is it still a secret?" She half-joked. "She knows I'm pregnant, but no. She has no idea who the real father is."

George caught what she said. "Real father? What do you mean by *real* father?"

"Yes. You see . . . that's what I needed to talk to you about. It appears . . ." she began with a slight stammer, ". . . everybody who knows . . . thinks the baby is yours."

"Then you need to tell them the truth."

She stood up again and paced near the chair. "Well now . . . that's easier said than done. You see, Sapphire has this thing for Maurice. I can't possibly tell her he and I slept together."

"Why not? Did he sleep with her, too?"

"No. I thought at one time something may have happened between them, but it seems she just has these dreams about them being together. She's one of the few people I know still saving herself for marriage."

"Theresa, don't you think you should tell her the truth? She's your friend. And what about B? Don't you think B should be told as well?"

"No. Neither of them needs to know the whole truth right now. They both automatically *assumed* it was yours. I mean, we *were* engaged to be married." She sat down and rubbed her temple. "They both knew I'd been celibate for years."

"So of course, they think you're pregnant by me." He stood up and shook his head as he stared out the window. A red bird lit for a minute on a tree branch nearby then flew—without a care—away.

"George, it's nothing personal."

He turned and looked at her. "Nothing personal? You're pregnant. Already showing. People naturally think I did this. It doesn't matter that I'm the pastor of this church. It doesn't matter that I'm telling people day in and day out to live a life pleasing unto the Lord. Now people find out you're pregnant. I look guilty. But it's nothing *personal*?"

"I know how this sounds, but—"

"But nothing! You just need to come clean, Theresa."

"I plan to."

"You plan to? When?"

She looked at her hands. "I don't know. But I thought it fair to warn you—"

"Warn me? Warn me?"

"Yes. *Warn* you. People are already starting to look at me funny. I'm sure they can tell something. Especially those older women with their old wives' tales and nosy noses!"

"Theresa, tell . . . the . . . truth. It's not fair you've involved me in your mess."

"George, in a weird kind of way, it's partly your fault."

He sat down and just shook his head. "And how do you figure that?"

"Well, if you hadn't gone trotting off to see about Johnnie Mae, I wouldn't have felt like I needed to turn to someone else. I wouldn't have needed to go somewhere else for attention."

"Theresa. You're not an animal. You can make decisions for yourself. Nobody caused you to do anything. And you're going to have to stop blaming everybody else for what you are responsible for."

"You're talking about Lena now, aren't you?"

"I wasn't, but since you brought her up, she's a great example. Lena has done nothing but love you. You can't even come up with a valid reason for mistreating her the way you do. You blame her for the way she looks."

"But she's ugly, George!" Theresa blurted it out before she could stop herself. "I can't help how I feel!"

"My goodness. You are something. You are really something! Some people are 'ugly,' as you put it, on the outside. Some are just rotten and ugly on the inside. Lena may have scars everybody can see when they look in her face and at her hands. You, on the other hand, apparently are plenty scarred, but on the inside where no one can see."

She stood up and grabbed her purse. "I didn't come for a sermon. I came to you as my pastor, my spiritual advisor. And I needed to let you know about my present condition. I'm not telling people you're the father—"

"You're just committing the sin of *omission*—not setting them straight that I'm not the father, either. Let me ask you something. Is this your kind of sick way of getting back at me?"

She stopped and looked straight at him. "George, I don't have time to be *getting back* at you. I've a baby to prepare for. I just wanted you to know what was happening. Just in case people do assume, as Sapphire and B immediately did. I'm not telling people you're my baby's father. I just wanted you to know."

He folded one hand over the other. "Have you told him?"

She smiled. "Don't you think that's my business, and thereby none of your concern?"

"As your pastor, I think you need to tell him. He has a right to know. Not counting he has an obligation to help you with this child. And he just might want to be a part of the child's life."

"What's wrong? Afraid I'll stick you with child support?"

"Theresa . . ." He shook his head. "Just forget it."

"Good," she said. "Well, Pastor Landris. You've been a wonderful listener. I'm really glad I got this off my chest." She walked to the door and opened it. "And, George, just to set the record straight, I'm not doing this to get back at you. It probably wouldn't have worked out between us anyway. You love this church and your God more than you would have ever loved me." She started out the door, then stopped. "George let me ask you: Have you ever loved someone that you never had?"

He stood up and moved toward her.

"When you said that, the day you went to Birmingham," she

said, "I didn't quite understand it. Now that I'm on this side, so to speak, I think I get what you were trying to tell me. You love Johnnie Mae, but she was never yours to have. Now, who can say? I loved you, but you were never mine to have. That's a hard reality to live with: loving someone you've never had. It hurts, doesn't it? Something fierce." She tried to muster, without much success, a smile.

"Thanks for listening. I suppose I'll be seeing you around, Pastor." She emphasized the word 'pastor.' "Oh, and George, should by chance I hear any, *any* details from this our private conversation, I'll know where to look. Then I'll know your true integrity. Just know this though: Should it ever come to it—at least for the time being—it would in actuality be your word against mine."

He glared at her, mulling the words she had just managed to say without saying. "But the truth would come out in the end. You do know *that?*"

"Oh yeah." She smiled, turned up her nose, and shook her head as she spoke. "But can you imagine the damage that could be done in the meantime? Like I said, I'm not trying to hurt you. I just need more time. That's all. Just a little more time." She then closed the door gently behind her.

George knew this was not something to be in the middle of. He prayed she would come clean and tell the truth before this got too far out of hand. He then whispered out loud, "And God, forgive your child. Help her. Right now I pray. And God . . . please help me to do . . . what is right . . . in your sight. Please . . ."

CHAPTER 28

Neither as Being Lords Over God's Heritage, but Being Examples to the Flock

"Pastor Landris," Mother King said. "First of all, like Elder Fuller said when he began, please know this meeting was not called for condemnation purposes. There is a situation apparently going on throughout this church now that we can no longer ignore."

Deacon Perkins stood to his feet. "Pastor, I'm not going to sugarcoat it like Mother King is trying to do. Sir, personally, I am *appalled* at your actions!"

"Now, now. Let's not accuse the man without giving him his fair say," Deacon Thomas said.

"Oh hush up, Bernard," Sister Murray said. "You're nothing but a little 'yes-man' to the pastor anyhow. Nothing he does is wrong in your sight."

"Sister Murray, please," Elder Fuller said. "We all discussed this, and we agreed we would give Pastor Landris time to speak his piece."

"Why? He's just going to deny it. Y'all know this! Anybody who could blatantly shove this in our faces . . . like we're a bunch of mindless fools—"

"Sister Murray," Elder Fuller said. "If you can't abide by the rules we have set, then maybe you should excuse yourself from this meeting right now."

"I'm not excusing myself from nothing!" Sister Murray repositioned her body better in her chair, then folded her arms across her full-sized chest. "Go on. Do your little meeting like you want. But if y'all think for one second I'm going to just sit here and let *this man* get over on me, y'all got another *think* coming!"

"Pastor," Elder Fuller said. "It has come to all of our attention that Sister Theresa Jordan, a member of our congregation, is with child."

"Hmph," Sister Murray said. "You can't help but notice it now! She looks to be about four months, I'd say. And I'm usually pretty right about these things."

"Sister Murray," Elder Fuller said. She flicked her hand at him for him to continue. "As I was saying, it is common knowledge that you and Sister Jordan were set to wed last year at the end of December. Although the details of why that marriage did not take place have not been disclosed—"

"And . . . it's none of our business," Mother King said.

"And, it is indeed none of our business, as Mother King so ably stated. But Pastor, people in the church are starting to put one and one together—"

Sister Murray leaned forward and looked dead in Pastor Landris's face. "And they're coming up with three!" she said, thrusting three fingers his way.

Elder Fuller rolled his eyes at Sister Murray and continued. "Pastor, many of the church members have figured you and Sister Theresa had to have had relations before marriage. And even though nobody can truly regulate things of that nature except God, this is not appropriate behavior for a pastor."

"Especially not the pastor of *this* church," Deacon Perkins said.

"Yeah," Sister Murray said. "We can't say about these other places and all that's going on with them, but we ain't playing that mess here! Not here! You gonna come before us saying you've been called by God, then we expect you to live a holy life! No ifs, ands, or buts!"

"At least, to try," Mother King said. "We don't believe anyone on this earth is perfect. 'And none is good but the Father.' But we do expect more from our ministers. And having *relations* outside of wedlock—"

"Fornicating," Sister Murray said, emphasizing it. "Having sex! Just call it what it is! I'm so tired of us holier-than-thou folks acting like we've been in the church all our lives and don't know the real deal. If we were outside these walls, we'd be calling it a whole lot worse! We get up in here and try to sanitize things. *Having relations.* They were sinning, apparently."

"Sister Murray," Deacon Thomas said. "We don't want to be here all day with this just because you've *apparently* got your own special issues to deal with—"

"What?" She began to fan herself with her hand. "You leave me and my old man out of this, you little—"

"Sister Murray!" Elder Fuller said. "Can you *please* hold your peace?"

"I do, and the rocks will cry out," she said.

Mother King leaned over and whispered something in Sister Murray's ear. No one heard what she said, but Sister Murray sucked in a big gulp of air and seemed to swallow it whole. It looked hard going down.

Elder Fuller looked over at Sister Murray and Mother King and knew Sister Murray would at least be quiet until it was a more appropriate time to speak.

"Pastor Landris, there is much murmur in and out of our church. The consensus seems to be that you're not a man of integrity. That you are one way when you're here, but entirely different in the unsupervised areas of your life. Had you and Sister Jordan gone through with your wedding plans, no one would have been the wiser of your . . . sin." He looked over at Sister Murray and could tell she was about to burst to say something, but she managed to hold her tongue.

"The other thing, Pastor," Elder Fuller said, "your leaving that woman at the altar, if that was the case, and certainly the speculation is running rampant, was not received well. Some folk . . ." he looked over at Minister Huntley, who had not opened his mouth throughout all this, ". . . feel it shows you don't have the heart of the people in your work of ministry, that you are only out for the profit and the recognition, and that you can't keep a vow or promise."

"Well, it's like I said before," Mother King said, "some things ain't none of our business. Quite frankly, Pastor, I think it takes a great deal of courage to cancel a wedding that close with that much expense put into it. Most folks would have gone through with it, even knowing it was a mistake. I don't hold the same views as to your engagement and your actual wedding taking place. I'm not concerned with your not having gotten married, as long as you did it the right way, and for the right reason. But—" She stood up and walked around the room. "I do have a problem with your being a pastor here . . . fathering a baby, apparently out of wedlock. And it appears you are not taking responsibility for any of these actions," Mother King concluded.

"And *I* have a problem with someone who is supposed to be an example to what is essentially God's heritage, making a mockery of it. What you gonna tell somebody when you evidently can't keep your pants up yourself?" Sister Murray said. "How you gonna counsel somebody on how to stay holy in the face of adversity, when obviously it doesn't work for you? And what else are you doing that we don't know about? This just happened to come out. For the most part, folks here thought you were sincere in your well-doing. But this done undermined all that!" Sister Murray sat back and interlocked her fingers together across her chest, glad to finally have her say without being beat down this time.

"Sister Murray is right in what she said," Deacon Perkins said. "We just want to know what you're planning to do about it now that it's on the table."

Minister Huntley, Minister Tucker, Elder Fuller, Mother King, Deacon Thomas, Deacon Woods, Deacon Perkins, and Sister Murray all sat there staring at their pastor, who had not opened his mouth. Some were attempting to read what he might say.

"Let me ask this," Pastor Landris said. "Has anyone spoken with Theresa Jordan about this matter? The matter you bring and have officially laid at my feet to address? I've done nothing wrong, so there's nothing for me to explain really." His audience continued to wait. He pressed his hands together in a prayer-like mode, bringing the tips of them up, and resting the two index fingers against his bottom lip.

"That's it?" Sister Murray said, not believing his nerve. "We're expected to believe you're not the father of this woman's baby from what you just said? Well, we did attempt to talk with Sister Theresa about it. She refuses to talk with any of us concerning 'her business.' Her friend, Sister B, suggested we speak with you if we wanted to know who the father was. So, if you're not the father, then tell us . . . who is?"

Pastor Landris looked at her. "Theresa Jordan is of age. She can speak for herself."

Elder Fuller sat forward. "Pastor Landris, that woman is with child. Somehow, the word is out that it's your baby. Must have come from her, and she ought to know. So, are you telling us you're not the father?"

Pastor Landris felt it really wasn't his place to discuss Theresa's personal business—her pregnancy or who the father of her baby was. He sat back against his chair. "That's exactly what I'm saying."

"Pastor Landris?" Deacon Thomas said. "Now you know I've been in your corner since that faithful thirty-seven when you first arrived. I've seen you work the pavements, seen you push yourself to see about somebody sick or in the hospital because you knew it would mean so much to them to know you cared enough. I've watched this congregation grow to over three thousand members now. I was there that day you were supposed to get married, when you delivered one of the most powerful sermons I've ever witnessed, forced us to look at what God has in store for us—promises that go well beyond just reaching or crossing over Jordan. Over seventy people gave their lives to Christ because you put aside what you were dealing with on that day and decided to use it to the glory of God."

"And what is your point?" Sister Murray said. "We're not here to give him a commendation."

"My point is," he said directing his eyes back to Pastor Landris, "if Pastor is telling us he's not the father, then we should believe him. But Pastor, can you please give us something to help put all this murmuring and gossip to rest?"

Pastor Landris stood to his feet. "You people know me. Most of you have seen me in action from the very beginning. When I was out in the world, I would tell people the truth. Even when they didn't want to hear it. Most of the people close to me today are close because they can count on me being honest with them. Anything I've told a person, I haven't had to produce evidence for them to know it was the truth. When I became pastor of this church, I made a promise—"

"Hmph," Sister Murray said.

"a convenant with each and every member who is, and will become, a part of this local body. I'm not perfect, and when I'm wrong, I'm not afraid to confess it and face the music. Mother King, I appreciate your pointing out that all things aren't other folks' business. Sometimes, people want you to jump hoops for them to take you at your word. I think I've proven myself here. I'm not going to prove it again on this matter.

"There are things in this situation that none of you are aware of. And truthfully, not my place to say. I know some of you believe you run this church. Maybe a few of you believe you can run me. When

I first came here, I already had money. Most of you know I'm not here for the money. I had a house, and yes, I bought a bigger house. But it's not because I misuse this church. I drive a nice car; you know this too. But it's not because I misuse the church. Check my giving record."

He hadn't told any of them, and didn't mention now, how he'd amassed his fortune back in the late eighties by purchasing two thousand shares of a then-unknown stock: Microsoft. Who could have ever guessed at the dividends, splits, and more splits. Or its value when he sold most of it last year before the downturn.

"I could leave right now . . . today," he said, "and start pastoring another church, if I so chose. You all are aware I've received my share of lucrative offers. Every day, it seems, I fight the thoughts and ideas of people who think all we preachers want is their money. Yes, I do know some preachers like that. They see so many hungry people—searching for the Word—and they end up abusing the situation. But believe me, there are scriptures that address those wolves in sheep's clothing. When God judges, He'll begin in *His* house first!

"Yes . . . people praise me, criticize me, talk to me, talk about me, want every ounce I have to give without thinking about what it takes to be able to do this. And yes, there are those who don't want to hear a word I have to say.

"None of you called me into ministry. Thank God. And I'm not trying to be difficult by not answering the question in the way you'd like it answered. But the Bible says, 'If you have aught against your brother or sister, you should go to them.' Your aught is not with me. That much I will say. And the easiest thing for me to do would be to give you what you think you need in order for you to support me. But right and easy aren't necessarily the same thing."

"Pastor Landris—" Elder Fuller said.

"Hold up, Elder Fuller. All I have left to say is this: I did nothing wrong. Whether I say flat out that I'm not the father, or just tell you I did nothing wrong, somehow, it still wouldn't be enough for some people. Now, having said all that, you can believe me and stick by me or . . . not. I can't force anyone to do or believe anything. I can only tell you the truth."

"Pastor, do you know how many people have stood and essentially looked us in our faces these past few years, and lied about doing nothing wrong?" Deacon Perkins said.

Pastor Landris laughed a little. "Yeah. But you know what? I'm not those other people. I am me. When you begin to judge everyone based upon your negative experiences with another, your ocean of life can become quite shallow. That's what I think, anyway. Now," he said as he headed toward the door with his briefcase in hand, "I thank you all. And since we have several members in various hospitals around the city who need to be visited today, I must bid you . . . adieu. Unless of course, anyone would care to come visiting *with* me?"

No one said a word. And with that, he walked out, gently closing the door behind him.

CHAPTER 29

Give and It Shall Be Given Unto You

On March seventh, Johnnie Mae arrived in Atlanta. The hotel was grand. Her suite was by the pool. She called Landris to let him know where she was staying. He asked to take her out to dinner. She declined for that night, but accepted his invitation for tomorrow after her two book signings.

"You look great," Landris said as they were being seated at a table by the fountain. Smooth R&B played softly in the background.

Her eyes appeared to dance to the rhythm of the beat. She smiled, then inhaled deep. "Thanks. You too."

His eyes locked with hers. "It's good to see you."

She looked down at her menu, but continued smiling.

As usual, they talked about how everything was going. He told her a little about the church meeting four days ago where they had literally accused him of misconduct. "They didn't even bother to ask me first whether or not I'd done it. They insisted that I *explain* my actions."

"And how did you respond?"

"I told them, in essence, I had done nothing wrong."

Having broken the crystalized sugar at the bottom of the glass of her Champagne Cocktail, it had already fizzed—creating a thick foam on top from the sugar infusion. She took a sip, being careful not to end up with a brown foam mustache. "Landris, that really *was* a vague answer. You do realize that, right?"

"I do."

"So why didn't you tell them more? What harm would it have been for you to have just flat-out denied it? Made them understand? To have told them what they wanted to know without mincing words? Allowed there to be no doubt?"

"You mean cause a scene? Act like *I* was appalled they would even bring something like that to me? Prove it, no matter the cost?"

"Yeah. Sounds like a good plan to me. And if you have information exonerating you, you should use it."

"Johnnie Mae, as a minister, I made an oath—somewhat like doctors and lawyers. When people come who are hurting, needing to be counseled, they're not looking to spill their guts and soul only to hear their business in the streets later. No matter what the reason."

"I understand. And I'd feel that same way myself, if I were to ever go to my pastor—which I wouldn't—but that's another conversation entirely."

"So you see, if I'm told something, even something that could benefit me, it would be wrong to take that confidence and use it. If I had made a scene, and believe me, I would have loved to, they wouldn't have stopped there. My telling them it wasn't true should have been enough. We'll just have to see."

"It's like being charged with a crime—you're supposed to be innocent until proven guilty, but instead you're guilty until you prove your own innocence?"

"Precisely." He took a swallow of green tea. "Apparently, it's common knowledge Theresa's pregnant."

Johnnie Mae stopped her sip in mid-air. "Pregnant? And you say—"

"Some believe it's my doing. I told the elders and board of directors I did nothing wrong."

"Okay," she said in a matter-of-fact tone.

He laughed and sat against the back of his seat. "Okay?" He smiled. "Okay?"

"Yeah. Okay."

"That's it?" He leaned forward. "You don't want to know why or what?"

The waitress brought out their salads. After she left, Johnnie Mae poured honey mustard dressing over hers and, without missing a beat, said, "Nope."

Landris fell against his seat. "You're something. Really something."

"No. But you said you did nothing wrong. You have your reasons for not saying any more." She looked at her salad. "Would you care to bless the food so we can get started?"

He laughed, and at the same instant he bowed his head to give grace, the power of Whitney Houston's voice filled the air with *I Will Always Love You*.

Sunday morning, March eleventh, Johnnie Mae attended Wings of Grace Faith Ministry Church. This would be her first time seeing and hearing Landris preach in person. She sat in the front row, thinking how good he looked—even if he wasn't wearing the traditional robe or standing in a traditional pulpit.

They had those carpeted steps that led up to a flat platform. But Landris, like many other preachers she had seen lately, usually walked the floor where the congregation sat. The service began with "corporate devotional prayer." They believed in praying in the spirit if you knew how, or praying with your normal language if you hadn't been "filled with the spirit." Everybody—all at the same time. She hadn't been filled, so she prayed using her regular language.

After about fifteen minutes of people praying at the same time, the Praise and Worship Ministry came up and led the people into songs of praise and adoration. Johnnie Mae liked what she was feeling. Pastor Landris had been out front when they had begun prayer. He was not visible during the brief announcement period, where, incidentally, they acknowledged a famous author was visiting with them this morning.

They said her name and everything. And to her surprise, the congregation applauded because she was in the service. They took tithes and offerings by passing golden buckets, and people were actually shouting for the opportunity to put their money in them. She'd never seen such excitement surrounding giving ever before in her life! The whole building felt electrically charged.

"God loves a cheerful giver. If you're going to give, give it because you're excited. Not because you feel you have to," a woman preacher, Minister Fulton, was saying as the buckets flowed down rows and rows of a sea of people. "God doesn't need your money. Get that straight right now. He has plenty! He doesn't need the farmer's seeds either. God has plenty of those, too. Yet the farmer is smart enough to know that one seed planted multiplies back to the sower. One seed—multiple seeds in return. Not a bad investment, I'd say. So if you want to give, then give. But if you want to grumble and mumble about it while you're giving, why don't you just keep it and see how far it will take you?"

Pastor Landris taught on "Truth or Consequences." Johnnie Mae enjoyed it because he brought out how people, Christians included, really don't tell the truth all the time.

"Even the Bible-toting, tongue-talking, Holy Ghost–shouting, 'on-my-way-to-heaven-anyhow' Christians don't always tell the truth. People lie to protect; lie to get ahead; lie to keep out of trouble; lie to get back a little more from their income tax; lie to not hurt someone's feelings. Some people even go as far as to categorize their lies. Like there are different levels of lies. One color lie is okay, which I suppose indicates another color lie is not. You got your white lies, but, of course, those also come in various sizes. There's the standard little white lie, implying there's also medium, large, possibly extra large, and jumbo."

Johnnie Mae thought he was outstanding. She could see why people came in packs to get a seat in this anointed place. At the end of service, she went forward and received the baptism of the Holy Spirit.

Her speaking and signing was at three o'clock. She felt good doing it. She'd forgotten how much she loved speaking to a crowd of people. The church was not packed like it was for the morning services. But Sister Thelma Miles, the woman who had coordinated everything, told her they had presold a thousand of her books. She prayed her hand wouldn't get cramped before she finished. Johnnie Mae had already planned on donating two dollars for each book sold toward the Community Development Center. That would be at least $2,000—essentially, her royalty on these books.

People were lined up to get their books autographed. It took about three hours before she could even see the end of the line. She still couldn't get over how people actually stood in line just to get her to sign their books. She was so humbled by them.

"Hi, Ms. Taylor. I love your books! I was so glad to hear you would be here. I loved your speech today! It really motivated me to not give up on my dreams."

"And who would you like your book autographed to?" Johnnie Mae said.

"Could you make it out to Christa, please?"

Johnnie Mae signed, smiled, and waited for the next person in line. Her hand was beginning to get a little tired, but fortunately there were only eight people left. She felt she would make it as she stretched out her hand between each signing time.

"Ms. Taylor." The voice had a chilling coldness about it. "I read your first book."

"Oh you did?" Johnnie Mae said with a warm smile.

"Yeah. Quite frankly, I didn't care for it. I'm hoping this one is better." She handed her the latest book.

Johnnie Mae was taken aback a little, but she maintained her smile. "Well, everything is not for everybody. Maybe you'll enjoy this one better."

"Hope so."

"And who would you like this autographed to?"

"B."

"Bee? Like the bumblebee?"

"No. B."

"Just the letter B?"

"Just . . . B."

Johnnie Mae signed and handed the book back to her. B didn't smile or anything. Johnnie Mae wondered, *What was that all about? But now, the world has all kinds. And there are plenty of critics to go around. Even when they can't string two sentences together themselves to form a paragraph, they can still tell you how you should have strung yours.*

"Hello. I enjoyed your speech," the woman with long dreadlocks said.

"Well thank you. And who would you like your books autographed to?"

"One to Maurice," she said. "The other to Sapphire. That's S-a-p-p-h-i-r-e."

"Sapphire. What a nice name."

"Thank you," she said as she walked away.

"Well, hello there. Oooh, are you expecting?" Johnnie Mae said, grinning.

"Yes," the woman said.

"When's your due date?"

"September eleventh."

"That's great. And who would you like these autographed to?"

"Could you possibly put my whole name in that one?" She pointed to the latest book.

"If you like." Johnnie Mae held the pen at the ready. "What's the name?"

"Theresa Jordan. That's Theresa with an aitch. Do you need me to spell all of it for you?"

While Johnnie Mae wrote, it was apparent Theresa had rattled her. At least now, Theresa was sure Johnnie Mae had heard of her, too.

Seeing Johnnie Mae in person, Theresa was shocked at how truly petite and beautiful she was: long black hair, beautiful, flawless, brown skin, a perfect smile. Her pictures obviously didn't do her justice. At forty, she could easily pass for a twenty-five year old . . . easily.

"Thank you," Theresa said. Her voice didn't move up or down. She began walking away.

"Theresa?" Johnnie Mae said, calling her back. Theresa came back over. "Might we talk? After I'm finished here?"

Theresa glanced at the remaining line. There were about five people left. "Sure, if that's what you want."

Theresa walked away and spoke briefly with B and Sapphire. Johnnie Mae pulled herself together.

"Hi, and this is to?" she said with her usual smile.

"Ms. Taylor, I just love your work! You are so great! I don't know how people like you do it. Could you make it out to Nicey? Like nice with a wye."

Johnnie Mae smiled. "Nice," she said holding long the 's' sound. "With a wye."

CHAPTER 30

Come Now, and Let Us Reason Together

When Johnnie Mae finished signing, she told Sister Miles she'd be back shortly. Sister Miles had stayed with her to make sure she was taken care of. Landris had other business he had to handle, and he had apologized for not being able to stay the whole time. But he knew she'd be there a couple of hours, at least, and he'd be back by the time she was finished.

Johnnie Mae and Theresa stepped out into the hall.

"Is there somewhere we can talk? In private?" Johnnie Mae said.

Theresa led the way to a room that was unlocked. "This is a conference room—it should do."

They sat down across from each other. Johnnie Mae began first.

"Theresa, first of all, I'd like to say how sorry I am about all that happened with you and Landris—"

"Landris? Is that what you call him?"

Johnnie Mae stopped for a second, not saying what she really thought about that comment. She smiled. "Yes."

"Hmph."

"Like I was saying, Landris has been a dear friend to me for a long time. We only see each other every now and then. But he's the type of person you can count on."

"Maybe *you* can count on him. I can't exactly vouch for that."

"Theresa, I'm trying to tell you what a genuine person he is. I don't know what happened between you two—"

"I bet."

"I don't. Really."

"How about, it started when he found out you were in that car accident, and he went flying out of here like his clothes were on fire?"

Johnnie Mae looked over at her. "Well that's understandable, don't you think? We're friends. If your friend needed you, wouldn't you go see about them?"

Theresa looked back at her. "Oh, you two are more than just friends. You might can get away with that innocent stuff with other folks, but I'm not impressed."

"Did you know I was married? I mean, before my husband passed . . ."

Theresa softened a little. "Yeah, I knew. I heard about him . . . dying and all. I'm sorry. But I'm surprised you and *Landris* haven't married yet. But I suppose that would be in bad taste, huh?"

Johnnie Mae leaned her head over to the side. "And what exactly do you mean by *that*?"

"Which part?"

"All of it."

"I mean, Ms. Taylor," she held the "Ms." long and was hard saying "Taylor," "he loves you. I know it. He knows it. You know it. I wonder if your husband ever knew it? It's quite clear to me. I would think, now that you're free, so to speak, the two of you would go on and begin your new life. Together."

"Theresa—"

"Has he asked you?"

"Asked me what?"

"To marry him."

"Theresa, look. I really wanted to talk with you so that I could let you know how sorry I am about all that happened. To apologize if something that was happening with me and my life, at the time, affected the two of you—"

"He has, hasn't he? I can see it in your eyes! He's asked you to marry him already." She began to shake her head. "God!"

"Theresa—" Johnnie Mae could see tears now blazing a trail down her face.

"I'm not surprised, you know. I'm just surprised that it still hurts so much." She began to massage her stomach. "I'm pregnant. Of course, you noticed that." She looked over at Johnnie Mae. "Did he tell you what happened? Tell you why he and I didn't marry that day? Tell you about . . . my baby?"

Johnnie Mae shook her head and pressed her lips firmly together. "No."

"I'm surprised. I would think he would tell you so you'd know the whole story. Did you know I was expecting? Before today?"

"Yes."

"So you mean to say, he didn't tell you any more?"

"No."

She laughed. "So aren't you worried in the least that this is his baby I'm carrying? Worried that he's not the person you believed him to be?"

"Theresa, why would you want people to *assume* that it's his baby?"

Theresa stood up and walked around. "It didn't start out that way. I told a friend I was pregnant. You met her earlier—Sapphire. You autographed her two books."

"Dreadlocks? Yes. Sapphire—I remember her."

"Well, when I told Sapphire, she automatically jumped to the conclusion that it was George's baby. I was trying to tell her, but the words just never came out. Then she starts to tell me about this guy she's interested in getting with . . ."

Johnnie Mae pulled her gently to sit down next to her. "And?"

"And . . . that's the guy I'm pregnant by." She looked up at Johnnie Mae and wondered why it was so much easier to spill her guts to a stranger than her family or friends. "So I can't even tell her now," she said.

"If you don't, then what if they end up together? Something like that could ruin your friendship."

"I know, I know. I keep making such a mess of my life! Then there's my other friend—B."

Johnnie Mae laughed. "Oh, yes. B. I remember B. She doesn't care for me too much, I gathered."

"Oh, that's just B. When she feels threatened, or feels like someone she loves is threatened, she comes out swinging. I wish I could say her bark is worse than her bite, but that would be a lie." She laughed. "Anyway, I couldn't tell B either."

"Why?"

"Lord, you ask a lot of questions!" She smiled. "But you're really easy to talk to. I tried to tell George some of this some time back. Went to him as my pastor, so I knew he wouldn't tell it. He's just like that: upright."

"Okay, but why can't you tell your friend, B, the truth?"

"Because . . ." she took a deep breath, "the guy I'm pregnant by is B's brother. Everybody thinks I hate him. How do you explain that, even to your best of friends?"

"You're right. Those are some tough ones. Have you told the father?"

"My father? God, no! My father's so upset with George, but at least he's handling it decently. But then, who can say what Daddy's plotting? He's nice, but if you ever cross him . . . look out. He'll let you have it with God's full force."

"I was asking had you told the father . . . of your baby?"

"Oh," she said, slightly embarrassed with her error. "No, I haven't. If he knew, he'd probably make a big deal about it. Then everybody would know."

"So you'd rather let Landris take the heat for something he didn't do?"

She looked up. "What do you mean, take the heat?"

"Did you know practically the whole church is talking about this? That the people on the board of directors at the church are calling him on it?"

"They are?"

"Yes."

"So why doesn't he just tell them it's not his?"

She took Theresa's hand, the one with the two-carat diamond ring prominently displayed. "Because, Theresa, you went to him in confidence. You went to him as your pastor. Whatever you told him that day, as far as he's concerned, is privileged information. And if I know Landris, he'll let this church throw him out before he will be disloyal to your confidence."

"Even though I'm the cause of his troubles?"

Johnnie Mae nodded.

"God! See, I keep getting deeper and deeper into mess. It's amazing how one little lie—even if it was a lie of omission—can snowball so out of control. Do you really believe the church might take action against him because of what people are believing? Nobody's come and asked me one thing. Nobody except Sister Murray, who was just trying to get all up in my business. None of the other people on the board have contacted me or asked me anything!"

"And if they had, what would you have said?"

"You don't really want an answer. You're just trying to prove a point."

"Yeah. Landris probably didn't say enough to save himself with the board because he didn't want them attacking you."

"And he even knows whose baby it is. So he didn't say *anything* on his behalf . . . in his own defense?"

"As far as I'm aware, nothing except 'I did nothing wrong.'" Johnnie Mae mocked the way Landris probably said it.

Theresa laughed because it sounded just like how George would say it. "Oh, that's him all right!" Theresa turned and looked at Johnnie Mae. "I sort of feel like an idiot asking you this. But . . . why won't you marry George now?"

"Look at *you* all up in *my* business." Johnnie Mae said, then smiled. She shook her head. "It's too soon."

"You can't get over your husband? Is that it?"

"That's part of it. But also, people wouldn't understand. How your husband whom you loved so much could die, and a few months later, you're happily off with someone else."

"So you're reacting and living your life based on what other people will think, instead of what's truly in your own heart? The heart God alone sees?"

Johnnie Mae looked at her funny. "Actually, I'm just trying to avoid any unnecessary complications."

"Like me, huh? But then again . . . I'm so wrong. So, do you think you'll ever marry him?"

Johnnie Mae rubbed her left ear. "To be honest, I don't know."

"Would you like to know what he said to me about you once? Right before he went traipsing off to find you in Birmingham after your accident?"

"What?"

"Have you ever loved someone that you never had?"

"He actually said that to you? About me?"

Theresa stood up to leave. "Yeah—when he called to explain you to me. I didn't understand it at first. But I do know he really loves you. And it looks like you've never been his. Personally, after talking with you today, I think the whole thing is kind of sad." She went to the door and held it open. "The two of you are going to miss out on a whole lot of life trying to please other people."

"Theresa, what are you planning to do . . ." she glanced down at Theresa's stomach.

"You mean about this mess I've created?"

"If that's what you want to call it."

"Honestly, Johnnie Mae, I don't know. I really don't know. But I hope you know I'm not purposely trying to hurt or get back at George. I probably should have. And if I were B, I definitely would have! But it's hard to stay mad at a person who is so real and genuine. Someone who might not be perfect, but who is at least trying to do right. Although losing me, if you ask my opinion, was pretty dumb on his part."

Johnnie Mae reached over and hugged Theresa. "Well, I believe you'll do the right thing because it's right to do it."

"I hope so," Theresa said, shaking her head.

"Don't hope—believe."

CHAPTER 31

Beloved, Think It Not Strange Concerning the Fiery Trial Which Is to Try You

The following few weeks, the Wings of Grace Faith Ministry Church was in a complete uproar. Some members were calling for a special meeting. They didn't care what the board had investigated and concluded; they wanted this out in the open so everybody could know what was going on. A few were talking about other things Pastor Landris might have done besides the Theresa Jordan situation. There were even murmurs about the church splitting, with the folks who insisted on keeping the "scoundrel" separating from the others who were tired of mess, scandals, and just wanted a "real-honest-to-God-fearing leader" for a change.

So an open meeting was quickly scheduled for Sunday, April the first, because many of the members didn't see a reason to come to church on another day when most of them would already be at church on Sunday.

"What don't come out in the wash, gonna come out in the rinse," Sister Murray said as the meeting got under way. "That's what Mudear used to say and I believe it. We gonna get to the bottom of this so we can all go on about the business of serving the Lord."

"Amen," said a few in the audience.

"They tried to hush me up when we met on this a couple of

weeks back, but now we as a people gonna have our say. They ain't gonna be able to hide this under a rock. The Lord said he was going to pull back the covers and expose all the folks trying to hide their misdoings."

A few people whispered, "Where in the Bible does it say that?"

"Listen people," Elder Fuller said. "There's no reason for us to get all excited. We can do this decently and in order, the way the Bible has instructed."

"Ain't nobody all excited. We just want to get to the bottom of the barrel and see what's been tainting the drinking water. If we have to clean it out, or throw it out and get a new one, we just need to know. I never was one to believe in that blind faith nonsense . . . not when it comes to following no man!"

"No woman, either." A woman's voice yelled out.

Pastor Landris sat on the front row, unable to believe this was happening. He looked ahead, wondering what he could have done to have avoided all this.

"I don't see any reason to discuss this. I think we ought to inform the church of what's going on. Throw out a few options once we've evaluated the facts. Then we just need to voice our votes. No need of us dragging this out."

Bishop and Beatrice Jordan suddenly appeared. "Praise the Lord!" Sister Murray said. "Here's Bishop and Mrs. Jordan now. Come on up front, dear hearts."

"This is supposed to be for members only," Elder Fuller said and stood.

"I invited them. I think they have a right to know what's going on. After all, it's their precious child that's having to bear through all this. Theresa Jordan? Baby? Where are you?" Sister Murray looked around the congregation. "Theresa Jordan?"

People started pointing when B began shouting, "Here! She's here! Over here!"

Theresa had been trying to get B not to do that. "I don't want any part of this. What is this about, anyway?" Theresa said. "What?"

"Come on up, baby. I know you've been through a lot," Sister Murray said. "We not trying to make this hard on you. God told us to watch for wolves around our sheep. You're one of our sheep. Somebody gotta stand for right at some point."

B pushed Theresa to get up.

"Stop it, B! I don't want to go up there! I don't want any part of this charade. Did you know about this? Is this why you thought I should skip church services today?"

"Well, while she's on her way, let's just go on," Sister Murray said. "As many of you probably already know, our dear precious sister is with child."

Gasps and murmurs went throughout the congregation. It was apparent some knew, but most had no knowledge whatsoever. Those who hadn't, could see where this just might end up being an interesting church meeting after all.

"Sister Theresa Jordan is the daughter of the Bishop Jordan. Many of us, she either grew up with or we watched her grow. Now she is a successful young businesswoman. Bishop and Sister Jordan have done an outstanding job in raising her to be a wonderful young lady. Y'all may also remember, she was to have married at the end of last year. Course, something happened, and *that* wedding never took place. Some folks say that it's none of our business—"

"Amen!" a chorus of voices sang loud.

Sister Murray rolled her tongue around inside her mouth, then began to speak again. "Like I was about to say, some say it's none of our business as to what happened, but what *has* become our business is a fact we can't ignore. Now I'm sure Sister Theresa will come before the church and ask forgiveness for her part of this sin of fornication. But in the meantime, we can't have a preacher saying one thing in the pulpit and living like Satan's grandchild when he's outside these doors. Only the Lord knows what the real truth is behind all this, but I can't see us having a pastor who has done this to one of our own. And he doesn't even seem to have the decency to be ashamed about it."

"Lord, have mercy," someone said. "Help us, Jesus!"

"At least the others who fell, and we know who they are, were decent enough to ask forgiveness from we who have been diligent in the faith. Bishop Jordan . . . Sister Jordan, I'd personally like to ask your forgiveness since we allowed the fox in the henhouse because somebody," she looked over at the row of deacons and fellow board members, "fell asleep watching the door."

Someone stood. "Sister Murray, I understand what you're saying. But we'd like to hear what Pastor Landris has to say about all this. You're accus—"

"Pastor Landris," Sister Murray said, smacking, "refuses to say much on this matter."

"Now Sister Murray, that's not true," Deacon Thomas stood and said. "Pastor Landris reassured all of us he hadn't done anything wrong."

"I suppose getting one of the members in a family way, without marrying her, is doing nothing wrong? See, that's my concern. Whose daughter will be next? Will it be yours? Or yours?" She looked around the room, pointing at various sections. "And does it matter what age they are? We don't know. Because the pastor of this great church believes there are *some* things he's not obliged to have to explain when questioned about it."

"Pastor Landris," Bishop Jordan said as he stood and walked to the front. "I've heard what the sister here has to say. I would have rather kept this a family matter and not brought it into the church," he continued in his heavy baritone. "I would like to hear from you, if you would so oblige me and my wife. I've heard many rumors about what is going on over here. Some people even labeled it a cult. Being a minister, I also know how people exaggerate and some just flat-out lie! God alone knows what all I've been accused of myself. My wife and I are aware of our daughter's situation. She hasn't spoken much to either of us about it, especially this much. And since she *is* grown, we're limited to how far we can take the matter. Please, Pastor Landris, I'd like to hear what you have to say."

Pastor Landris looked at Bishop and Mrs. Jordan. He turned and looked in the direction Sister Murray had spoken when she was calling for Theresa to come up. Theresa sat there with so much pain on her face. He walked to the front, and the place was as quiet as a last breath breathed.

"You all are not strangers to me. As many of you as there are, you know I've always made myself available to you and your families. I came here to make a difference. Not only a difference in your lives, but hopefully, to instill the confidence back to the office of pastor. I'm not pointing a finger at any particular minister or person because, at some point, all of us have sinned and fallen short of the glory of God. The wonderful thing is that Jesus already paid the price. And each day, we get brand-new mercy.

"God says if we'll ask, He is faithful and just to forgive. And He will throw our sins into the sea of forgetfulness. No, that doesn't mean we can sin because we know forgiveness is available for the asking. But we, like sheep, have gone astray. There have been times I myself have had to leave the ninety-nine, just to go after the one. Jesus left heaven—just to get the one: the Church. And if you or I had been the only one, he would have died for that one. Am I perfect? No. Have I done some things I wish I hadn't? Oh, of course. But in this particular case, and because of a commitment I've made that I intend to honor, all I can say here today is that I did nothing wrong. Now, should you feel in your heart you can't believe me, then there's nothing I can do—at this time—to cause you to."

Pastor Landris sat down. Rumblings spread throughout the sanctuary.

Sister Murray hurried back up. "So, members. You can see! Pastor Landris takes us for fools! He denies it, but gives us nothing to hang our belief on except his word. In light of this, I'd like to bring to the floor and move that we vote on the suspension if not dismissal of this—"

"Wait a minute!" fifteen-year-old Jalil said. "Y'all gonna just sit here and let the Pastor go out like that?" He looked around. "Nobody gonna stand and say nothing on his behalf? Well, I want you to know that Pastor Landris got me off the streets and kept me out of the gangs. Many of my old friends are either incarcerated, dead, or somewhere mutilated, if not paralyzed. It has never mattered what Pastor Landris had going on, he has always taken the time to let me know he cares. I don't know about some of you, but I needed and still need that.

"I don't have a daddy to tell me he's proud of me. But Pastor Landris told me a long time ago that I did have a Father. That He sits high and looks low and He would never forsake me. But Pastor Landris didn't stop there. He said whenever I needed an earthly father figure, to let him know. I might need a pat on the back or a word of encouragement. Someone to go to a game I might be playing in. He said if he wasn't available, there would be someone here to do it. Then he began a ministry in the church where young men and boys pair up with the seasoned men, as he put it. The young women and girls have seasoned women. Deacon Thomas up there . . ." he pointed to the front, "he's my seasoned buddy. We go fishing and stuff. He comes to my basketball and baseball games and cheers me on. He goes to parent/teachers meetings to meet my teachers. But you people want to just vote Pastor Landris gone when he just stood and told you he hadn't done anything wrong? That's not right! It's wrong! Plain wrong!" Jalil sat down; a few people reached over and patted him on his back.

"Hi, my name is Sandra. And I remember when my mother was in the hospital with cancer. Pastor Landris came by to see her. He never knew how much that meant to her. I found out later from other people, most pastors of a church this size hardly ever visit their members. Some say it's not because they don't want to, but because it's too much for them. Well, Pastor Landris manages somehow. That might change in the future because I wouldn't want him to wear himself out. But I want people to know how much it meant to my dear mother."

People, one after another, got up. Some had been on drugs, were alcoholics, had been on welfare, depressed, released from prison with no job—the list went on and on. But the biggest bulk came from plain folks who were just blessed beyond measure by the Word of God—the life-enhancing Word of God! Not one person had anything negative to say about Pastor Landris.

Sister Murray was beginning to get uneasy. She stepped back up to take control of the madness brewing. "Okay, people. Nobody said Pastor Landris wasn't a good person or a good pastor. And yes, he can teach and preach the Word. But that's not what we're here about right now. So I move we vote—"

Theresa stood up. Something wasn't right. She started running and didn't stop until she reached where her father and Beatrice sat. He was slumped over.

"Somebody call 9-1-1! Please hurry!" Beatrice was saying.

"Daddy!" Theresa yelled. "Daddy!" She shook him. "Daddy!"

A doctor in the congregation was hurriedly making his way over to them. He examined Bishop Jordan. "He's had a stroke!" he said.

"Does anyone have an aspirin on them?" one woman said.

Another woman, wearing a gray wig, shouted out, "I've got Tylenol. Extra strength."

"No, we need an aspirin. A plain old aspirin!" the first woman said.

"No aspirin!" the doctor said. "We're not sure whether or not there's any bleeding in the brain. If there is bleeding in the brain, an aspirin could cause it to bleed faster." He continued working with Bishop Jordan until the ambulance arrived; Beatrice rode with the Bishop. Sapphire drove Theresa in her SUV. B drove her own car.

The meeting and the vote were postponed, against Sister Murray's objection, until another time. Sister Murray insisted they had enough time to at least take the vote, and then they could adjourn.

"Bertha!" Mother King said. "Stick a sock in it, then wrap a girdle around it! I believe you've caused enough trouble for one day! And to think . . . you call yourself a Christian!"

Pastor Landris was due to pick Johnnie Mae up from the airport in about thirty minutes. There was bad weather where she was headed, and all flights had been diverted to other areas until the weather stabilized. Her flight was being routed to Atlanta.

Landris decided he'd go to the airport, pick up Johnnie Mae, drop her off at his house, then swing by the hospital afterward.

"Dear Lord," he began to pray en route to the airport, "let Bishop Jordan be all right. By Jesus' stripes, he's already healed; your Word in Isaiah declares it. So let your Word be true, and let everything contrary to your Word be a lie. I thank you that all is well. Now. Right now! In Jesus' name I pray . . ."

CHAPTER 32

Behold, I Have Refined Thee, but Not with Silver

Landris picked Johnnie Mae up from the airport. Fortunately, the flight arrived on time.

"Johnnie Mae, I know we were planning to get a bite to eat while you were here, but something has come up."

"Oh, that's okay. Something wrong? Anything I can do to help?"

"Theresa's father had a stroke just when the church was about to vote on whether they should keep me as the pastor or send me on my way."

Johnnie Mae looked concerned, then laughed. "Oh, I get it. April fool. But Landris, that's not funny. And you shouldn't be joking about somebody having a . . ." She saw the look on his face. "You're serious, aren't you?"

"Yes."

"Is he all right?"

"I don't know. It happened about an hour before I came to pick you up. I left five minutes behind the ambulance that took him to the hospital."

"Oh Landris, you could have gone with them. I could have done something different. I'm so sorry I—"

"Stop that. It's not a problem." He glanced at her, then back to the road. With a sigh he said, "I'm not even sure they want me there. Considering . . ."

"Considering?"

"The meeting at church was because of Theresa's pregnancy."

"My goodness."

"One of our good sisters invited Theresa's parents to the meeting. A meeting no one, at least I didn't, seemed to know we were having until Elder Fuller announced it right before benediction. They were about to vote when—"

"Theresa? What about Theresa? She must not have been there."

He looked at Johnnie Mae then back at the road. "She was there."

"And she didn't say anything to stop their voting or them from accusing you? She knows—"

"No. She didn't say a word."

"Landris, if you don't mind. I'd like to go to the hospital with you."

"But Johnnie Mae—"

"It'll be okay. Trust me." Her eyes pleaded her case. She hadn't mentioned to him anything about her talk or having met Theresa that day.

"All right. If you're sure?"

"I'm sure."

Fifteen minutes later, they arrived at the hospital. Landris had overheard where they were taking Bishop Jordan before he left for the airport. This was one time he was glad to be so familiar with the hospital; he knew exactly where to go.

"What are *you* doing here?" B said as soon as she saw him walk in. "And how dare you bring *her!* You selfish, insensitive—"

Theresa walked over to where they were. "B, it's okay." B started to object; Theresa put her hand on her arm. "I said . . . it's . . . okay." B stomped off.

Theresa looked exhausted. "Sorry," she said to them both. "Johnnie Mae, how are you?"

Johnnie Mae nodded. "Just fine." She and Theresa embraced.

George looked like he was in shock. "I didn't know you two knew each other."

"I met her when she signed my book a few weeks back—at the church."

"You were at the church?" George said to Theresa. "I didn't realize you had come."

"Yes," Theresa said. "And the two of us had a nice talk."

"How's your father?" Johnnie Mae said.

Theresa let out a deep sigh. "He had a massive stroke. They're doing CAT scans, MRIs. You name it, looks like they're doing it. I went in at one point. His eyes are so weak. He can't talk. He can't move his left arm or leg. The whole left side of his face is drooping." She began to cry. Johnnie Mae held her. "They say it looks like there might be bleeding in his brain. It's all my fault! God is punishing me now!"

"Theresa, that's not true," Johnnie Mae said.

Theresa held her head up. "It is. I sat right there and let those people say all those things about George. And I wouldn't open my mouth. I was too proud. God hates a prideful heart. I'm sure Daddy was under a lot of strain. That was my fault, too. I've just been biding my time, allowing everybody else to suffer while I get to look like the one who's being mistreated. God is punishing me!"

"No," George said.

"Yes, George. It's called reaping what you sow. I've been planting seeds for years. Now, it's harvest time. Only I'm taking people down with me."

Johnnie Mae hugged Theresa while she continued to cry. She signaled for Landris to go away and give them some time alone together. He went over to meet Beatrice when he saw her slowly walking down the hall. B rolled her eyes just as he walked past her.

"Sickening," B said so he could hear her. "Just plain old *sickening!*"

When George reached Beatrice, he wasn't sure how she would feel about him being there. Her smile reassured him. They immediately hugged.

"Thank you for coming."

"How is he?"

"Not well. I'm trying not to tell Theresa everything, but it's not looking good at all. I already called for Lena to come."

"Lena?"

"Yeah. I think she needs to get here. The bishop was trying to say her name. I asked him if he wanted me to call her. He nodded that he did. Then he said 'wallet,' and when I pulled it out of my purse, he started crying when I got to the article, then that picture of him and Lena. The doctor says it's common for stroke victims to experience crying spells. I've just never seen him cry before."

"I'm sorry all this happened."

"Why should you be sorry? None of it was your doing. His blood pressure has been up for a while. We found out during one of those in-the-mall blood pressure screenings. He knew it, but wouldn't take a few minutes to go see a doctor. He kept putting it off. I tried to tell him, you can't tell when your blood pressure's up—not by the way you feel. Every time he said he was going to the doctor, he found an excuse not to go. Now, he's in here—and no more excuses."

"Theresa believes it's her fault."

"Where is Theresa?"

"With Johnnie Mae."

"Johnnie Mae?"

"Yeah—a friend of mine. I picked her up from the airport. That's why I'm just now getting here."

She patted him on the back. "You're a good man. I'm sorry you're having to go through so much yourself. There's something Theresa hasn't told her father and me about this baby business. I don't know if it had anything to do with why you two didn't get married. But I do know, you're a good one."

Theresa sat limp like a stalk of wilting celery, telling Johnnie Mae how she was the cause of all this trouble visiting her father now.

"If God will just let my daddy be all right. I promise, if I have to, I'll go before that entire congregation on Sunday and tell them the truth. I promise. Oh God, please forgive me. Punish me, if you need someone to punish. Just don't let my daddy die," she cried.

After Theresa calmed down, she stood up. She and Johnnie Mae started back toward the large emergency room waiting area. So many memories came back as Johnnie Mae recalled all the time she herself had spent in the hospital, not that many months ago.

The elevator dinged just as they walked past it. "Theresa!" A man's deep voice called out from inside it.

She turned. "Maurice? What are you doing here?"

"B called—real upset. Said your father had a stroke. The whole community is talking about it. How it was Pastor Landris's fault all of this even happened." Maurice walked alongside Theresa, Johnnie Mae having already walked on ahead.

"Maurice," she said as her faucet of tears began to flow again, "this wasn't George's fault at all. Not at all! It was mine! Me. My fault! Maurice, there's something important I need to tell you. And Maurice, I need to tell you now. . . ."

CHAPTER 33

My Grace Is Sufficient for Thee

Lena got a flight out immediately. It was only about an hour-long trip. She had never flown anywhere before. Beatrice had given her a number to call when she arrived. Beatrice wondered out loud where Theresa could be. Johnnie Mae told her she'd left her talking with someone getting off the elevator.

George volunteered to pick up Lena after she called.

"Johnnie Mae, would you like to ride to the airport with me? Or if you like, I can drop you off at my place."

"I'll ride. I don't mind."

They walked quickly to the car and headed for the airport. He smiled. "You're a real trooper, you know that? You're also pretty good at this stuff."

"What *stuff?*"

"Helping me. So I'm not spread so thin. I still can't get over how you and Theresa appear to have hit it off. It's amazing. David Copperfield amazing!"

"Why so amazing?"

"Well, it's just . . . I've learned how Theresa can fly off at times. When she's upset, anyway. Are you *sure* you want to go? It wouldn't be a problem to take you to my house. You could relax. I could stop real quick, pick you up something good to eat—barbecue from Clyde Houston's maybe? Oh," he said, looking her way quickly with a grin, ". . . there is this fabulous restaurant I know you'd love. That's where I had planned to take you today. It's called, are you ready for this? Veni Vidi Vici." He smiled and stole another look at her. "Seriously. I kid you not. They have the most wonderful food, too."

"Serious? Veni, Vidi, Vici? Your trademark Latin phrase: I came, I saw, I conquered." She laughed. "Well, as tempting as all that sounds, I think I'll just hang out with you. I kind of like watching you work. But, now, that B woman . . . I just might have to haul off and slap her. Let *her* turn the other cheek!"

He started laughing. "Now, you know you're wrong. What kind of a Christian are you, anyway?"

"Well, I've been trying for the longest to figure out what the B stands for. Other than the word I've concluded from all my previous encounters, that is."

He turned off onto the airport exit. "Oh, before I forget. Let me kind of warn you—about Lena. She was burned in a fire a long time ago. She still has the scars. I just didn't want you to be caught off guard."

"And who's Lena again?"

"It's sort of complicated. But the short answer is: She's Theresa's real mother."

"Real mother? But I thought Beatrice Jordan was her real mother."

"No. And I don't know all the details, but seems Lena and Bishop Jordan had her, and somehow Theresa ended up with him. I suspect it had to do with Lena's recovery period. But then, there's a lot I have no clue whatsoever about."

"How does Theresa feel about Lena?"

"It's strange. Theresa doesn't want anyone to know Lena's her mother. I don't even think her friends know."

Johnnie Mae frowned. "But why?"

"Now that's where it starts to get complicated."

She clamped her hands together. "In other words, you don't want to tell me any more."

He looked over at her. "Let's just say, Theresa has plenty of issues of her own to work through. Trust me."

"I believe she's going to. Work through them, that is. Her father's stroke has definitely gotten her attention. I tried to tell her it wasn't necessarily anything she did. But she feels, or knows rather, she hasn't done right. 'Touch thou not my anointed one,' she kept quoting. Says she doesn't feel right asking God for anything at this point. Feels she can only ask Him about making her father well on credit, although she does plan to settle that account next week."

Landris and Johnnie Mae found Lena standing near baggage claim.

"This place is so big," Lena said. "I would never have found my way out of here if I were alone." She hugged George. He got her bag and took it to the car.

"So." She sighed softly. "This the woman you left my daughter for?"

Johnnie Mae looked at Landris, then back at Lena. "Excuse me?" she said as they got into the car. "Oh, we aren't together-together." She smiled.

"I'm sorry. It's just . . . George here was carrying a torch for somebody. Now, he didn't tell me that. But I sensed it in my spirit." She looked at them both. "Based on how you two are when you're together, not-together, I figured, it must be you. But then, I could be speaking out of place. Wouldn't be the first time."

George laughed. "Ms. Patterson, you're too much."

"Well, I just hope you remember what I told you back at Christmastime. Nothing can take the place of true love—not money, not houses, not prestige. True love doesn't come along every day either." She looked out the window. "How's Richard?"

George looked to the back as he pulled out. "Not too good."

"I didn't think so. Beatrice sounded like I might not make it in time even with a plane. They know I don't fly nowhere. She said she thought this was one time I should."

"Mrs. Jordan said he was trying to talk . . . to tell her some things he needed her to do."

"That's Richard. How's Theresa?" She looked back over at George.

"She's not taking this well at all. Somehow feels she's responsible."

Lena nodded. "What did he say your name was again?" she asked.

"Johnnie Mae."

"Johnnie Mae. Did George here tell you what my daughter thinks of me?"

"No, ma'am, he didn't." Johnnie Mae looked at Landris and grinned like she wanted to stick out her tongue and say, *Nah!*

"She thinks I'm ugly. I embarrass her. She didn't even want me at her wedding. Imagine that. I was going to go home, but George here talked me into staying. Then he ups and messes things up. So I still didn't get to go." Lena was calm and talked freely. George looked surprised by her words. "Yep. That's life for you."

When they arrived at the hospital, Theresa saw them coming down the corridor. She ran to meet them. "Lena, Daddy's been asking for you. Please hurry."

Lena tried to walk fast, but she had a slight limp that slowed her down. Landris and Johnnie Mae stood back out of the way.

B started walking toward Landris and Johnnie Mae. Johnnie Mae spotted her coming and turned her back to her. "Here comes the B woman," she sang.

He smiled. "You need to stop." He said it through clenched teeth, as though they were secret agents on a mission. "Because I'll tell you, B don't play. I know some three-hundred-pound men right now . . . today . . . who shake, and I mean *literally* shake, when she comes their way."

"Pastor Landris?" B said.

He turned toward her. "Yes? Why, Sister B." He smiled pleasantly.

She cleared her throat. "I just wanted to come . . . and first off . . . apologize."

"Apologize? For what?"

"Well, it appears . . . I . . . may have jumped to conclusions about Theresa and her . . . baby. I'm still a little shocked, but I'll be okay." B smacked as she spoke. "I would also like to thank you for all you seem to have done for my friend. I sat in church today, ready to vote that they send you packing. But I learned that you truly take what you do seriously. And the fact that you still didn't say anything damaging about Theresa, although you knew the whole truth and could, if not should, have, even while you were about to be nailed to the cross. Well, you're okay with me."

"Why thank you, Sister B. Coming from you, that's *definitely* something."

"Anyway, I just thought it only appropriate that I take care of this now." She began to walk away. Johnnie Mae started grinning at Landris. B turned back around. "Oh, and Ms. Taylor? I guess I owe you a slight apology as well. Also, I really didn't *hate* your first book. But honestly, I really didn't understand it either."

"That's quite all right, Ms. B."

"Oh please, just B."

Johnnie Mae smiled. "Of course."

B went back over to the other side of the emergency room waiting area and stood next to Sapphire.

"So. What do you think *that* was all about?" Landris asked.

"I think your girl, Theresa, might be trying to make a change."

Landris pursed his lips as he gazed at B and Sapphire chatting in the corner, then back to Johnnie Mae. "What exactly did you say to Theresa?"

She smiled. "Essentially, that God's grace is sufficient. 'That His strength is made perfect in weakness'."

Landris looked at her. "Second Corinthians, 12:9. You go, girl! You *are* good!"

She laughed out loud before she could catch herself, then bowed her head, smiled, and said a quick, silent prayer of thanksgiving.

"But the real test," Landris said, "will come with her father and her mother, Lena." And with that, his face seemed as hard and unmoving as stone.

CHAPTER 34

To Proclaim Liberty to the Captives

Beatrice took Lena in to see Richard. He looked real bad. Hollow. Drained. Weak. When he saw Lena, he started trying to talk.

"Bishop Jordan, now don't you be trying to do too much. We still got some more tests to do," the nurse said loudly, like he was hard of hearing. "Try and squeeze my hand," she said, taking his hand. "Can you feel my hand?"

He shook his head. She pinched him a little. "Can you feel that at all?" He shook his head. "Okay, then. Somebody's here to see you. Do you know who these people are?" She was still speaking loudly.

"My wife," he said, and his voice could barely be understood.

"That's right. And do you know the other person there? Is that your sister?"

"That's Lena," he said. "Lena's from North Carolina." He started to cry.

"All right, Bishop Jordan." She patted his arm. "I'm going to leave you with them for just a few minutes. I've got to get you another IV started, okay?"

He nodded.

"Beatrice," Richard said in a mumble. "Give it to Lena."

Lena walked over beside him. "Look at you. What are you doing in a place like this?" Lena said. She smiled. "How you feeling, Richard?"

He shook his head.

"Not good. I know. But you're going to be all right. You know that, don't you? You're a fighter. Just like me."

"Lena . . ." He tried to point to Beatrice.

"You want me to have this?" Lena said, looking at what Beatrice held.

He nodded. She took the article she'd forgotten when she left before, and the picture of the two of them Richard apparently had decided to keep.

"Lena . . . tell Theresa," he said.

"Richard, there's plenty of time for that—"

He shook his head. "Tell her now . . ." he mumbled. "Today. Now."

"I'll do it."

"Promise me."

She smiled. "Why, you old fox. You think you're slick, don't you? Asking me to promise."

"Promise . . . me."

Lena turned and looked at Beatrice. "Why today?"

"Because, Theresa is in a bad way. For one thing, she's pregnant."

"Oh, my. Why didn't anybody tell me? How far along is she?"

"A little over four months, I believe."

"Pastor Landris's baby?"

"We don't know for sure. But—"

"She out of control," Richard said. "She need to be stopped. From hurtin' people."

"Why does he think my telling her this now will affect anything?" Lena said. She looked at the article again.

"She got away with treating you like she did all of her life," Beatrice said. "Now it's become a way of life. We were at George's church today when the bishop had the stroke. Of course, his blood pressure was way up, and he wouldn't go see about it. But I'm also sure, it upset him to see how Theresa was sitting there allowing an innocent person—again—pay the price for what she wanted for herself. I've been telling you both for years, she should be told. Years ago, I said this."

"No lecture, Beatrice," he said. Only the word "lecture" didn't come out right at all.

"Richard, are you sure this is the reason you want me to tell her? You're not plotting to check out and leave me and Beatrice holding the bill, are you?" Lena looked lovingly down upon him.

"Lena, I sorry . . . sorry for all the pain I caused you," he said, slurred.

"You didn't cause me no pain."

"You lie . . ." he said, then started to cry. Lena took his hand.

Beatrice walked over and rubbed his face. "Sometimes when he cries, he thinks he's laughing. It's hard to tell. It bothered me too, at first."

"Lena, tell her the whole thing. Don't leave none out . . . don't spare me."

"Sure, Richard."

"You promise?"

"Yes, Richard. I promise. Now I'm going to go so you can work on getting better." Lena stepped back. "You promise, you'll get better?" He nodded.

"Bishop, I'll be back in a minute, okay?" Beatrice said. He nodded. "Now, you be good while I'm gone." He nodded once again.

Beatrice and Lena stepped outside the room. "Lena, tell her. All of it, please. The bishop can't. He was going to after that meeting today. He whispered to me that Theresa wasn't being honest. He knew it was because she had always gotten away with hurting folks who hadn't done her any harm. He told me he would tell her about the way she had treated you, and how wrong she was. And why. He was going to make her see she couldn't continue to ruin other people's lives because it was convenient for her. She could be ruining a promising minister's ministry, if Pastor Landris becomes at all tainted."

"Ruin his ministry? What do you mean?"

"Some people at his church think he hasn't been living the life appropriate for the office of a pastor. Theresa knows the truth, but she sat right there and didn't open her mouth! Probably didn't want to be embarrassed. As soon as the bishop heard George speak, he knew George was somehow protecting Theresa. He possibly spoke with her in confidence. Theresa knows George takes his oath seriously. The bishop also knows George had a good reason not to cause a scene and hold that congregation together. George isn't the type to allow division or conflict to take root in that church.

"So, Bishop watched her sit there while those people were about to vote and possibly get rid of him. Of course, he was fuming. We know she's scared because the bishop's in here right now. And she might even take a few steps to get God to help with her desire for the moment. But I also know Theresa well enough to know that before a few days pass, she'll forget she was going to do better. And she'll slip right back to her old self-centered way of life."

"So, Theresa didn't say anything to straighten out what was happening?"

"Not one blessed word. She sat there like it had nothing whatsoever to do with her."

"I see. I understand now why Richard wants this today. All this time when I thought I was helping to make her life better, I was giving her permission to treat people any old way. I thought it was okay when she treated me with such indignation. I was wrong there, too. I'll tell her, Beatrice. Nobody deserves to be mistreated by another. I don't care what's wrong with either of them. Lord forgive me for having allowed things to go on like this for apparently far too long."

CHAPTER 35

Behold the Bush Burned with Fire, And the Bush Was Not Consumed

"Theresa, could I speak with you a minute?"

Theresa was talking with B and Sapphire. "Lena, is it important? Can't it wait? I'm talking with B and Sapphire at the moment. And you know I'm upset about my father."

"I wouldn't ask if I didn't think it was important."

"Well, can't we do it some other time—"

"Theresa, as your mother, I would like to talk with you. Right now."

B and Sapphire exchanged looks and smiled. They knew how Lena wanted to be Theresa's mother. But they knew *this day*, Theresa was about to set this woman straight!

Theresa looked at Lena like she couldn't believe she had said that. It had been over twenty years since Lena had said something out loud while anyone was around. "Lena, I don't believe you're acting this way in front of my friends."

"Tell your friends to get over it! You and I need to talk. Now!" Lena said and started limping away. Theresa stood where she was. Lena turned and looked back. "If you prefer, I can just as well do it in front of your friends here. Makes no nevermind to me. Because

I'm not in a 'play-mama' mood today. Are you smelling which way the wind's blowing now?"

Theresa hurried to catch up with Lena. They rode up the elevator to a quiet outdoor space located within the hospital.

"What got into you back there?" Theresa said. "I've asked you to be considerate of—"

"Hush up and sit down! I'm not in the mood for your foolishness today."

Theresa was stunned. She eased into a chair.

"Look at my face," Lena said. Theresa had already turned away. Lena grabbed her by the jaw and turned her face toward her. Theresa closed her eyes. "I said, look . . . at . . . my . . . face."

Theresa opened her eyes and looked, by now on the verge of tears. "Why?" she asked.

"You still think I'm ugly, don't you? Just like when you were little."

"Look, I don't want to talk to you. I made a promise to God I'd try and do better, but I don't want to talk to you. Okay?"

"Do you know how I got like this?" She held out her hands, then pulled up her long sleeves so Theresa could see how badly she had been burned there too. "My face, my hands, my arms . . . they were the worst places for the most part."

"I know you were burned in a fire. I'm sorry about that, but what do you want me to do about it? Your scars have stared me in the face all of my life. As a little girl, people teased me because of *your* scars. I don't want to see them, Lena. Can't you understand that? I don't want to see them!"

Lena pulled out the article. "I gave this to your daddy once. A long time ago. It was a week after I'd been in the hospital with those third-degree burns."

"Can we go back inside and downstairs now?" She stood up. "What if Daddy's looking for me and they can't find me?"

"Theresa!" She moved her face in closer to Theresa. "The world does not revolve around you and what you want." She grabbed her by the wrist and pulled her down as she sat in the chair next to her. "You can just sit, because you're going to hear me out this time!"

"Well, hurry and get it over with. Then, will you do me a favor? Just stay out of my life and leave me alone!"

Lena started smiling as she relaxed her entire body. "Beatrice said I was making a mistake. Now I see just how right she was." She held the article back out again. "Like I was saying, I gave this to your father once. I hadn't planned on bothering him after the fire—didn't wish to be a burden on anybody. But then, this nurse . . . I don't even remember her name, gave me this piece of newspaper. I saw where they said I probably wouldn't make it, saw the extent of what had really happened to me that day." Lena smiled. "Here. Read it." She shook it toward Theresa, who was slow to take it.

When Theresa finished, she twisted her mouth. "Okay. So you apparently went inside a house to get some children out. It says two children. What happened with the other one?"

"The other one? Oh, yes. What happened with the other one? Interesting, isn't it? You asked about the other one, but not the one who was brought out."

"Look, if you don't want to tell me, it's fine. I just want you to hurry and be done so I can go back downstairs and see about my daddy."

"I was thirteen when I met your father. We were so much in love. When I was sixteen, my grandmother died. She raised me because my own mother was 'more interested in changing men than changing diapers.' That's what Big Mama used to say. I've never *formally* met the woman who gave birth to me—not to this day. She didn't make it to Big Mama's funeral. But she did manage to come get what she claimed was 'her inheritance.' That was my first and only time I remember her having anything to say to me."

"Speaking from personal experience, I wouldn't worry too much about it if I were you," Theresa said.

Lena nodded as she continued. "Richard and I had planned on getting married when he graduated from college. I won't go into all the details with you . . ." She looked over at Theresa. "You probably could care less anyway. Your father was on his way to Fayetteville State University, a fine institution, when I learned I had gotten pregnant that first and only time he and I were ever together. I didn't tell him I was pregnant. You see, your father was the type of man that he would have married me and worked three jobs if it took it to take care of us. So I chose not to tell him. Just let him go off to college without a care in the world. Then I managed to avoid him during the later time I carried you.

"When he was due home, I'd tell him I would be gone. We lived far enough from each other that I didn't have to worry about anyone accidentally revealing my secret. Once, he even tried to surprise me. I watched him knock on my door from a window. Now, that was truly a hard thing for me to do. I did love him so. . . ."

Lena looked at Theresa, who seemed more interested in her story now. "After I had you, he had been in college for about a year. I pretended like I was always baby-sitting you for this well-to-do couple who just liked to party all the time. He never suspected you were his child. I was going to tell him. Just after I was sure he saw how important it was that he finished college. He loved you, even with him not knowing you were his own. He would say how we'd someday have a baby just like you. And you were a good baby, too. Smart. A beautiful, sweet child. No trouble at all."

"Really?"

"Oh yes. You didn't cry unless there was a real reason. You knew how to play by yourself. And you were such a beautiful baby. I thought I was going to burst trying to keep that you were really his from him. He even asked, since you and I seemed to be together every time he visited, if your parents might consider letting us adopt you. I would laugh. I could hardly wait until the time when I could tell him the truth about who you really were to us."

"So what happened?"

"You were about three. It was around Christmas time. You loved the lights on the Christmas tree. You would stand there looking at them and say, 'Lights, lights.' And of course, I loved to hear your little voice. Richard came over Christmas Eve night. He used to smoke every now and then, and when he came in the house, he was about to light a cigarette but remembered I didn't like people smoking around you. He put his pack of cigarettes back up, along with his fancy lighter. Then the two of you played for hours while I cooked us this wonderful little Christmas Eve dinner. You and I lived in a tiny, hunter green, duplex house."

"Duplex?"

"Yeah. Two houses built side-by-side. Sort of like a small house divided in the middle with two separate front and back door entrances."

"I've seen those before."

"The rent was something I could afford. We didn't have much, but we were happy back then. I used to have to work split shifts at this convenience store some ten blocks away. By then, I had told Richard the truth about you being his daughter—just six weeks earlier. I had to, since he insisted on meeting this couple who didn't love their child any more than they apparently did. He said he wasn't leaving until they came to pick you up. So I told him the truth. He couldn't have been happier. He had six months left until graduation. Everything was finally coming together for us. Finally."

Lena readjusted herself in the seat. "Richard had planned to keep you while I worked my four hours on Christmas Eve. Then we had planned the rest of the night for our special dinner and to wait on Santa Claus for the first time as a real family. Don't get me wrong . . . Richard and I weren't sleeping together then. We were saving ourselves for when we got married. That first and only time happened only because Big Mama died and we let my grieving get in the way of our better judgment. We were planning to get married the day after he graduated—only six months away. But something came up and for some reason, Richard had to leave. Something unexpected. All he said was, something special. There went our planned special dinner."

"So he had to leave that day unexpectedly?"

"Yeah. At the time, I didn't know what it was that came up. He was sneaking and working odd jobs, I did know that. Trying to give me some extra money to help out. But when I left, he was going to watch you. I wasn't worried; he loved you so much even then. Whatever it was called him away, he stopped by the 7-Eleven to tell me he had gone next door and gotten Amy, the sixteen-year-old who sat with you from time to time, to watch you until I returned. I only had two hours left. No problem. He'd paid her in advance. Said he'd be back no later than Christmas morning for sure. 'With a *special* surprise,' he said. 'Something really great!'"

"Just like Daddy."

"I was walking home when I saw that dark smoke climbing and rolling toward the sky. I didn't even realize I had done it, but I had thrown down my bag of items I had purchased, and I started running. Faster. Like I knew already, in my spirit, it was my house."

"Your house?"

"Yes. When I got there, the firemen—they called them firemen back then before they became gender sensitive and changed it to firefighters. Anyway, they were there, trying without success to put the fire out. I was frantic. Crying. Screaming. About to lose my mind. I didn't see you anywhere. I found a fireman and asked if they'd gotten the child out. He said, 'Yes.' I was relieved. 'There she is. Over there.' He was pointing at Amy. I said, 'There were two! A three-year-old. Did they both get out?' He says, 'Ma'am, we just know about that one. She got herself out. Maybe she can tell you where the other one is.' Then he asked if I was sure there were two. And who was I? But I didn't have time to hold no conversation. I had to find my baby."

"Me," Theresa said softly. "It was me who was still inside? That must be where those fire dreams I've had in the past come from. It actually happened?"

Lena kept going. "I ran over to Amy. 'My baby,' I said. 'Where's Theresa?' She said she couldn't find you, thought maybe you'd gotten out. I asked her what happened? She said she was talking on the phone. You kept looking at the Christmas tree, pointing, and saying, 'Lights, lights.' She didn't say this, but I know she wasn't paying you any attention. That's when you must have found Richard's lighter. It must have fallen out of his pocket. Apparently, he lost it when you two were playing. It was his lighter. An investigator found it next to the tree remains. A fancy lighter someone gave him in college. It's something you even figured out how to work it, especially at that age. Like I said, you were smart."

"Lena . . ." Theresa cried. Lena found a packet of tissues, then wiped her tears while handing some to Theresa.

Lena wondered what good reliving the past was doing or whether she should tell Theresa about the surprise Richard had gone to get that night: a white rocking horse for his baby, and an engagement ring for her. Or how he'd gone to work when they agreed to pay him double-time—in advance—if he would work Christmas Eve night. The money was just the amount he needed to get that horse and ring for Christmas. Maybe she'd said enough.

She looked over at Theresa. Maybe not . . .

CHAPTER 36

And the Truth Shall Make You Free

"They think you must have lit the Christmas tree, and it went up in flames so fast it scared you. Because I knew you, I knew when Amy said she couldn't find you and thought you were outside, you had to be under the bed with your favorite teddy bear—Cocoa. That's what you named him. 'Where's Cocoa?' you'd say. The house was burning something fierce. I tried to go in, but they stopped me, said it was too dangerous. I told them you were in there. I could tell they felt bad. They knew you would be a statistic before the night was over." Lena shook her head.

"Not my baby, I said to myself. And I would have fought off ten men if I would have had to. If I perished in the fire, let me perish. But I was gonna try. I wasn't gonna hear nothing about how I could always have another child. What kind of foolishness is that? Each child is unique. It's not like losing a doll or some toy . . . if you lose one, you can always get another one."

"So you broke loose," Theresa said looking down at the article again.

"Yeah. And I got inside, God only knows how. I know an angel had to be in there already, protecting you with his wings until I could make it over to you, guiding me through the smoke, flames, and fallen debris. It was so hot in there, but I didn't think about it. I found my way to our bedroom. You and I shared the same bed back then. I got down on my knees and crawled, trying to find your body. And I did find you. Glory to God, I did find you! Couldn't tell if you were alive or dead. But I wasn't gonna just let you be consumed by no fire."

Theresa couldn't stop crying. She kept looking down, then back up at Lena. And each time now when she looked at Lena's face, she could see just how beautiful she really was.

"I could tell the fire had gotten worse. Snatching an army blanket off the bed, I tried to wrap you up so that the flames couldn't touch you. You were limp. Didn't know whether you were alive or dead. As I made my way out, I felt my skin burning. Figured my clothes had caught fire. I prayed like I've never prayed before—nor since. A beam suddenly fell, almost hitting us, then blocking my path. It was burning tall with flames. There was no other way; we had to go through to get out. As I jumped over the beam, I hurt my left leg. The blanket fell open. Got caught. Hung. I had to let it go. Flames roared up at us like some wild animal. I took my hand and face and covered your little body and face that were now exposed to the flames.

"The flames were so intense. Painful. It felt as though my whole body were literally on fire. Burning. Still, I wouldn't let go. I pressed my body tight . . . hard against yours, refusing to let go. I kept those flames from you, and pressed my way through. And now today . . ." Lena reached over and lifted Theresa's face, arms, and hands as she inspected each area, ". . . today there's not a mark on you anywhere. Not one." She smiled . . . proud.

Theresa cried out. Lena pulled her into her thin body and rocked her. Just like when she was a baby.

"Lena," Theresa said. "Lena, I'm so sorry! I didn't know. I promise . . . oh, God! I promise. I . . . didn't . . . know!"

"I held and covered you, and it didn't matter how much it hurt, I refused to let go. And I wouldn't have ever let you go either, except for that hospital. Someone had to take care of you while I got better. But I never wanted you to know hurt the way I had. I told a nurse at the hospital how to contact your father. I had to be sure—no matter what—you would always be all right. Your father loved you, this much, I knew. I made him promise he wouldn't drop out of college either, if he could at all help it. Because if he did, all my sacrifices would have been for nothing. He promised he'd take good care of you. And he kept his promises. Every . . . single . . . one . . . of . . . them."

Theresa continued to cry as Lena stared out and continued to rock her.

"Oh, yes. He took real good care of you. Did a fine job, too. A fine job. But I always intended to come back for you. And I did. But the fire had changed my skin. My looks. People weren't just cruel to me—oh, I could have taken that. It was seeing my baby having to deal with it. I didn't want to let you go then either, but sometimes we have to do what is right for another. Even when it hurts. I never thought you'd hate me, though. Never. Not *just* because of the way I look. Not that." Tears fell from Lena's face. She tried to wipe her face dry with her bad hand, but the tears kept coming.

Theresa looked up, reached over, and took Lena's right hand. She touched it . . . caressed it. And for the first time, she saw what Lena's hand had taken instead of her own face. Theresa touched Lena's face. Saw the side Lena had pressed against her to cover her body, and the side she had left exposed for the burning flames. She witnessed the damage Lena had suffered in her place, sparing her body to still be beautiful. Theresa shook her head and continued to cry. "I treated you so horribly. All these years. Oh God, look at the person I ended up becoming. But I never knew . . ."

"And I never wanted you to know," Lena said. "Never. Hey." She tried to get Theresa to stop crying. "I've something else to show you." She took out the photo Richard had kept. "Your father asked me to give this to you as well."

Theresa looked at it. "This is the picture I found Christmas Day in that shoe box. I told him she was gorgeous. Daddy told me he had asked her to marry him seven times. Said she turned him down six." She let out a laugh.

"Actually, it was eight times he asked. He probably forgot about the very first time when he tried to impress with his rap. 'Hey, sweet mama. You look just like my wife.' 'Your wife? You ain't got no wife.' 'I will when you say *I do*.' It was eight times. I remember. You see, I turned him down seven."

Theresa looked at the picture then back at Lena. "This is you?"

Lena struck a pose. Hand on hip, head cocked to one side, with a smile that would melt cheese. "A little clearer now?" Lena grinned.

Theresa laughed. "You're really quite a character."

"When people give me a chance and stop judging first by what they see."

"That's what George told me about you. I thought he was just looking for something to aggravate me."

"I like Pastor Landris. Too bad you two didn't make it down the aisle. And speaking of which, this baby? My grandchild? Who's the father?"

"It's not anybody you know," Theresa said softly.

"Then that answers my question, since I only know Pastor Landris when it comes to you. So what's the deal with you letting people think this baby's his? That church mess that shouldn't have ever happened? Theresa, that man don't deserve to be going through mess. I went through a whole lot of mess myself—"

"Because of me," she said, apologetic.

"I'm not gonna lie. You made that fire seem like a day at the beach. And I didn't think I could ever feel any more pain than I did from that. Third-degree burns. Shoot! Pain I wouldn't wish on my worst enemy. But you definitely gave me a run for my money. Now, please do the right thing about Pastor Landris. He doesn't deserve what's happening to him now. And you know it."

"I know. I know," Theresa said. She looked at Lena. "You appear to be so well-adjusted. And I seem so messed up." She wiped tears that still flowed.

Lena held out her hands. "My scars . . ." she said, placing her hand on her face. "Your scars." She placed Theresa's hand over her heart and on her forehead. "Both are scars. First you must deal with it, then allow it to heal. The healing process may hurt sometimes, but in the end, you'll be all right. 'I count not myself to have apprehended: but this one thing I do, forgetting those things which are behind, and reaching forth unto those things which are before—' "

" 'I press toward the mark for the prize of the high calling of God which is Christ Jesus,' " Theresa said completing the quote from Philippians 3:13-14.

"You remember? Just like we used to do it when you were little," Lena said with a smile, then sighed.

"Yeah." She smiled and looked into her eyes. "Lena, can you ever forgive me?"

"Forgive *you?* No," Lena said shaking her head. She got to her feet, brushed down her clothes. "No."

Theresa looked at the ground. "I understand. Well, I can't say I blame you."

Lena stooped down, pulled Theresa up by her shoulders, and gave her a tight hug. "There's nothing to forgive. You're mine. Good, bad, or indifferent. I think somebody once said, 'Love means never having to say please forgive me.' "

"I don't think that's the way it goes."

"It's the way I do it. So that's how it goes. Now, let's go check on your daddy. He owes me another promise." They started back inside—arms wrapped around each other's waists. Some looking at the two together might have thought *the beauty and the beast*. Yet there appeared to be hope, for the beast, in Theresa . . . after all.

"Sure," Theresa said, "Mama. Sure."

Lena stopped, pulled back, and looked at Theresa with an approving smile. "My beautiful little girl. All grown up and about to have a little one of her own. I hope I get to be part of this one's life, since I missed so much of yours."

"You will, Mama. You will. And *that's* a promise. From *this* Jordan."

CHAPTER 37

Let the Redeemed of the Lord Say So

"The doors of the church are open. If you'd like to make Jesus the Lord of your life, if you died today and you're not sure where you'd go, then come. There's no reason for you to leave here today without knowing where you'll spend eternity," Pastor Landris said. "Maybe someone wants to rededicate their life. You want to begin anew—a fresh anointing. God will wipe your slate clean, and it will be as though your sins were no more. 'Whom the Son sets free is free indeed!'

"Or just maybe you're interested in making this church your home. Visiting a place is nice, but everyone should have a place they can call home. If you'd like to become part of this body, then come now."

Sister Murray sat near the front with her arms crossed, waiting for this part to be over. The meeting might have been interrupted last Sunday, but she was not giving up so easily. She had a surprise for the good pastor. It wasn't over!

No one was coming forward. Then suddenly, a person got up and began walking to the front. When she got there, she whispered something into Pastor Landris's ear. Pastor Landris gave her a handheld microphone.

She turned toward the audience. "Good afternoon. For those of you who don't know who I am, my name is Theresa Jordan. I realize I've been the topic of discussion for the past few weeks. First, I want to give honor to God who has allowed me this opportunity and has already forgiven me my sins. Next, I want to ask Pastor Landris to forgive me, for in many ways, I have wronged him. Then, I'd like to ask you, this wonderful congregation, to forgive me as well." She paused.

"Without going into too many details, I have sinned, in more than a few ways. Besides fornication, as Sister Murray put it, I allowed people to think the baby I carry was Pastor Landris's doing." She looked at Maurice, who smiled and winked at her. "This is not the case. I didn't start that rumor, but I didn't stop it either. And that was just as wrong. Sometimes things get uncomfortable, but that's no excuse for us to shirk our duties. Not that this is anyone's business, but I would like to say that I talked with Pastor Landris back in February as a pastor. I told him the truth about what was going on in my life."

She began to cry and looked up. "I said I wasn't going to cry, but it's hard. You see, we have a pastor that when you tell him what is supposed to be kept confidential, he keeps it that way. Last week, Sister Murray, when you were so adamant about getting rid of him, you didn't know he could have told everything just to save his own hide. But he didn't. And he was willing to be humiliated for what he believed to be the right thing to do—no matter what. Whether we agree or not, how many of us are willing to put our all on the altar for God? As for why we didn't marry, I'd just like to say: That's truly nobody's business. So let's get our focus off the negatives, and get our eyes back on God."

She turned around. "Pastor Landris, again . . . please forgive me. And thank you for coming to the hospital and being such a blessing to me and my family." She turned back around. "For those of you who know my father, I'm happy to report he's in rehab. He has a long way to go, but he's a fighter, my dad. And he believes in the power of prayer and divine healing. Just like my dear, sweet, beautiful mother. Mama . . . will you please come up here with me?"

There was total silence throughout the entire sanctuary as Theresa's mother came and stood next to her.

"This is Lena Patterson—my mother. Not 'play-' . . . real mother. A very special lady I'm looking to have around quite a lot in the future. I just wanted you all to know who she is. Mama, I love you . . . and I thank you." Theresa held her close and kissed her as the congregation applauded. "People, if you have a mother, let her know how much you love and appreciate her. For it may never be revealed to you how much she has gone through . . . just for you. That goes for daddies too."

Lena leaned back and looked at her daughter. "Thank you, baby." Theresa pulled her close and hugged her again.

Pastor Landris walked over, took the microphone, and hugged them both.

"She done good, huh, Pastor?" Lena whispered.

He looked at her and winked. "Well, what else do you expect? Look at the people she's hanging out and surrounding herself with these days."

After Theresa's confession, Pastor Landris opened up the altar for all who wanted to privately confess their sins, wipe their slates clean, and begin anew. Over 2,000 people came forward, and there was shouting like nobody's business as people individually—and collectively—laid their burdens on the altar of God, and left them there.

When service was over, Pastor Landris went to get in his car. Standing beside it was Johnnie Mae with Princess Rose. He hadn't seen Princess Rose since she was in the hospital. He smiled as she stood next to her mother, rocking back and forth, twisting and turning.

"Wow, look who we have here," he said. "You must be Princess Rose?"

She nodded.

"Go ahead, baby. Do it like we practiced," Johnny Mae said.

"Because you've been so nice, I picked you something with my Mommie's help. May you always leave your fragr . . . fragrance on everything you touch." She pulled a flower from behind her back. "Just like this flower. This is my Mommie's favorite. And I . . . and *we* wanted you to have one from our very own garden."

"Wow," Landris said. "That is so pretty. Just like you."

"Say thank you."

"Thank you," Princess Rose said.

Landris inhaled slowly and deeply into the petals of the flower. "Moroccan Rose," he said to Johnnie Mae.

"Yes. The brown rose—you always know love, joy, and gladness is there."

He smiled. "You remember."

"How could I ever forget? You told me what all the color roses meant. Red, white, pink, yellow, and brown."

"So what brings you way up here today?" Landris said.

Johnnie Mae started to bounce a little on the tips of her toes. "I found a house." She radiated with a grin.

"Here? In Atlanta?"

"Yes!"

"I didn't even know you were in the market. Why didn't you tell me? I could have told you about a few homes I knew about."

"Well, I found one I really like! And I'd love for you to see it and tell me what you think."

"Sure."

"Can you go now?"

He looked at his watch. "Let's see, I have an engagement in about an hour and a half. Can we do it within that time frame, or should we wait until afterward?"

"It's only about twenty minutes from here. Your engagement? Who is it with?"

"Some weirdly named group I've never heard of before. Jocelyn scheduled it against my normal Sunday—only church engagements—policy. They invited me to a function they're having over on Peachtree Street. She said it would only be about a forty-five-minute deal. They begged, she said. Had to have an anointed preacher to come pray a special blessing. It had to be *me*. Go figure."

"Good. Then we'll hurry. Why don't you drive your car? That way, you'll be ready to leave for your appointment."

"That'll work."

"Oh you know . . . the house is not all that far from where you live. Why don't we just drop your car off at your place? Either I can take you back home to pick it up, or I can carry you over to Peachtree Street if we find we're pushing it."

"That's fine."

They went to his house, left his car, and he rode with them. Leaving his neighborhood, Johnnie Mae made a few turns as she continued to rattle on and on about how excited she was about this and that, how different it would be to live in another state. Landris alternated between what she was saying and where they were going. She finally turned and drove into a subdivision.

He started laughing. "I hope you do a better job of finding your house after you move than you're doing today. Do you realize you just drove right back into my neighborhood?"

"I did?" She looked slightly concerned, then popped in her Yolanda Adams CD. *Open My Heart* began to play as she parked the car in his driveway. She got out. The song was still playing as she walked around to the back and took Princess Rose out of her car seat. Landris watched her while patiently waiting in the passenger's seat.

"Johnnie Mae? *What* are you doing?"

"Well? Are you coming? I told you I wanted to show you my new house."

"Johnnie Mae. This is where *I* live."

"I know, and I *really* like this house. I'm thinking the owner may be willing to negotiate a deal; work out something. I'm going to speak with him about it."

Landris got out of the car. "Johnnie Mae? *What* are you up to?"

"You see, I heard a rumor that the owner might be in the market for a woman, oh about yay high, preferably with her own child. And if the child happened to have Rose in her name, that would be even better. You see . . . he has a thing for roses. The only catch: the owner is some old fuddy-duddy who has this obsession with God, church, love, romance . . . and oh yeah, the institution of marriage. But he's so charming . . ." she paused and grinned, "and about . . . the best friend—male or female—anyone . . . could ever . . . ask . . . for."

He looked at her and smiled. "Johnnie Mae? Are you saying . . . ?"

"Are you asking?"

"Yes."

"Well . . ."

He kneeled down on one knee, took her hand, and looked up into her big brown eyes. "Johnnie Mae, I love you. I've always loved you. I always will." He shook his head and smiled. "I always envisioned me asking you this in a much more romantic setting than . . . this. Although *Open My Heart* as background music does tend to cast quite a special touch. Johnnie Mae Taylor, will you do me the honor of being my wife?"

"That depends," she said, smiling down at him.

"Depends?" He looked confused. "On what?"

Her eyes softly followed his as he stood up—tall above her. "Have you ever loved someone . . . that you never had?" she said.

He looked deep into her eyes. "Well, there was this one woman I met back in '93. She happened to be vacationing—as was I—on the beach. In the Bahamas. Alone. I fell in love with her the moment my eyes brought her into focus. She was beautiful both inside and out. I wished I could simply freeze time. I never even entertained the idea she might be married. Else I might have guarded my heart a little better. I mean, she was so lovely there was no way in heaven—if she were married—a husband would not have been glued to her side." He smiled as he bit down on his lower lip.

"But the type of man I was back then, my knowing she was married, possibly wouldn't have mattered. The moment I saw her, I was a goner. And I vowed right there, should I *ever* be blessed with the opportunity, I'd spend the rest of my life showing this nubian angel how much she meant to me and how much I loved her. I knew even then she was, in some way, my soul mate.

"But wouldn't you know, she refused to give me any information about herself—other than her first name: Johnnie, after I heard her being called J. M. As only fate could orchestrate, we ran into each other again some years later, then again in '98. My heart beat just knowing someone like her existed—a woman of integrity. She completed me . . . my friend. Oh, *how* I loved her. Still—she was never mine to have. I went forward with my life. Yet the heart loves whom the heart loves.

"So, yes, to answer your question. I have loved someone that I never had." He then smiled at her and spoke words he'd said to her when he left Birmingham back in '98. "*Alaiyo, Mee saloby you, langa alla mee hatty, so langa mee leeby.*"

Johnnie Mae smiled back. "*Alaiyo* is a Yoruba word. It means, 'one for whom bread . . . food . . . is not enough.' The other is Surinam. It means—"

" 'I will love you with all my heart, so long as I live'," Landris said, hugging, then kissing her with years of pent-up passion.

After a few minutes, she gently stepped back from him. "Landris?" she said. "That meeting you have over on Peachtree Street today? Well . . . I'm Destination Forever, Incorporated. And I think I'd like to change the meeting place to here. It appears you and I have an agenda requiring some serious discussion. Something that will benefit *our* destination forever. And truly, we need to fervently pray for God's will and guidance if this is to be all it can be. The God-kind-of-way: Blessings, with no sorrow added."

Landris looked into Johnnie Mae's eyes and laughed. "Woman, you are too much! What am I going to do with you?"

"Love me. That's all, just love me: the way Christ loves the church."

"You know . . . I believe I might can handle that," he said, nodding, while stepping back closer to her. "Oh yes! I do believe I can, J. M.—Johnnie . . . My love."

He picked her up and twirled her around. "Put me down," she screamed, then laughed.

Princess Rose began to giggle and clap.

"God is *so* good!" Landris yelled. "So, *so* good!"